Please address questions and book requests to: Harlequin Reader Service
U.S.: 3010 Walden Ave., P.O. Box 1325, Buffalo, NY 14269
Canadian: P.O. Box 609, Fort Erie, Ont. L2A 5X3

Marriage, Inc.

CATHY GILLEN THACKER
FATHER OF THE BRIDE

Harlequin Books

TORONTO • NEW YORK • LONDON
AMSTERDAM • PARIS • SYDNEY • HAMBURG
STOCKHOLM • ATHENS • TOKYO • MILAN
MADRID • WARSAW • BUDAPEST • AUCKLAND

HARLEQUIN BOOKS
225 Duncan Mill Road, Don Mills,
Ontario, Canada M3B 3K9

ISBN 0-373-30119-7

FATHER OF THE BRIDE

Copyright © 1991 by Cathy Gillen Thacker

Celebrity Wedding Certificates published by permission of Donald Ray Pounders from *Celebrity Wedding Ceremonies*.

A Letter from the Author

Dear Reader,

Although there have been many songs, stories and poems celebrating it, I'm not sure I believe in love at first sight. Maybe this is because the pragmatist in me always wonders how you can "love" someone you don't even "know."

But I do believe with all my heart in the chemistry and the mutual spark of interest that precedes every strong and enduring love. I felt it the first time I met my husband; I had only to look into his eyes and gauge the warmth of his smile to know he felt it, too. And though it took us nearly a year to get together, once we did, we've never been apart.

Of course, we were lucky. We had the support of our family and friends. Mutual interests. We attended the same high school and college and were active in many of the same extracurricular activities.

But what if we hadn't been blessed with such support, I have often wondered. What if our families had worked to keep us apart instead of wished us well? Would we have successfully overcome such obstacles? Would the courtship have been simple and short? Or would it have taken years? Just as it took years for Ethan Holbrook and Amanda Stratton to find each other again....

After twenty-five years of togetherness, there's no doubt in my mind what would have happened to Charlie and me. Some loves are destined to make it through thick and thin and endure a lifetime.

I hope you enjoy *Father of the Bride* as much as I enjoyed writing it. And once again—I can never say this often enough!—thank you for all your cards and letters; they've touched me more than you know.

With warmest regards,

Cathy Gillen Thacker

Chapter One

"Amanda, you can't seriously be thinking of consulting on this wedding!"

Amanda sent her older sister a chagrined look and with effort bit back the wry retort on the tip of her tongue. She'd known Mimi would react this way the moment she heard about the job and had braced herself accordingly for the tirade sure to follow. "Do you have any idea what kind of money we're probably talking about?" she responded calmly. "Thousands!"

"I don't care," Mimi countered stubbornly, pushing back a lock of her bobbed auburn hair. "I remember the way that guy hurt you, even if you don't. You don't need Ethan Holbrook's business, Amanda."

Amanda only wished she had the luxury of turning down jobs. But as the sole source of support for her fifteen-year-old daughter and herself, and the founder of her own bridal consulting business, Moonlight and Memories, she needed every penny she could bank. What they didn't need to live on, she deposited in a savings account earmarked for Babe's college expenses. Her mind made up, she enunciated clearly and firmly, "Regardless of what happened in the past, this is a job—a job I am well qualified to do. A job that when all is said and done should cement our reputation as *the* bridal consulting business in the Dallas metropolitan area. I've got to take it."

Mimi followed her around the office, cup of herbal tea in hand. "At least let one of your other consultants handle it, then."

Amanda faced her sister wryly, amused by what she wasn't saying. "I notice you're not signing up for the job?"

Mimi finished her tea in a single draft. "I'd rather spit on the man than look at him."

Mimi never had been one to hold back an opinion or feeling, no matter how outrageous. Whereas Amanda had learned early on it was safer to control and conceal her feelings, present a cool, collected face to the world, unlike the other members of her highly emotional clan. People couldn't hurt you if they couldn't pinpoint your vulnerabilities.

"At least give it to Laura or Rochelle—" Mimi continued persuasively.

Amanda perched on the edge of her desk and picked up the file of notes she'd already made on the job. "I can't," she said, crossing one slim ankle over the other. "Ethan's secretary insisted Ethan and his daughter would only meet with the company's top consultant. And I can't blame him. For the kind of money he's going to be paying to make his daughter's wedding the social event of the season, he should have the most experienced person on the staff arranging it."

"The Holbrooks are so cruel!" Mimi mused. "They always have been."

Not Ethan, Amanda thought. Not at first. His father, however, was another matter. She was sure that man had ice water running through his veins.

Mimi sighed. "Mom and Dad will be livid when they hear."

Amanda successfully fought an embarrassed blush, not easy for someone with her fair coloring. "What happened between Ethan and me is history."

"Yeah? And what about what his father did to Dad? Can you forget that, too?"

"No, I can't." Her father's firing had devastated the entire Webster family. In some ways, even after twenty-six years, her father had yet to recover from the blow to his professional reputation that the senior Holbrook had precipitated. She knew emotionally he'd never forgiven him. Nor was that likely to happen in the future, either.

Mimi sighed, still caught up in the trauma of the past. She shook her head disparagingly. "I knew Ethan was trouble from the moment he first kissed you in high school."

Caught off guard by that remark, Amanda did blush this time. Leave it to Mimi to bring up what had first brought Ethan and her together. "It wasn't a kiss," she countered, unable to prevent the stiffness in her voice. "It was an acting exercise for our theatre arts class." And if it hadn't happened, if they hadn't been pushed into it by a teacher, they might never have gotten together, even briefly. Certainly the fact that Ethan had been a senior and she a freshman had worked against them.

"Acting exercise, my foot!" Mimi scowled and made a dissenting sound. "From what I heard that was a real, bend-you-backward-from-the-waist kiss—that went on and on and on—"

Amanda's cheeks heated up even more. "So he got carried away," she countered evenly. That occasionally happened when novices were trying to be dramatic . . . didn't it?

"I'll say he got carried away! The kids at school didn't stop talking about the red-hot embrace for weeks. They thought the two of you were a real Romeo and Juliet. And I guess you two did, too. Because it was after that the two of you started dating on the sly."

Amanda's thoughts drifted back to that thrilling and complicated time of her life. "We didn't have any other choice," she said softly, remembering how unexpectedly intense her feelings for Ethan had been. She smiled wanly. "We knew how our folks would feel if they found out." After the senior Holbrook had fired her father, her parents had despised him. And vice versa. Contact between the two families had been forbidden.

"They found out, anyway, when he asked you to his senior prom."

Amanda shook her head ruefully, her strawberry-blond curls falling in tousled disarray around her head. "I should have known better than to accept." But Ethan had so wanted to take her. At least she'd thought he had. Later . . . later it was rumored the whole thing had been a joke from start to finish, a senior prank on a stupid freshman. Just remembering how humiliated she'd been made her stomach roll.

As usual, her sister thought she—and indeed all the Websters—were as close to perfect as it was possible to get. "I'd still like to kill him for standing you up that night!" her sister swore.

Amanda got up wearily and tossed the file down on her desk. "Mimi, it's a lot more complicated than you know." Had Ethan's father not gotten into the act . . . maybe she would have had the courage to confront Ethan about what he'd done to her . . . but he had . . . and the night of the prom, she'd known it was as hopeless a situation as the elder Holbrook had tried to tell her. Not that it mattered now. What happened then was over, long over, she told herself firmly.

"You're not still carrying a torch for him after all these years, are you?" Mimi stared at her incredulously.

Amanda lifted her head and fastened her clear blue eyes on her sister's face. Having a crush on Ethan would be unlikely after the number of years that had passed. "No, of course not," she said in a drained voice. She walked across the plush white carpet and sat down on the ice-blue satin brocade sofa across from her polished teak desk. "It's just all this talk about the past has made me feel...I don't know...confused." And upset, angry, lonely.

"I just don't understand why he would ask for you, of all people, to handle his daughter's wedding," Mimi murmured.

Amanda didn't, either.

"Maybe he doesn't realize it's me," Amanda speculated with a shrug. "Although I've retained Webster as my middle name, I always go by my married name, Amanda Stratton, professionally. We don't exactly run in the same social circles."

"What if he does know it's you?" Mimi asked, a worried frown creasing her face.

"What if he does?" Amanda parried dryly. On a strictly professional level, she knew it shouldn't be a big deal even if he did know with whom he was dealing. It had been over twenty years since they'd seen each other from a distance, over twenty-four years since they'd talked. In the interim, both of them had been married to other people. Both of them had children—one daughter, each. There was no reason to let a teenage grievance, an old family feud, influence their lives now. Was there? Especially when he had a job for her that, old grievances aside, she would like to do.

"When's he meeting you?"

"I've been invited to the Highland Park Country Club this evening for a preliminary meeting with Ethan, his daughter and her fiancé."

"Couldn't you have insisted they all come here, to your office?" Mimi said.

Amanda shrugged, long used to putting the client's wishes above her own comfort or convenience. "For the kind of money he's going to be paying, I have no choice but to let him call the shots. It'll be fine, Mimi, really. I can handle this." She wasn't the same trusting, naive girl she'd been when she'd first become involved with Ethan so many years ago.

"I hope so," Mimi said slowly, looking troubled. "I really hope so."

Nevertheless, during the next hour, Amanda couldn't stop thinking about Ethan. She'd been so intimidated by him when they'd first met. A major football and basketball star at their school, with a fabulously wealthy father, he'd commanded the attention of every girl there.

She probably never would have even gotten close to him if it hadn't been for a scheduling problem that had landed Ethan in her freshman theatre arts class. He'd made it clear from the beginning that he didn't want to take it, and was only suffering through it to get the fine arts credit he needed to graduate. Their teacher had not been delighted about his beleaguered attitude. She no doubt felt if she could change Ethan's attitude she could change anyone's. She tried everything under the sun to get Ethan to put everything he had into the class, to be an example to other students. She begged him to try out for a part in the spring musical. When her efforts hadn't worked, when he'd continued to refuse to even read for a part because he knew he couldn't carry a tune, she'd gotten angry and had begun humiliating him in class by giving him roles she knew he hadn't the capacity to handle. It was a petty action on the part of the teacher, and Amanda had felt sorry for Ethan because he'd been singled out.

But he'd handled it well, at least initially. Refusing to be embarrassed about his lack of acting talent and/or life ambition in that area, Ethan had done what he had to to get by in that class. He memorized the lines when required, and participated to the extent of his limited ability whenever asked. Although he eventually excelled in farce or physical comedy, he had continued to bomb miserably in anything the least bit dramatic. Given a part like that, he would look like he wanted to crawl under a desk and mumble and stumble his way through it. The other students in the class, amused by his inability, would usually get the giggles. And their overbearing teacher would get angrier and angrier.

It all came to a head one spring afternoon. The casting was still going on for the spring musical. Perhaps hoping Ethan might be persuaded to read for the romantic lead of *South Pacific*—and thus assure a healthy box office for opening night—she assigned him the part of the glamorous and sexy Emile de Becque, and for reasons unknown to Amanda, she selected Amanda to play the part of the down-to-earth navy nurse Ensign Nellie Forbush.

She'd been trembling when they started the climactic scene, knowing there was a kiss at the end of it. For his part, Ethan didn't look too thrilled, either. As usual, he read his lines with all the emotion of a stone. Amanda did her best with the poignant lines, but under such stressful conditions, she wasn't much better. The class was giggling like mad at their inept performance, the teacher furious. She stopped them and made them start over, swearing they would have to keep doing it until they got it right, if it took all week! Not surprisingly Ethan's reading of the lines got even more succinct, unemotional—to the point it was almost hysterical it was so funny. She was stuttering, continually losing her place. And only when he got to the part of the poignant kiss, did he put any real energy into it. And that effort, too, Amanda was sure, had been meant to be comical, to totally disrupt the class out of spite for what the teacher had put him through.

And it had been funny. The class had laughed and laughed as the hot, searing kiss went on and on and on and on. A mere freshman to his senior status, she hadn't known how to handle the unexpectedly amorous embrace. And it hadn't helped matters that, unbeknownst to everyone else in the class, she'd never been kissed before then. When he'd bent her backward and delivered that heartstoppingly ardent kiss, she'd been first dumbfounded and then helplessly caught up in the heat and fervor of the moment. She'd known what it was like to be swept away by passion. Only after their theatre arts teacher had literally pried Ethan away had Amanda come out of her fogged state of mind. She could still remember how mortified she had been that day, and how aroused.

And Ethan, well, he'd looked as stunned and moved as she felt. She would never forget the look on his face before they took their seats. She'd seen real gentleness there, apology, and a kind of vulnerable need that had let her know at heart he was as lonely as she. After that, he'd begun calling her, stopping by her locker, occasionally giving her a ride home or meeting her in the library. Within a month, they had considered themselves in love. He'd asked her to his senior prom. She'd agreed to go. And then the real troubles began.

But she didn't want to think about that, Amanda realized as she turned her car into the country club parking lot. Not when she had a meeting with Ethan and his daughter. The past was over. It was over to stay.

IT WASN'T THE FIRST TIME she had been in the Highland Park Country Club. Amanda's firm had consulted on a number of wedding receptions there. Nonetheless, her legs felt like jelly as she greeted the maître d' and was led to Ethan's table. Neither he nor his daughter and her beau had arrived yet, so she had a moment to compose herself.

There's no reason to feel like the poor little match girl looking in, she schooled herself firmly. Her black suit had a Donna Karan label and pure silk lining. Her heels were Italian. Her jewelry real gold.

But she still felt that way. . . like she was on the outside looking in.

Ethan walked in, his tall broad-shouldered figure unmistakable even after all these years. He moved with the same confidence and easy grace she remembered so well. His hair was just as white-blond, his skin lightly tanned, his features appealing and handsome in the boy-next-door way. She saw him speak to the maître d', then turn in her direction. Amanda's heart seemed to stop as his eyes rested on her. Initially he didn't move, either. For a moment he looked as stunned as she, and then he was recovering, striding casually toward her.

She used the time to pull herself together.

Easy now, she thought, I can handle this.

"Mrs. Stratton."

His voice was deeper than she remembered, soothing. "Mr. Holbrook." To her satisfaction, there wasn't a hint of breathlessness in her voice—although at the moment she felt strangely unable to draw air into her lungs.

He paused, gray eyes narrowing. "It is Amanda, isn't it?" A questioning note underlined his voice. "Amanda Webster from my. . . high school days?"

She nodded, aware of the way her pulse had speeded up and still refused to slow down.

He kept his eyes fastened on her face, pulled out a chair and sank into it with the casual yet economical motion of an accomplished jock. "I'm sorry I'm staring," he said, still drinking in the sight of her as his long legs straddled either side of the chair. He shook his head as if that would clear it. "I had no idea the Mrs. Amanda Stratton of Moonlight And Memories was you."

She smiled, watching him visually try to sum her up, and make the years that had separated them disappear. "That's the problem with a name change."

"Yeah, I guess." Turning, he signaled the waiter and, noting she'd already ordered an iced tea for herself, ordered a bourbon-and-branch. He turned back to her, still looking fascinated and surprised. She used the brief interim to take a better look at him. He had aged well. There were faint lines on his forehead, around his eyes and mouth, a certain rough-and-tumble quality to his face and skin, true; but he also had the supremely healthy aura of a dedicated outdoorsman, the firm, well-muscled body of a person who worked daily at keeping physically fit, and the inner assurance that came from spending nearly two decades in the work force and raising a child.

She knew from a recent article in the business section of the *Dallas Morning News* that he had spent the last eighteen years heading up the Atlanta branch of HCI—or Holbrook Computers, Inc.—and had recently returned to Dallas to take over as president of the family company. His father was due to retire in June. He had one daughter. There'd been no mention then of any woman in his life, but in the two-month period since the article had appeared, literally anything could have happened.

He glanced down at her hands, which were clasped together primly on the white linen tablecloth in front of her. His white-blond brows furrowed as he looked at her ringless fingers. "Stratton," he repeated softly, thinking aloud. His eyes lifted to hers, and held. "You're married, then?" he asked, no emotion readily definable in his low southern drawl. Yet she thought—hoped—she saw the barest twinge of disappointment in his pewter-gray eyes at the knowledge she might be unavailable.

"Was married," she corrected in a voice that was a lot calmer than she felt. There was a slight tremor in her hands, an airy feeling in her head. This whole interview, the ordeal of seeing him again, was exhausting her from the inside out. "I'm divorced now."

He nodded his understanding, the corners of his mouth lifting ever so slightly. "But you didn't return to your maiden name?" he pressed, seemingly as hungry for details on the time they'd spent apart as she was.

"I have a daughter." Amanda smiled, thinking of her lively teenage daughter. Seeing he was still puzzled about the Stratton, she explained, "To avoid confusion and make it easier on her at school and so forth, I kept my married name."

"I see." He paused.

Now that the shock had worn off and he'd adjusted to her presence, she had the distinct impression he would not have called her firm had he known she was the founder. On a strictly emotional level, she couldn't say she blamed him. Things had ended badly between them. Their families were feuding, albeit impassively, to this day. Any association with each other was bound to be awkward, at least initially. He also probably felt embarrassed and ashamed about what he'd done to her back then. She was no more eager to remember the humiliation he'd put her through. And yet . . . looking at him now, seeing what a nice man he'd become, it was hard for her to believe the past.

She'd been right earlier, she could put the past behind her. Besides, she needed the work and the revenue his daughter's wedding would bring in. Realizing he still looked uncertain, torn, she took charge of the situation. The sooner they got this meeting back on a businesslike footing, the better, she decided firmly. "How did you happen to call us?" she asked, careful to keep her tone casual.

He shrugged indifferently, the motion drawing her gaze to the gray Armani suit, the light blue shirt and the coordinating pure silk tie. "I asked around. Your firm's name came up more than any other. You were also highly recommended by my daughter's friends at SMU. She's a senior there." His words were easy, positive. Nonetheless, now that he knew exactly whom it was he was dealing with, he seemed to have some reservations about going on.

To tell the truth, Amanda had them, too. Maybe this wasn't such a good idea, after all. Maybe the past was stronger than they knew . . . she didn't want to get caught up in the emotional strife that had surrounded them years ago. Not with her family or his. And arranging his daughter's wedding would mean running into his formidable father…something else she hadn't given nearly enough thought to.

She was about to tell him it was all right if he wanted to back out when he glanced back at the maître d'. Amanda followed his gaze and saw a lovely girl coming their way.

As he watched her approach, Ethan's glance filled with fatherly pride and love. He looked back at Amanda and frowned, seemingly about to speak, then after another brief pause abruptly changed his mind. "That's my daughter, Heather," he said after yet another moment, his deep voice resounding with all the affection Amanda would've expected him to feel for his child. "She's the one getting married. And her fiancé, Tim, is with her."

Evidently in Ethan's mind the matter was set, Amanda thought. She would handle his daughter's wedding after all, if for no other reason than he didn't want to get into explanations of the past when it concerned the two of them anymore than she did.

Perhaps that too was wise.

"Hi, Daddy." Oblivious to the undercurrent of tension still flowing between her father and Amanda, Heather bent to give Ethan a kiss before she slipped into a seat beside him. She was cheerful and pretty with his Nordic blond looks, extremely outgoing and down-to-earth, Amanda thought, pleased to note that there didn't appear to be a spoiled bone in her body. Ethan was lucky to have her. And he obviously loved her very much. Her fiancé was dark-haired and handsome in a rough-hewn sort of way, and obviously very devoted to her. Together, they made a striking couple.

Amanda noted the two men didn't greet each other. Which was odd, she thought, since the two of them were soon to become family. She had no chance to dwell on the odd noncontact between the two men any further, for Ethan's daughter was already babbling on excitedly about her plans. She wanted to be married on Valentine's Day, and she wanted all her friends to be included in the happy occasion, which added up to an enormous wedding.

"That doesn't leave us much time to put everything together," Amanda warned, making notes. Five weeks to be exact. "Although it can be done if I put in a lot of overtime and you're willing to make occasional substitutions if the musicians you want are already booked or whatever."

"That's what I told her." Ethan frowned, looking vaguely uneasy. He glanced at his daughter. "You're sure I can't convince you to wait until June—after you graduate?"

Heather shook her head, her long blond hair glowing like silk in the subdued lighting of the clubhouse. "Not a chance, Daddy. Tim and I are getting married on Valentine's Day, no matter what. I promised him that when I said yes to his proposal...didn't I, Tim?"

"You sure did, honey."

Ethan grimaced slightly at the voiced endearment from his future son-in-law, then took his first—and only—sip of his bourbon-and-branch.

"Besides, I don't care if everything isn't perfect!" Heather continued elatedly. "I just want everyone to have a good time."

He doesn't approve of this wedding, Amanda thought, watching as Ethan's face quickly became impassive again. Although he is doing his best to hide it, he doesn't like Tim! The knowledge brought a certain déjà vu to the moment, because Ethan's father hadn't liked her, either. It was all Amanda could do not to shudder at the sense of history repeating itself.

"Tim," Ethan said with what Amanda was sure was a false cordiality, "you're a sensible guy. Maybe you can convince Heather it would be better to wait until after she graduates."

To Amanda, Ethan's carefully worded request seemed like some kind of test. One Tim was determined to fail.

"Why would I want to do that," Tim countered just as civilly, "when I don't want to wait to get married, either?"

"Maybe because you know it would make her family happy," Ethan said, his words heavy with meaning.

Tim shook his head in silent bemusement, not about to give in on this point. "I don't care what makes Heather's family happy. I care about what makes her happy. And I am what does that." Looking smugly victorious, he reached over and linked hands with his fiancée.

Heather looked like she wanted to strangle both men, for the way they were subtly dueling it out. Amanda shared her sentiments wholeheartedly. Not that she should have been surprised, she reminded herself firmly. Ethan's father had acted precisely the same way—autocratic, omnipotent, uncaring about anyone's wishes but his own.

"For now, the *romantic idea* of marriage to you makes her happy," Ethan amended with a cutting smile directed solely at Tim. "But what about when that dream changes to the reality of taking out the garbage and trying to stick to a budget?"

"I have a very generous allowance from my father that will support the two of us quite nicely until I get my MBA in June and go to work for Summerfield Construction. My salary there will also be quite generous," Tim countered, just as autocratically. "So we won't have a budget and we'll hire someone to take out the garbage."

Unconvinced, Ethan shrugged. "Fine. And until then?"

Tim spread his hands broadly. "We'll flip for it."

Ethan's gaze narrowed. "Okay then, tell me this. What happens when Heather takes her first job, too, with some interior design firm and is struggling just to keep her head above water, never mind make a marriage work, and you need her to go out to dinner with an important client and his wife? And Heather, who's on a deadline on a job herself, has to say no and the client is insulted and you lose an important job. What then?"

"We'd probably have a fight," Heather cut in dryly, annoyed at the question. "But all married people fight, Daddy. I don't expect things to be perfect. And neither does Tim."

Didn't she? Amanda wondered, studying Heather's rosy glow. As much as she hated to admit it, for fear of sounding aligned with Ethan on this, Amanda knew what Heather's father was trying to say to her. Ethan had valid points. Marriage wasn't easy. And the first year tended to be a literal mix of heaven and hell for everyone, as husband and wife tried to adjust to living together as a single unit and deal with the many, many compromises that entailed. Heather and Tim were both so young and in love they had blinded themselves to the nitty gritty of that.

"You're making marriage seem like a real grind. It's not that hard," Tim countered defiantly. "In fact, if you love each other as much as Heather and I do, it's probably damn easy to get along . . . a joy to share space—and a name."

Heather smiled adoringly at the romanticism in Tim's words, while Amanda did her best to hide a worried frown.

"I know on the surface it looks that way, Tim, but neither of you has ever been married—"

Having heard enough, Heather rolled her eyes and glanced at her watch. "Daddy, you promised me you weren't going to do this," she reminded him plaintively.

"I know." Ethan's mouth compressed grimly as he gave her a protective look. "But I couldn't help it. I have to speak what is on my mind."

So had his father, Amanda remembered unhappily.

"And I don't think the two of you are ready."

"Well we do. And now that you've said what's on your mind, and Tim's refuted your arguments successfully, you don't have to say it again," Heather retorted sagely. She glanced at Tim. In silent agreement the two of them got to their feet.

Heather turned back to her father, all sunshine and smiles, since she had obviously won her battle. She was going to do what she wanted, regardless of what Ethan thought or felt, Amanda noted, with something akin to respect for the pretty young girl. Heather might be indulged to a fault, but she wasn't weak....

"Listen, Daddy," Heather said, bending to give her dad a quick kiss, "we've got to run. We've got a party to go to over at SMU at my sorority house."

Ethan nodded, unable to completely mask his relief to be rid of his future son-in-law as he said a polite goodbye to Tim. "Call me tomorrow, first thing, Heather, so we can get started on this...wedding." He finished in resignation.

"I will." Heather turned to Amanda and took her hand. "It was nice to meet you, Mrs. Stratton." She smiled, for a moment looking so much like her father in his youth that Amanda thought her heart would break. "I'm delighted your firm can handle my wedding on such short notice. I've been to a few weddings Moonlight And Memories has arranged. They were wonderful! If mine is even half as nice, I'll be beside myself with bliss!"

Amanda grinned, appreciating the young woman's exuberance and enthusiasm. There were times when she would give anything to have that kind of unencumbered joy back again. But perhaps that was impossible at her age, knowing all she did about how hard, how down and dirty, life could sometimes be. But for Heather, there was none of that yet. Feeling everyone deserved at least one carefree period of their life, Amanda was determined to let her hold on to her illusions a little while longer. "We'll work very hard to make sure your wedding is everything you want it to be," Amanda promised gently. After all, that was her specialty, making dreams come true.

The young couple departed.

Silence fell when she and Ethan were alone again. Suddenly Amanda wanted very much to get out of there, away from the dynamic man across from her, away from the memories his presence was generating. She'd had a tremendous crush on him once, had pinned all her hopes and dreams on him—to disastrous result. She wouldn't let herself get involved with him again, not even the tiniest bit. Not as a friend, an acquaintance, nothing. As for the way he was acting toward his future son-in-law, that was none of her business. Nor would it ever be. In a hurry to conclude their business and get out of there, she said stiffly, "I'll need a retainer."

To her relief, he took no offense at her clipped, businesslike tone. Instead, he seemed relieved she didn't comment on his near-argument with Tim and Heather about the wisdom of the wedding date they had selected and were stubbornly refusing to change. "No problem," Ethan said, reaching into his jacket pocket for his checkbook.

Unexpectedly, the action reminded Amanda of another time, another place....of Ethan's father getting out his checkbook...the way she'd felt then and every time she remembered it...humiliated, disgraced and angry.

Bile rose in her throat as Ethan gave her a sweeping, curious glance. Knowing she couldn't stand another minute with him, for fear of what she might blurt out in her misery, she got up with a start, panic welling up inside her.

She could handle his business—but only from a distance and only under her terms. That didn't include taking a check from his hand—or from any Holbrook's. "Send it to the office," she directed crisply, hating the vulnerable way he made her feel and knowing she had to get out of there or risk losing her composure completely.

What we had once is over, she thought to herself, long over. She wouldn't let him dredge up the memories, dredge up the pain, dredge up the grief for what might have been, what could have been if only they'd both been smarter, older, wiser, kinder. It hadn't happened then and it wouldn't happen now.

Without so much as another word to him or even a glance in his direction, she walked off. And only as she left the club did she become aware of just how hard and how frantically her heart was pounding.

Ethan Gilbert Taylor

picking up minutes tucked into hospital bags I plan. and
sheating the vessel out forth those anguish me was, he wasn't to
everything the next an old wed Carlton on would be worse
pictures.

Chapter Two

Ethan remained in his chair for long moments after Amanda had left. He was still in shock, seeing her again after all these years.

She hadn't changed in looks, except perhaps to be sleeker, more sophisticated in terms of dress, hairstyle, makeup. As for the rest of her...she still had the same heart-shaped face and naturally curly strawberry-blond hair—although it was coiffed to chin-length now. Her skin was fairer and more translucent than he remembered, dusted with golden freckles. Her eyes were a clear light blue, her gaze direct and self-possessed now—almost too direct, he thought uncomfortably—instead of the shy and vulnerable gaze he remembered. As for the rest of her...she was still slim and femi-nine-looking, with curves in all the right places and long, long legs.

And she distrusted and resented him with all her heart and soul. Why, he had no idea. If anyone should be angry, it was him. Considering what she'd done to him...

But that was in the past. Years ago. They'd both grown up. There was no reason he should let *her* mistake affect the quality of wedding his daughter was going to have.

He could get through this wedding. And after that...he'd never have to see Amanda again.

The thought should have comforted him. It didn't. Why, he had no idea. Maybe it was because she was his first love, the first girl he'd ever dared give his heart to. Maybe it was because he hadn't expected her betrayal and because he didn't understand it even now. Maybe it was because she was still beautiful and, on the surface anyway, everything he had ever wanted in a woman. But looks could be deceiving. And that was a lesson, he schooled himself firmly, he would not allow himself to forget. Not this time. She'd hurt and disillusioned him once. She wouldn't get a second chance.

Frowning, Ethan glanced at his watch. He'd better get moving or he'd be late with his second command performance of the evening, dinner with his father.

"I can't believe you're supporting Heather's decision to marry Tim Summerfield," Harrison Holbrook said an hour later as his housekeeper served them dinner in the homey, masculine study in the eighteen-room Highland Park mansion where Ethan had grown up.

"I don't have much choice," Ethan countered as soon as they were alone again. "She's over twenty-one, legally able to do as she pleases." And that meant, like it or not, he was out of it.

"She cares what you think," his father insisted.

Ethan looked at his father patiently, for a moment seeing beyond the formidable exterior of the famed Dallas businessman—the starched white shirt and obligatory red tie, the carefully combed snow-white hair and sharp steel-gray eyes—to the loving father beneath.

How many times had he sat in this cream-and-deep-blue study, the two-story stained-glass window at his back, a fire roaring in the wide stone hearth in front of him, his father seated across the Chippendale table, since he'd returned to Dallas three months ago? A half dozen? More? How many times would they have to argue—about everything from HCI business to their personal lives—before his father accepted the fact that he was no longer a kid in constant need of parental wisdom and guidance?

It would have been easier if he could have just spoken what was on his mind, to hell with the consequences. He hadn't hesitated to do so in the past when the two of them had disagreed. But he couldn't do that now, knowing his father's time with him was limited. He was getting older—he was nearly seventy—and the recent onset of Parkinson's disease gave him tremors of the hands and head, stooped posture, muscle weakness, and a decreasing ability to move and retain his balance. Currently his father was on medication that had slowed down the debilitating progression of the disease, but the future looked bleak.

Ethan understood that his father didn't want to become an invalid, that he was fighting to remain as active and vital and involved as he'd always been. However, his father's renewed enthusiasm for meddling in his family's life was something Ethan hadn't had to deal with during those years he'd lived with his family in Atlanta.

He'd gotten used to doing what he pleased without suffering parental comment. Now, back in Dallas once again, he was struggling to deal with his father's attempted "guidance." It wasn't easy holding his tongue, especially when his father was so blunt-spoken, but he knew he had to at least try to remain tactful, since, as Dr. Newman had indicated, stress would exacerbate his father's condition, perhaps irrevocably. As irritating as his father could be sometimes, Ethan loved him, and wanted him to be there forever. Which meant he had to tred carefully. "I know what you're saying, Dad. I admit I have a few reservations myself about this marriage—part of me thinks they're rushing into it needlessly—but I can't stop the wedding." That didn't mean he wouldn't try and talk them out of it, as he had done, but his efforts had failed. There really was no choice now but to go along with his daughter's plans if he wanted to maintain a close relationship with her, and he did.

His father watched him shrewdly, disapproving of Ethan's unwillingness to get further involved. "Are you going to sit there and tell me you'll do nothing about this wedding . . . even if it means your daughter will end up with a broken heart?"

Ethan fought back a sigh of exasperation. His father saw everything in black and white. Ethan never had. "There's no way we can know that—" he disagreed calmly.

"Isn't there? The apple never falls far from the tree, son." His father took another sip of Perrier and dug into his delicately sauced veal. "We both know how amoral Phil Summerfield is. The man's been known to do anything to get work for his firm—lie, cheat or steal."

Ethan couldn't argue with his father on Phil Summerfield's lack of integrity. But Tim wasn't his father, any more than Ethan was his. In this instance he'd have to count on his daughter's inherent wisdom and solid upbringing to see her through. "Heather is a smart girl. She'd know if Tim was a jerk."

"Maybe not. You've sheltered her, Ethan. She's an heiress in her own right. Tim Summerfield knows that."

"Tim stands to inherit a fortune, too."

"But he hasn't been accepted here socially. None of the Summerfields have. Heather could be his entrée to Dallas society."

Ethan knew there was truth in what his father was saying, however snobbish it might sound to an outsider. Phil Summerfield and his wife Gloria were a loud, flashy couple who'd long been shunned by polite society. Thankfully their only son Tim had adopted none of his parents' often grating flamboyance. "I've talked with Tim at length about a variety of things." Tim irritated Ethan on a variety of subjects, but... "I don't think he gives a damn about Dallas society."

His father arched a dissenting brow. "Don't kid yourself, son. Being shunned the way he has must've hurt. It'd probably delight him no end to see the people who for years have excluded him from their A-list parties have to come crawling on their bellies to attend his wedding to Heather."

Ethan could see Phil and Gloria Summerfield acting that way. But not Tim.

"Add to that the fact he plans to work for his father. You know what an unsavory reputation their construction firm has."

Privately that bothered Ethan, too. "Perhaps that'll change," he prophesized hopefully, unable to realistically see any way Tim could work side by side with someone as unscrupulous as Phil Summerfield, and keep his own integrity intact.

"How could it change?" his father queried disbelievingly. "Unless...you're planning to set Tim up in his own business. And even if you did, what would stop him from doing business exactly the same way his father has? Or at least developing the same sleazy reputation?"

Ethan shook his head. He had his doubts, too, but he couldn't, wouldn't, interfere in his daughter's life. Especially not the way his dad had interfered in his. He had expressed his opinion, more than once as a matter of fact, and Heather had steadfastly refused to listen to him. If he kept it up indefinitely, he knew he would create a permanent rift between them. And that he didn't want, any more than he wanted to argue with his father. Knowing nothing positive would come of this conversation, he said wearily, "Dad, I don't want to talk about this."

His father looked at him with acute disapproval. "At least check into the boy's background, Ethan. Find out if there's anything unsavory you should know about."

"You're suggesting I hire a private detective?" he asked incredulously.

His father shrugged. "I can't think of a quicker way to break up this engagement."

Finished with his meal, Ethan got up from the table. This conversation was bringing back a wealth of unpleasant memories, none of which he wanted to face. All of which had to do with Amanda. Lovely, deceitful, greedy Amanda. "No. I won't hire a detective." He wouldn't sink that low.

"At least think about it—" his father said, trying to persuade him.

"No. And that's the end of it, Dad."

Obviously disappointed, his father sighed and moved slowly, his gait awkward, to the leather settee in front of the fire.

Not wanting to argue with his father further or risk endangering his precarious health, Ethan changed the subject to business. "I've been negotiating with the Japanese."

"And?"

Ethan watched his father settle on the sofa with the help of his cane, aching inwardly as he saw how difficult it was for the once-energetic man to get around these days. Dissatisfied with the outcome of his efforts, Ethan reported tersely, "There's still no progress on getting them to share their technology. There's only one group here in the States that could give us what they have."

His father nodded sagely. "Webster's firm."

Ethan nodded, knowing full well how his father felt about Amanda Webster's father, Lloyd. The two detested each other. "Webster's built up quite a think tank there since he stopped hiring his people out for contract programming and started concentrating solely on development work three years ago." Rumor had it they were on to something big that could one day mean millions for all those involved. Rumor also had it that Webster was almost out of the cash he needed to keep the new lab going. And that was where they came in.

His father looked at him with interest. "What are you proposing?"

"That we try and work a deal with them, maybe absorb them back into our firm."

His father shook his head in mute remonstration. "It'd never work. Lloyd Webster's too emotional—brilliant certainly, but no businessman. We need someone tough enough to handle the competition, someone who'll be a team player and make the hard decisions when they need to be made. That isn't Lloyd Webster."

Ethan was silent. He'd felt that would be his father's answer, although for the sake of the company, he'd hoped against it. After a moment, he nodded his agreement. "I'll keep trying with the Japanese," he said.

"You do that," his father said. "Because without a technological edge, the future of our company is very bleak."

"Yo, Mom. Snap out of that dream world!" Babe's merry voice interrupted Amanda's thoughts. She turned to face her daughter, who was studying her, and the mess around her, curiously.

"What are you doing?" Babe continued, then grinned mischievously, adding, "Or maybe I should ask who's the guy?"

Amanda blushed, embarrassed, as her fifteen-year-old-daughter draped her lanky six-foot-two frame across the white satin coverlet on Amanda's bed. "There's no guy. I'm just checking out my wardrobe, that's all."

Babe's light brows furrowed. "Why would you need to do that? You know all your clothes are in perfect condition. Did you gain weight over the Christmas holidays?"

Unfortunately, according to her scale, yes. "About five pounds," Amanda admitted, turning sideways to check the profile of her tummy and hips. The good news was, wherever that five pounds had gone, she couldn't see it. The bad news was that it was there.

"Everything still fits, doesn't it?" Babe said, around a yawn.

"Yes."

"So what's the problem?"

Amanda turned back to the mirror and studied herself critically. "The problem is I have a very special, very wealthy client I'm working with tomorrow." Heather Holbrook. "I want to look exactly right, and I've been trying to decide what to wear."

Babe screwed up her mouth in a problematic frown. "You've worked with rich people before. I don't remember you ever worrying about how you were dressed."

That was because none of the wealthy people had been the daughter of Ethan Holbrook. Amanda didn't know why exactly—maybe it was a matter of pride—but she wanted him to think she'd done well. She didn't want either Ethan or anyone in his family ashamed he had hired her. And maybe, too, she wanted to flaunt her success in Ethan's face. She doubted he had ever expected her to have her own business or be doing so well at it. His tyrant of a father probably hadn't, either. No doubt they'd heard of her business; they just hadn't realized the Amanda Stratton who ran it was the Amanda Webster who'd once been foolish enough to get involved with Harrison Holbrook's only son.

Amanda turned sideways and studied her silhouette in the mirror. The navy Anne Klein suit was very sophisticated—almost stark in its clean lines. "What do you think?" she asked. Maybe with a single strand of pearls...her pearl earrings...her navy pumps...

Babe wrinkled her nose and shook her head no. "Too businesslike. You look like you're trying to impress someone. Either that or you're over the hill." She rolled over on her tummy and propped her chin on her upraised palms. "Go with something...I don't know...younger...sexier..."

"Babe!" Amanda said, shocked.

Her daughter continued dispensing advice unperturbably, "Like that pink Escada. You know, the silk dress you always wear when you're really happy?"

"It's not the season for it. It's a spring dress."

"How about the flowery mauve Ralph Lauren dress with the circle skirt and the white cashmere sweater you always wear with it?"

"Too...girlish."

Babe rolled her eyes and frowned. "If you're not going to take any of my suggestions, why'd you ask for my help?" she demanded petulantly.

Immediately chastened, Amanda started to apologize. She hadn't meant to take her own lingering insecurity where Ethan and his family were concerned out on her daughter. "Honey—" But it was too late, Babe had already jumped to her own conclusions.

"You don't think I have any sense of style, any panache, do you?" Babe rolled clumsily to her feet and moved to the mirror. She stared at her reflection unhappily. "You probably think I'm ugly, too."

Amanda was aghast. "That's not true. You're a beautiful girl." She couldn't imagine where her daughter got the idea she was homely.

Babe crossed her arms against her chest, her expression stormy. "Yeah, right. Mom, face it, I'm a six-foot-two geek!"

Amanda couldn't bear hearing her daughter put herself down like that. "You're not a geek," she said firmly, giving her daughter a stern glance.

"Don't humor me, Mom."

"I'm not."

"Oh, what's the use? I'm going to bed." Babe whirled and stomped past, her shoulders slumped dejectedly forward.

"Babe, wait." Resisting the urge to tell her daughter to straighten her shoulders and maintain good posture, Amanda caught up with her daughter before she could leave the room. Aware nothing could be gained from discussing Babe's unusually tall height—they'd gone over it before to no avail—she let that subject drop and concentrated on what they could discuss, without fighting. "Is everything all right?"

There were times these days, like right now, that she felt so alienated from her daughter. Oh, they talked, they joked and teased, but the truth was Babe never confided in her anymore. Amanda knew, intellectually anyway, that perhaps that was to be expected. After all, her daughter was in high school now. She was growing up. She had a close, very loyal circle of friends. It was only normal she'd want to cut the apron strings a bit. But it hurt, just the same, being shut out of her daughter's life. Especially at such a critical time of her development.

"Sure. Everything's fine." Babe shoved her hands into the pockets of her sweatpants, looking decidedly unladylike. "Why wouldn't it be?"

"You seem down."

"Too much homework."

"Is that all?"

Babe's eyes darkened. For a moment, she seemed so vulnerable, so young, so in need of a mother. And then, as had happened so many times lately, her expression became closed and unreadable.

"Yeah. I can handle it. I better get back to my reading, though. I'm supposed to have the first fifty pages of *Silas Marner* read by tomorrow and I've only managed the first thirty so far." She slipped out as unexpectedly as she'd come in.

Amanda stared after her, wishing she could do or say more, yet knowing she had to be patient. Babe would talk to her when she was ready, and not before.

Amanda spent the rest of the evening trying on clothes. Finally, after much hemming and hawing, she decided on a cream-colored silk-jersey dress by Ralph Lauren. The long dolman sleeves, turtleneck and calf-length skirt presented a cool sophistication. The wide alligator belt hugging her waist would be her only adornment.

At six the next morning, she slipped out of the house and headed for Neiman's. The saleswoman was waiting for her in the bridal salon promptly at seven, as they had arranged, although the store would not open to the public for three more hours. Ethan wanted his daughter to be able to try on wedding gowns in privacy.

"Heather here yet?" he asked, when he came in moments later.

Amanda shook her head no. She had expected the two of them to come in together. "Is she coming from school?"

Ethan nodded. The saleswoman appeared, silver tray in hand. She poured coffee and offered croissants. Ethan accepted both and sat down on one of the sofas. To Amanda's relief—she would have preferred not to spend any time alone with Ethan, period—Heather arrived soon after. They got straight to work. With Amanda's help, Heather picked out several gowns to try on and went into the dressing room with the saleswoman.

Ethan seemed both restless and aloof. She also had the strange feeling he resented her presence there, why she didn't know. Nor was she sure she wanted to find out. Concentrate on business, she schooled herself firmly. Think of what the commission on this job will mean for Babe and just get through it.

Meanwhile, Ethan was pacing back and forth. "You don't look quite comfortable here," she noted after a moment, wondering if there was anything she could do to make him more relaxed.

He turned to her with a half smile. "I guess I am a little tense. This is the sort of thing my wife always used to handle."

She knew he had married. And not just anyone, but a lovely debutante from Fort Worth . . . just as his strong-willed father had predicted. There was no reason the thought of his marriage should make her feel so . . . devastated. He was the one who had suffered a tragic loss, she reminded herself sternly. She met his gaze straightforwardly and said softly, "I read about your wife's death in the paper. I'm sorry."

He nodded, accepting her condolences. Sighing wearily, he ran a hand through his thick white-blond hair, which was still worn a shade too long—against the back of his collar—for the nine-to-five set. "It's been hardest on Heather, of course. Losing her mother when she was just eleven." He shook his head in obvious regret.

Amanda wasn't sure why—maybe it was because she suffered her own share of doubts when it came to parenting—but she felt the need to comfort him. She moved closer, so there'd be no need to shout. Her heels digging into the plush carpet, she crossed her arms at her waist. "She seems to be doing okay."

His glance lifted. Briefly he seemed reassured. "Thanks," he said, smiling softly, and reminding her of what a nice man he could be when he wanted. "I think so, too." He paused, then amended wryly, "Most of the time."

There was a flurry of movement behind them. They turned in unison as Heather came out to show them a lacy gown designed in a Gibson-girl style, then, after eliciting comments all around, disappeared into the dressing room to try on another.

Watching her float off, Amanda smiled. Ethan had reason to be proud; despite whatever shortcomings he suffered personally where she was concerned, he had done a beautiful job raising his daughter. She was warm and delightful.

"How old is your daughter?" he asked her.

She turned to him, surprised he'd be interested. "Fifteen."

He nodded. "You and your ex-husband must be very proud."

Unwittingly he'd hit a sore spot. Amanda did her best to hide her resentment for her ex as she related, "Babe hasn't seen or heard from her father in several years. He walked out when she was three." With effort, she made her voice light. "The last I heard he was living the good life in Hawaii." And the two of them had learned they couldn't count on Alex at all.

"I'm sorry."

Amanda nodded, knowing as difficult as it was sometimes, her divorce had been for the best. In retrospect she realized she had confused the excitement she'd felt whenever she was with her unpredictable ex for love, and that she had married the Colorado playboy for all the wrong reasons. Maybe it had been out of a need for security, stability in her life, and maybe it had been to prove she was worthy of or could hold the attention of a man who could have any woman he wanted. A man like Ethan. Unfortunately the ill-thought-out marriage had been flimsy from the start. By the time Babe had been born two years later, any hope she'd harbored of being the loving wife her husband had wanted or living happily ever after had died. Yet stubbornly she had persisted trying to make the match work for Babe's sake. She had wanted her daughter to grow up with two parents. Unfortunately her husband hadn't shared her devotion to their daughter, then or now, or her commitment to their marriage. And though she'd done her best to make it up to Babe, she ached for what she couldn't give her—the unconditional love of a devoted father. The kind of love Ethan obviously had for his daughter.

She wondered if Babe would feel more secure now about her height, her potential appeal to men, if she had a father who doted on her, instead of one who ignored her for two-to-three-year periods.

Ethan was watching her carefully, an enigmatic look on his face. She ducked her head, aware he had been staring and that she had been too caught up in her own retrospective thoughts to notice.

His next question caught her off guard.

"What made you decide to become a bridal consultant?"

She shrugged, suddenly feeling as if she were being looked at with microscopic intensity. "Weddings are happy occasions. I enjoy planing them, ensuring everything goes off as envisioned." Doing so gave her a chance to believe in the happily-ever-after she'd never found for herself.

"And that's all?" He continued to watch her curiously.

With effort, she held his gaze unflinchingly. Why did she have the feeling he was putting her through some sort of test? It was she who should be examining him for signs of reliability. After all, he was the one who'd stood her up on prom night, not the other way around.

Gathering her composure, she answered his question. "It was also a business I could start without a lot of capital. Plus, I wanted a job with flexible working hours, so I could be with my daughter as much as possible. It gave me both."

"You've done well for yourself."

To her surprise, she saw respect, even admiration, in his gray eyes. "Yes, I have," she said softly, wondering why he should care now what she'd done with her life when he had treated her so callously in the past. Was it possible he had changed? They had both changed? The idea of them picking up their friendship where it had left off before the breakup was as tantalizing to her as it was out of the question. Like it or not, the two of them were still from two different worlds. That hadn't and wouldn't change. She had to remember that.

Heather came out of the dressing room, diverting their attention once again. Over the course of the next two hours, she tried on over a dozen gowns. None of them would do. Ethan grew first exasperated, then resigned. "Look, maybe you should consider waiting until June," he said. "That way we could have a special dress made for you by Priscilla of Boston. You could help design it."

"Oh, that does sound wonderful." Heather bit her lip in consternation, tempted; then shook her head, her mind made up. "No. I don't want to wait to get married. Tim and I want to be married on Valentine's Day."

"You could always get married on Valentine's Day of next year," Ethan said.

Although his tone was jovial, Amanda knew, as did Heather, Ethan wasn't joking. He really wanted his daughter to wait. A shiver went down her spine at the hint of parental interference and the unwelcome memories it evoked.

Heather tossed her father a wry look and shook her head silently, letting him know his latest ploy wouldn't work, either. Nothing would. "A gown isn't that important, Daddy; the commitment I'm making to Tim is," she said in a voice laden with underlying meaning before turning back to the dresses and inspecting them with a practical eye. "I'll take one of these. I just have to decide which gown I want."

"If you're sure—" Ethan said with a sigh.

"I am." Her chin set stubbornly, Heather disappeared into the fitting room again.

Watching, it was all Amanda could do not to shake her head. Like his father, Ethan just wouldn't give up. But unlike the girl she had been back in those days, Amanda thought with admiration for the young bride-to-be, Heather wouldn't fold.

As the process of selecting a gown continued, Ethan paced and looked increasingly anxious. "You don't have to worry," Amanda assured, assuming he was worried about making this work. "The time frame is short, but I'm sure we can manage everything, nonetheless. I've put weddings together in as little as two weeks. We have five."

"I'm not worried about that." His eyes met hers for a long second before he spoke candidly, one parent to another. "I'm just concerned that she's rushing into marriage unnecessarily. If I could do something to stop it or at least delay the marriage—" he paused, fighting some inner battle with himself before finishing with a kind of weary resignation "—I would."

His words shouldn't have jolted her. It was natural, even admirable, to want to protect his daughter from making a lifelong mistake. Amanda knew she would do the same for her own daughter, yet she couldn't help recalling what great lengths Ethan's father had gone to to keep the two of them apart. Even now she could remember how frightened she'd been when he'd sent his limousine to pick her up at school.

Harrison Holbrook's downtown office had been even more imposing and formal than the plush chauffeured car. And it hadn't helped Amanda to realize that her father had been fired from the Holbrook company just a few short months before.

Her knees had been knocking together as she walked into the senior Holbrook's office and took a leather chair in front of his desk. He hadn't wasted any time in getting straight to the point. "...You understand that the two of you are from different worlds," the senior Holbrook had said in his gentle patrician voice. "It'll never work. Better to end it now before you get even more hurt."

Only, fool that she was, Amanda had refused to end it. She'd been so caught up in her feelings for Ethan that she was sure they would eventually conquer whatever stood in their way. And then Ethan had ended it for her. Prom night, he'd failed to show up. She'd never forget the hurt and humiliation she had felt that night. What a fool she had been, she thought ruefully, remembering her pain. Of course they were just kids then. There was no reason she shouldn't be able to put the whole heartbreaking incident behind her.

"Amanda? What do you think?" Heather asked, jarring her from her introspective reverie once again.

Amanda turned. Heather was a vision of loveliness in an ivory silk-taffeta gown with beaded alençon lace. "I love it," she said, checking out the high collar and fitted sleeves and cathedral train. It was perfect for her.

"So do I!" Heather exclaimed jubilantly. She turned to Ethan. "Daddy?"

"I love it, too," Ethan admitted in reluctant defeat.

"That settles it, then, this is it. This is the one I want!" Heather said. She and the saleswoman went back to the dressing room, where a seamstress was waiting to fit her.

This time, Amanda went back, too, to make sure everything was done to perfection. It was, and, delighted with the progress they'd made, Heather began to dress.

"Everything all right back there?" Ethan asked nervously when Amanda emerged from the dressing room.

"Everything's fine," Amanda reassured him in her most professional tone. "Heather will be out in a second."

"Good."

Once again, Ethan and Amanda were alone in the silence of the empty department store. Amanda felt even more uncomfortable. And she stayed tense until Heather emerged from the dressing room, her coat already on, her purse slung over her arm. "I've got to run, Daddy! I'm due over at the university." She pressed a quick kiss to Ethan's cheek, said a cheerful, "Thanks, Amanda!" and was on her way, dashing toward the elevators.

Relieved that had come to an end, Ethan glanced at his watch, then said brusquely, as if in a hurry to be on his way, also, "I'd better get going, too. I've got a meeting in an hour."

So did Amanda. "There's just one more thing." She tactfully broached the subject she liked least; money. Her voice felt very dry as she said warily, "We need to talk about the overall cost of the wedding, set an amount you want to spend, whether it be two or twenty or one hundred thousand dollars." She assumed that he, as did most of her wealthy clients, would prefer to talk to her about this without his daughter being present.

At the mention of money, he stared at her, and this time she had the sharp sensation he was the one struggling with déjà vu. Why on earth, she didn't know. His look turned even angrier, his eyes a more bitter hue. She suddenly had the feeling she was on trial and that he was the judge who was ready to hand down a life sentence. For what despicable act, she had no idea.

"I'm sorry," he said abruptly, shaking his head as if that would clear it. "I thought I could handle this ... put the past behind me ... but ... if I can't even discuss money with you, it's obvious I can't. I'm going to have to get another consultant to handle this wedding."

Amanda stared at him, stunned. "Wait a minute." He had not only fired her without any prior warning or reason—so far as she could tell—but was acting as if she had wounded *him* in some very unforgivable, intimate way. Panicking, furious, Amanda blocked his way to the exit. "You can't just walk out on me like this, not without giving me any explanation as to why. What happened just now? What did I say? What did I do?"

"Think back about twenty-four years," he said tersely, his eyes hurt and accusing. "To another discussion of money, one I was kindly excluded from."

At the brittle sound of his voice, her pulse picked up. With effort, she held her ground. "I don't have a clue as to what you're referring to!" she said, though icy fingers of dread had begun to encircle her heart. Ethan couldn't know about that—could he? His father had promised he wouldn't tell anyone—ever!

His eyes narrowed treacherously and he leaned closer. "Then allow me to enlighten you," he whispered harshly, his fragrant breath warm on her face. "I know about the money you accepted from my father, Amanda," he said in a voice so thick with anger it made her tremble. "I know about the twenty thousand dollars my father paid you to stop seeing me!"

Chapter Three

Amanda faced him in astonishment. "Wait a minute. I never took money from your father to stop seeing you."

He looked down at her coldly, the suspicions he harbored etched in the grim lines of his face. "But you did take money from him."

She flushed with embarrassment. "Technically yes—"

His pewter-gray eyes glittered even more dangerously as he affirmed in a husky voice laced with contempt, "Twenty thousand dollars' worth."

"—But it wasn't for me. It was for *my father.*"

He shook his head in disgust. "You really expect me to buy that?" he asked incredulously.

Pain filtered through her as she met his accusing look. "At this point, I don't care what you think," Amanda retorted emotionally, having had more than enough of his doubts and his third degree. Picking up her coat and briefcase, she spun on her heel and stalked out of the bridal salon. He wasn't going to listen to anything she had to say, she thought, as she shrugged into her black suede balmacaan coat. And why should she care what he thought about her? What they had was over, long over. A crazy teenage love affair that was never meant to be.

She was nearly to the parking lot when Ethan caught up with her. His face still set, suspicious, he fell into step beside her. "Tell me what happened," he ordered gruffly.

She sent him an angry sidelong glance and kept walking. "Why? You won't believe me."

He shrugged into his buff-colored cashmere overcoat and kept pace with her. "Maybe I will."

She met his assertion with stony silence, aware they were almost to her car, and that he looked remarkably handsome in his Armani suit and tie, his overcoat open, the cold January wind whipping color into his cheeks.

He thrust both hands in his pockets, stopping as they reached her shiny blue BMW sedan. "If there's been a misunderstanding between us, it's time we got it straightened out."

The urgent plea in his low voice got to her as no angry demand ever would. Slowly she spun around to face him. She gave him a clear, direct look, letting him know wordlessly she wasn't taking any more guff from him for any reason. He was silent, waiting. They continued to stand as they were for a moment, assessing each other, rethinking their positions.

This wouldn't be over until he heard the truth. She knew that. They both did. She swallowed hard. She was doing this for her father. Not him. In a voice shaking with repressed pain, she explained how she'd come to see his father in the first place, how without any warning at all his father had sent his limousine for her at school, and then once she was in his office, had tried to talk her out of seeing him.

"And?"

"I refused, of course. I couldn't be bought off or scared off."

"I don't understand," Ethan said, looking relieved but wary. "The money—"

Amanda sighed. "That was another matter altogether, something we discussed only after we'd finished talking about you and me." She ran a hand through her hair, not sure where to start. Shaking her head in bitter bemusement, she continued self-effacingly, "I should've realized the next part was too good to be true. Your father wouldn't have offered to help my father without an underlying reason after the bad feelings that had passed between them when he was fired from the company. But he was so nice to me that day, Ethan, so gentle, despite our difference of opinion about what was best for you. And when he said he was sorry for what had happened with my father, that he felt badly and wanted to help my father with a loan to start his new contract programming business, I listened. I knew that he was right when he said that my father wouldn't accept the money from him and couldn't get it from any bank because he didn't have enough of a track record or sufficient collateral. I knew my father had been turned down to get a start-up loan, and he wasn't having any luck with any of the other banks he tried."

"So my father gave you a check for twenty thousand dollars." His voice sounded as hollow, as numb, as she felt inside, then and now.

Amanda nodded wearily, unsure what was worse, the anger or the despair. "Yes, he gave me a check, written out to me. And then I endorsed it and turned it over to one of the banks where my father had been trying to get a business loan—the specific bank your father told me to go to. Arrangements had already been made. They loaned him the amount he had asked for without ever letting him know where it came from." Because she wanted to cry, her voice and eyes were hard. "My father still doesn't know to this day, Ethan. And I'd prefer he didn't." He would be furious with her if he found out.

She paused, feeling exhausted by the truth-telling session, but curiously relieved, too, now that the truth was out, and she no longer had to bear this secret alone.

She studied him resolutely, some of her fury returning as she thought about how they'd gotten at this place. "How did you know about the money?" she asked, aware that it was barely 9:00 a.m., and it had already been a grueling day. She watched the wind toss his Nordic-blond hair about, sweeping it down across his forehead in soft disarray. "Your father promised me he'd never say a word about that—"

"Obviously it was a promise he never meant to keep," Ethan said grimly. "He showed me the check the day after it was cashed and intimated he'd bought your cooperation, that if I showed up to take you to my senior prom as we'd agreed, I'd be stood up. I was so hurt—" His voice caught; he couldn't continue.

"So was I." Amanda's voice trembled slightly as she met his eyes and the years faded away. "I couldn't understand why you didn't show up that night." She closed her eyes briefly, remembering the humiliation, the pain, the bewilderment she'd felt. A chill wracked her body, and shivering she drew her suede coat closer to her body. "My father was livid. He thought it was proof you'd been toying with me all along. And then there were all the rumors floating around school after that, the kids saying you'd only asked me as a joke. Only I was too stupid to realize it."

"And what did you think, Amanda?" he said softly, brushing a strand of hair from her eyes.

She shrugged helplessly, aware of the terrible ache in her throat, her heart. "I never believed in the joke theory. I just assumed your father had gotten to you the way he'd tried to get to me and talked you out of seeing me." It had been easy for her to picture that. Harrison Holbrook had been such a strong, formidable man—a man obviously used to getting his own way. A bottom-line person, he cared more for the final result than the means or methods of reaching it. "I couldn't forgive you for not calling me, though, and telling me you weren't going to show up."

Ethan let out a ragged breath, apparently damning himself now, not her. "I should have checked with you. But when I saw your signature on the check..." His voice trailed off once more. She knew how disillusioned and confused and lost he must have felt then because she'd felt the same.

Unbearably weary, she leaned against the side of the car. "Oh, Ethan, all this time I've resented you so."

"I resented you, too."

The silence between them was laced with mutual regret.

She tilted her head back to look up at him. "So what now?"

His mind made up, he straightened his shoulders. "I see my father."

At the hint of trouble, she tensed. "Ethan—" She didn't want any more unpleasantness. Confronting his father would create friction and dredge up the past again.

Ethan must have realized that, but he didn't seem to care as he continued gently but firmly, his face mirroring the determination he felt. "And then we get a fresh start and try to put the past behind us."

Was that possible? Amanda reflected cautiously. So much had happened between them, so much animosity still existed between the two families.... But already, old feelings were stirring deep inside her, pushing her to see where this new turn in her life led, to see if the vibrant chemistry between them—a chemistry she had felt with no other man—was still there. But she also realized that getting involved with Ethan again—even superficially—could carry with it an enormous potential for conflict on many levels. She didn't want to be hurt again, and she knew there was still so much separating them—their families' intense dislike of one another, their different life-styles, even the way he viewed Heather's marriage to Tim. She wasn't sure any of those issues was something they could overcome.

But in typical Holbrook fashion, he gave her no chance to debate further. "I'll call you," he said autocratically. And then was gone.

"SO YOU LIED to me," Ethan said furiously as he confronted his father in the executive suite.

Harrison Holbrook sat imperiously behind his desk, his hands clasped together, temple-style, in front of him. "I was doing what was best for you, whether you believe that or not," he retorted unperturbably.

The rage and betrayal Ethan felt grew. How could he have been so foolish, he wondered. "You let her be humiliated," he accused.

His father's voice grew blustery and defensive. "I'm sorry about that, but let's face facts. It would've happened sooner or later at your hands, anyway. She was too young for you, Ethan. Much too young. You were about to head off to college, and she still had three more years of high school to go through. I didn't want you breaking her heart. And then there was her father's animosity toward me. It hasn't lessened to this day. What do you think your chances would've been of ever forging a successful relationship with her?"

Ethan paced back and forth, feeling caged. "I don't know, but I sure would've liked the chance to try. Dammit, Dad, you've taken your meddling too far." At the irritation in his voice, his father's expression grew unexpectedly contrite.

"I know. I'm sorry. I guess I knew it at the time, but I wanted to protect you."

Protect him! He'd ended up hurting him even more. Ethan had never really recovered from that disillusioning experience. It had made him wary, distrustful. But he also knew, as a father of a twenty-one-year-old daughter who was about to make a lifelong mistake, what it was like to watch your child going headlong into potential tragedy and have to stand there and do nothing about it. His father had acted incorrectly, but he had acted out of love. Even in his anger at having been so cleverly manipulated, Ethan understood that.

"How did you find out about the check, why it was really given and to whom?" his father asked curiously after a moment.

"Amanda."

His father stared at him, speechless. "You saw her?" he finally bit out.

Ethan nodded, his feelings becoming incredibly confused as he thought of her. "A few times. Her firm is consulting on Heather's wedding."

His father blinked. "Well." A wealth of emotion seemed summed-up in that single word. Ethan heard resentment, astonishment, perhaps even a bit of grudging admiration for Amanda and her coup de grace, in finally revealing the truth. And then . . . nothing.

Ethan stared at his father, amazed at his lack of reaction. The man was incredible. He thought he could bend the rules to suit himself. But all that was going to change. "I'm still mad as hell at you, Dad," he warned softly. And at this point he wasn't sure when he would get over it. He didn't like being made a fool of, and the fact Amanda had been hurt in the bargain made it all the worse.

His father made a futile gesture with a hand that trembled. "I expect she is, too."

Ethan saw no remorse in his father's hawklike gaze, only regret he'd been caught. Frustration made him ball his hands into fists. "After what you did, how would you expect her to feel?" *How do you expect me to feel?* He wanted to punch something. He wanted to turn back the clock. He didn't know what he wanted, and if his gauge of Amanda's present feelings was correct, neither did she.

Silence fell between Ethan and his father. Finally his father sighed. "Well, it's over."

Was it, Ethan wondered bitterly, thinking how different the course of his life might have been had his father not interfered.

"Not quite," Ethan corrected him blandly. "I'm going to get to know her again, Dad." He didn't know why exactly, only that he was compelled to do it. And without any meddling this time. "I won't tolerate any interference from you."

His father surveyed him briefly, then shrugged as if Ethan's warning mattered not in the least to him. "All right," Harrison said, his voice quavering slightly as he spoke. "I'll stay out of it this time."

Ethan didn't trust his quick agreement, but he also knew he couldn't go around slinging accusations of interference before the fact. Hard as it was, he'd just have to wait and see what developed. But if his father made another misstep, this time—ill health or no—he would walk out and would never come back. He would not tolerate any more meddling in his life.

IT NEARLY KILLED HIM, but Ethan waited until five o'clock to drive over to the offices of Moonlight and Memories. Located in a black glass high-rise off the Central Expressway, Amanda's business occupied most of the fifth floor. There were half a dozen consultants busily working with clients. Amanda was on the phone when he arrived, and it was nearly fifteen minutes before her secretary allowed him to go back to her private corner office to see her.

She was waiting for him when he got there, looking both pleasant and efficient. "Mr. Holbrook." She greeted him cooly as she drew him in and shut the door behind her. "What can I do for you?"

Her businesslike tone carried a hands-off warning, which he just as determinedly ignored. "I'm not here about my daughter's wedding, Amanda. I'm here about us." About this incredible mix-up. He paused, watching her clear blue eyes widen as the meaning of his words sunk in. "I'd like to take you to dinner."

Her slender shoulders stiffened, and she looked at him like he had just insulted her. She moved gracefully but deliberately away from him, to sit behind her desk. "I can't, I'm sorry," she said, putting him off with a curt smile as she scooted her chair all the way in. She picked up a pen. "As you can see, I'm swamped."

He knew when he was being given the brush-off; he didn't like it. What his father had done to him had not been his fault. They'd both been victims here. They'd both suffered. And somehow, Ethan felt it was up to him, maybe because their mutual unhappiness had been generated by his family, to right this wrong. The first step to doing that was to end this cold war between them.

"I can wait until you're done with your work," he offered casually.

"I wouldn't want you to waste your time."

"It won't be wasted." He, too, had a briefcase full of papers in the car in need of his attention. Used to utilizing every spare moment, he could easily while away an hour...maybe two. Any amount of time would be worth it, if he could somehow undo all the misery brought on both of them.

But that wasn't all that was motivating him here. No, the truth was he wanted to know if his instincts were on target, that the electricity between them was still there, waiting to be tapped. Or if his elemental reaction to her was just a memory, built up over time, and exaggerated because of the loss. To do that, he had to be with her. Alone. When they weren't doing business or talking about the highly emotional subject of his daughter's wedding. But he could see Amanda was reluctant to grant him even that much of her time.

"A simple dinner, what could that hurt?"

Looking as if she felt all the more vulnerable, Amanda said with a sigh as she ran a hand through her hair, "It's not that easy. I have a fifteen-year-old daughter to get home to and feed, remember?"

Although Amanda's voice was purposefully light, he couldn't help but notice the underlying tension in her slim frame. She looked harried, wrung-out emotionally. Like she needed to be nurtured, held. "Tomorrow then," he pressed.

"No," she said, her blue eyes steady. "Ethan, you hired me to do a job. And I will do that. I won't see you socially."

This, he hadn't expected. Keeping his hurt feelings to himself, he merely lifted a brow. "Why not?"

"I've had time to think about what happened to us." Head down, she shuffled through the papers in front of her. "Maybe your father was right. Maybe it was for the best."

He moved closer, until only the wide, cluttered desk stood between them. "You can't mean that."

She swallowed hard and lifted her chin, her blue eyes brimming with determination. "I do. Our lives are very different."

He held in a sigh of exasperation with effort; she was beginning to sound like his father. "Maybe not as different as you think," he said tersely, annoyed she was playing so hard to get. Not as some sort of game, obviously, but because she really thought it was best they not see each other socially. Because she really thought that he might hurt her again.

Amanda bit into her lower lip, sidestepping an argument she was bound to lose, then continued carefully, "I have a daughter to consider, and all I can handle is just taking care of her and working full-time. There's no room in my life for socializing, at least not right now."

"When then?" He felt his impatience rise as steadily as his heartbeat. It annoyed him to know she thought he was a jerk. He was motionless, waiting for her answer.

"I don't know." She gestured vaguely. "Ask me again when she goes off to college." As restless as he was now, she got up to file a sheaf of those papers she'd been sorting through.

Determined to end this lingering angst between them, he followed her to the filing cabinet and stood to the side, watching while she tried to file the Jones folder under the *S*'s. "Your change of heart goes back to what happened before." She was judging him unfairly, and that rankled.

Realizing her error, she shut the third file drawer and opened the second. "How could it not? The pressures that drew us apart then still exist."

He watched her slide the Jones file in the appropriate place with quick efficient motions of her slender hands. "But we're older now."

She shut the drawer with a bang and turned around to lean against it. She viewed him with womanly exasperation. "Right. We are older now. Too old to be chasing a fantasy of something that might have been if, and only if, we'd been very, very lucky." Her voice dropped another husky notch, and for a second he could have sworn there were unshed tears shimmering in her eyes.

"What we had then was special, Ethan." Shaking her head in rueful memory, she pushed away from the filing cabinet and moved away, roaming restlessly around the lavishly appointed room. "You were my first crush, my first serious boyfriend, and I'll always cherish the memory of the brief time we spent together. Always. But I don't want to go back," she said, turning to face him. "I can't."

He heard the remembered pain in her voice and knew she meant it. "You won't even let us be friends?" It had never occurred to him she would react this way. Or that it would be so important to him that he regain some sort of camaraderie again, something to replace the hurt and sorrow that had lingered over the years. He wanted that chapter of their lives to end, and he knew it wouldn't unless they moved on, to a new plateau.

"No." She shook her head, resolutely, unable to completely mask her sadness that their lives had turned out so differently. "I don't see how that's possible, other than on a very cursory level.

I'm sorry, Ethan. I don't mean to hurt or offend you, but I know it's best to refuse you."

He knew from the stubborn yet proud tilt of her chin there was no changing her mind. Not now. Maybe not ever. Depression filled his soul and colored his low tone. "I'm sorry, too," he said softly, sadly, wishing she weren't so damn stubborn. "More than you know."

THERE OUGHT TO BE A LAW about trying to drive a car when wearing a formal gown, Amanda thought wryly. She had tucked her full skirt and petticoat up around her knees so they wouldn't get tangled in the gas pedal or brake. Now she turned her BMW into the circular drive leading to Ethan's Highland Park home.

The classic slate-gray Colonial was as elegant as she had expected. The black shutters, white trim and wine-red front door all gleamed with new coats of paint. The weathered gray cedar exterior shingles on the three-story abode were all in perfect repair.

Two tuxedoed valets stood at the entrance, ready to park her car. Amanda smoothed her glittering black-and-gold skirt with her left hand as she braked and put her sedan in park. No sooner had she stepped out of the car than the front door opened and Ethan emerged from the covered portico. She hadn't seen him in over a week, wouldn't be seeing him now if it weren't for the engagement party he was throwing for Heather and Tim. She had to remember that.

"Glad you could make it," he said, taking her arm as she started up the three steps to the porch.

Apparently they were on cautiously friendly terms again, although he'd made no bones about being annoyed and disappointed she refused to see him outside the demands of her job as consultant on his daughter's wedding. "Everything okay with the caterers?" Amanda asked, working hard to keep the edge of unaccustomed breathlessness from her voice. There was no reason she should be so ill at ease around him, so jittery.

Ethan nodded, his eyes skimming her face, lingering on her mouth, before returning to her eyes. "Come in and see for yourself."

He led her inside. As they stepped into the formal front hall, with white Carrara marble floor and sweeping circular staircase, Amanda caught her breath. His home was absolutely stunning.

"You like it?"

Amanda nodded, wondering why it seemed so important to him she do so. It wasn't as if he needed her approval on anything. "Very much." It was also way too rich for her blood, way too rich. And that made her uncomfortable. She'd made a very cozy niche for herself in this life. She didn't want to start feeling like Cinderella again.

"I'd like to show you around."

He looked magnificent in black tie, the snowy-white shirt gleaming against the soft golden luster of his skin. She was close enough to inhale the after-shave he wore and identify it as Obsession. Close enough to know she had never gotten over him, and maybe never would.

Feeling vulnerable again, unnecessarily so, she glanced away and saw his father standing next to the exquisitely carved fireplace in the next room. Although Harrison Holbrook's home was on the opposite side of Highland Park, she had known he would be here as a guest. Harrison sent her a glance, then turned away, dismissing her pointedly.

Amanda didn't know whether to feel relieved they hadn't confronted each other, or hurt at having been ignored by him. She did know she didn't want to talk about the past and the deliberate misunderstanding he'd machinated any more than Harrison Holbrook apparently did.

His back to his father, and therefore not privy to the glances and feelings that had been exchanged, Ethan took her elbow. Over the next several minutes, he showed her the billiard room, walnut-paneled library, lavishly appointed formal living and dining rooms, a solarium that overlooked the swimming pool and exquisitely landscaped grounds, his exercise room and sauna. They bypassed the maid's quarters in favor of the kitchen, where the caterers were busily preparing for the seventy intimate friends Ethan had invited to his party.

"Would you like to see the rest of the house?" he asked, his voice cordial but aloof.

Knowing there were two more floors to go, and on one of them was bound to be Ethan's bedroom, Amanda shook her head. Her own condominium was nice, and comparatively, very small, less than fifteen hundred square feet, but it suited her and Babe's needs perfectly. She couldn't imagine living in this mansion, never mind alone. How did Ethan stand it, she wondered, rattling around all these empty rooms?

"I'd better supervise from here," she said.

He hesitated, measuring her for a moment. "I'd rather you helped me greet the guests."

At his conciliatory look, Amanda felt a tinge of guilt. He was being so nice to her, so polite. And yet she wanted nothing more than to run away. It was too confusing, being so near to him again. All sorts of feelings and emotions had been dredged up. She didn't know what to do or say, and she hated feeling so inept. Worse, she hated the coldly dismissing way Harrison Holbrook had looked at her when she had entered Ethan's home. She knew if she got close to Ethan again, that was something she would have to deal with all the time. She wasn't sure she was up to Harrison's continual disdain. She wasn't sure she wanted to be up to it. And until she was...

"I'm not sure that's appropriate," Amanda said in response to his expressed desire.

"Maybe not," he admitted with a matter-of-fact shrug, "but guests tend to arrive in bunches, and with my father unable to get around very well and Heather off somewhere with Tim, that leaves only me. I have no one else to help me."

Technically Amanda knew this still wasn't part of her job description. All she'd been hired to do was arrange the party beforehand. She was just here tonight in case of any emergency, in case Heather needed her, and had planned to spend most of the night in the kitchen with the caterers. On the other hand, Amanda hadn't gotten where she was in this business by refusing to go above and beyond the call of duty now and again. "I suppose I could help out," she said at last, stifling her reluctance as best she could.

The smile he gave her reached his eyes. "Thanks," he said gratefully, escorting her back out into the front hall.

In their absence, Heather and Tim had arrived, as had countless others. "Amanda!" Heather said, rushing over, her long taffeta skirt rustling. "Everything is just perfect, right down to the canapés. I don't know how to thank you enough! And that dress you're wearing. It's to die for. Where'd you get it?"

Amanda smiled, relived to know someone beside Ethan thought she looked as terrific as she felt she needed to look for this evening. "Neiman's."

"Well, I love it!" Heather said, her glance running down the black velvet bodice, cut square across the front and low in back, and the glittering black-and-gold full skirt. "That color is wonderful on you."

Ethan looked at her approvingly. "I think so, too."

Even though his tone was casual, not intimate, Amanda's heart speeded up a little more. Defiantly she schooled herself not to take any compliment he might give her, however offhandedly, to heart. She wasn't going to get involved with him again. She wasn't going to let herself be hurt again, and any liaison between them would end in her getting hurt. She knew it with a certainty as solid as gold.

Oblivious to the tension flowing between Amanda and Ethan, Heather turned to her father. "When will we make the announcement to the guests?" she asked excitedly.

"After dinner," Ethan said, looking about as eager to do that as Amanda had been to help him greet the guests.

Tim looked at Ethan, a rebellious light gleaming in his eyes. "You don't have to do this, you know. Heather and I could make the announcement ourselves."

For one tension-filled moment, Amanda thought Ethan was going to respond in kind. Fortunately he got a grip on his soaring temper and said evenly to Tim, "I am doing this for Heather."

And not Tim, Amanda thought.

Tim glared at Ethan. Heather looked ready to burst into tears.

Not wanting a scene, Amanda stepped in. "Did any of you get any negative RSVPs for this evening?" The group looked at one another, shaking their head in a collective no. Amanda wasn't surprised. A sumptuous A-list party was too enticing to resist. "Which reminds me," Amanda said, eager to get away now that the tension between Ethan and Tim had been momentarily broken. "I'd better check the buffet."

Guests had been arriving in a steady stream. She estimated at least fifty people were scattered across the formal front rooms. Many of them she recognized from the society page. Others were friends of Heather's and Tim's who'd been asked to join the wedding party.

"Need any help?" Ethan asked, almost hopefully.

Amanda was about to reply when the screeching of tires and screaming of car brakes cut her off. Outside, car doors were slamming. Voices were rising. The front door was flung open.

Seconds later one of the valets followed a disheveled heavyset man in a rhinestone-studded tuxedo into the front hall. He had an open silver flask in his hand, a ten-gallon hat crookedly on his head, and a walk that weaved slightly as he moved forward. He was accompanied by a nervous-looking older woman in a beaded gown adorned with ostrich feathers that clung to her full figure. Both the man and the woman wore several diamond rings on each hand. In contrast to her companion, the woman seemed stone-cold sober and greatly embarrassed by the antics of her partner.

"Put that away," she hissed, elbowing her companion in the side.

"Can't, it's my liquid courage," the man replied cavalierly, then swung around to give Ethan a big grin. Conversation among the guests came to a halt as everyone turned to see what the ruckus was about. Tim looked very upset, as did Ethan. And then the heavyset man was striding drunkenly toward Heather, his arms outstretched. "Well, hey there, Heather darlin'. Welcome to the family, honeybunch!"

Chapter Four

A muscle worked convulsively in Ethan's jaw as he regarded his inebriated guest. "Mr. Summerfield," he said coldly.

"Now, there's no call for the two of us being so formal," Mr. Summerfield said, slapping Ethan on the back. "We're going to be family, Ethan. Family."

Amanda stepped forward, between the two men. Out of the corner of her eye she could see Harrison Holbrook in the background, an I-told-you-so look on his face. Recognizing the old man's snobbery for what it was, Amanda was even more determined to save the moment.

Swiftly she introduced herself to Tim's parents, adding, "I've been wanting to meet you. We need your input on the menus for the rehearsal dinner and the wedding reception. Ethan, you wouldn't mind, would you, if I absconded with your guests for just a minute?"

His expression still looking as if it had been carved in stone, Ethan nodded.

"Where are we going?" Mr. Summerfield asked.

Amanda linked arms with him. "To the kitchen, where my catering staff is set up." In an effort to keep him distracted and at ease, Amanda continued chatting up a storm. Beside her, Mrs. Summerfield sent her a look of gratitude.

Once in the kitchen, Amanda wasted no time having Mr. and Mrs. Summerfield sample three different kinds of coffee, plus a number of other dishes. As Mr. Summerfield got food in his stomach, he began to sober up. By the time Tim came in half an hour later, his father was looking and feeling much better. "Hey, Dad. How about a game of pool?" he asked easily.

"They got a billiard room here?" Phil Summerfield perked up.

"Oh, yeah. And you ought to see it," Tim enthused. "It's great."

The two men walked off together, with Mrs. Summerfield trailing behind them.

Heather came over to Amanda. "I don't know how to thank you enough, Amanda," she whispered, as soon as Tim and his family were out of earshot. "That could have been a real disaster."

Amanda knew. "Just see he doesn't get any more whiskey tonight, okay?" she whispered back.

Heather smiled. "Not to worry. Tim planned to keep him busy playing pool. And I'm going to go and get his mom, introduce her around, try to make her feel comfortable."

"Good thinking," Amanda said, smiling.

No sooner had Heather left than Amanda looked up to see Harrison Holbrook walk into the kitchen. He headed straight for her, his countenance tight and unreadable as he reached out and gripped the back of a chair for balance. She barely had time to brace herself before he started in on her. "I imagine you're pretty proud of yourself, coming to Summerfield's rescue like that," he began with characteristic bluntness.

"Someone had to do something," Amanda returned just as pleasantly. Although Harrison's underlying tone was deceptively civil, she felt his animosity to the quick. "I didn't want a scene."

Harrison frowned, looking even more unhappy, as he eased his stooped frame onto a nearby chair with a great deal of difficulty. "Maybe it would've been better if there had been a scene. Then Heather would've known what kind of family she was marrying into."

Amanda watched him grip the handle of his cane with a hand that trembled badly. She pitied him his disease-ravaged body. "You'd wish for your own granddaughter to be humiliated?"

"Better now than a thousand times later on," Harrison retorted around a gruff sigh.

Was that what he'd told himself about Ethan, too? she wondered. Was that how he had managed to lie to his son about the check he'd given her and still live with himself later?

"I heard you were married—and divorced," Harrison continued conversationally. "To the son of a prominent Colorado family. Into banking, weren't they?"

What was he getting at now, Amanda wondered uneasily. Harrison's voice might be pleasant, but his intentions were not. "Yes."

"You did very well for yourself. Financially."

Tension stiffened her shoulders. Unhappily it wasn't the first time someone had implied she was a gold digger, but she sure wanted it to be the last. "Money had nothing to do with my marriage. I married my husband because I loved him." Or thought I did.

"Ethan married for love, too—a woman from a similar background." Harrison spoke as if underlining every word. "They were very happy together. In a large part, I think, because they did have so much in common in the way they were both reared, and so forth. Perhaps, had you married someone whose life experiences more closely mirrored your own, Amanda, your marriage would've lasted, too."

He was getting his message through loud and clear; she wasn't good enough for his son.

"A shame your marriage had to end, though. Divorce is so ugly."

She couldn't miss the note of disdain, or the none-too-subtle warning to stay far away from his only son. She determined not to let him see how much that rankled. "Mine was very civilized," she countered conversationally with a pleasantness she couldn't begin to really feel. Years before, she would've run from a confrontation like this. Not anymore. The years running her own business had taught her that she could hold her own with people like Harrison anytime.

Harrison nodded, not bothering to mask his surprise at her strength in light of his constant badgering. "Well, good. I know how conservative a man my son is, how fiercely he loves his only daughter. He wouldn't want any hint of unpleasantness to touch Heather or her wedding."

Amanda met his gaze and said bluntly, meaning it, "I don't, either." Furthermore, she was really beginning to detest Ethan's father.

"In that case," Harrison continued smoothly, as if he had every hope of gaining her cooperation, "perhaps you would be willing to step down from this job, let another firm handle it. Or at least have one of your assistants work with Ethan."

"I can't do that." *I won't do that. I need this job for my firm. Furthermore, absolutely no one could tell her what she could or could not do.*

Harrison's eyes darkened. "Surely you can see it's not going to be easy or comfortable for Ethan, having you here all the time."

It wasn't easy for her, either, especially with Harrison around. But the job was a good one, and she wanted the money the work would bring into her firm. "He seems to be handling it," she countered smoothly.

"On the surface, but you're aware, of course, had he known who you were, he never would have hired your firm in the first place. He would have gone with another wedding consultant. He stayed with you only to avoid having to make explanations to Heather."

Amanda knew there was a grain of truth in what Harrison was saying about his son, but she also knew Ethan had a mind of his own. If he had wanted to fire her, he would've done so. It was just that simple.

Unable to hold on to her flaring temper any longer, she retorted, "Our avoiding each other would never have been necessary if you hadn't told him those lies about me. How could you say I accepted money to stop seeing him?" Amanda demanded furiously.

Harrison's face turned white then red before he responded civilly, "I thought I was doing the right thing!"

Like Ethan was doing the right thing by continually trying to circumvent Heather's relationship to Tim, Amanda thought contemptuously. "A lie is a lie, Mr. Harrison."

"And you can't make a silk dress out of cotton."

Silence fell between them as Amanda's breath halted in her chest. "Ethan understands that now."

Amanda felt the double-bladed insult as sharply as a hard slap in the face. "I don't see the point in this," she said between tightly clenched teeth, wanting nothing more than to get away from him.

Harrison latched on to her wrist and wouldn't let go. "I heard you out. Now it's time for you to hear me out. Ethan has a conscience. When he sees an injustice or something he perceives to be an injustice, he often bends over backward to try and make amends."

Amanda shrugged free of Harrison's detaining grip. "So?"

"So I would hate to see you perceive his . . . kindness . . . to you now, as anything other than what it is, a way to make up for what he considers to be my affront to you and your family in the past."

Amanda held on to her composure with considerable effort. So now they were getting down to brass tacks. The check, the feud, the friendly if aloof interest Ethan exhibited toward her when she arrived. His father was really worried. Worried they might both rediscover the passion of their carefree youths. Only because she didn't want him haranguing her anymore did she relieve his worries by saying stiffly, "Our relationship is strictly business, Mr. Holbrook."

Harrison studied her coldly, finally coming to the conclusion she was telling the truth. "I'm glad," he said with quiet satisfaction. "You'd be wise to see it remains that way."

Or what? Amanda wondered, sensing an implicit threat behind the cool words.

"Dad—" Ethan walked into the kitchen, interrupting them. "Some of the guests are asking for you."

Harrison cast his son a glance over his shoulder. "Thanks."

Not feeling up to Ethan's close scrutiny after the run-in she'd had with his father, Amanda busied herself arranging petit fours on a tray. "How's Mr. Summerfield holding up?"

Ethan thrust his hands in his pockets. "Okay for the moment. Tim's keeping him busy."

Good for Tim.

He moved slightly closer. "What were you and my dad discussing?"

What could she say? That Harrison was determined to prevent something as innocent as a simple friendship from developing between her and Ethan again? Sure, she could tell him what had been said, but it would only cause a fight between Ethan and his father and subject her to even more harassment from Harrison. Pulling Heather's wedding together in less than five weeks' time was going to be hard enough, without adding further tension. As much as she would've liked to blow the whistle on Harrison, she knew she couldn't do so now, not without hurting Heather. And that she couldn't and wouldn't do. Enough innocent people had been hurt

by the continuing animosity between the older Websters and the
Holbrooks. She wouldn't subject the twenty-one-year-old bride to
it, too. "Nothing much," she lied evasively, telling herself her unaccustomed duplicity was for the best. "He just wanted to catch up
on old times and thank me for sobering up Tim's dad."

He didn't believe that was all that had been said; it was evident
in the tense expression on her face.

Nevertheless, Amanda knew now was not the time to discuss
Harrison's snobbery toward her—if there ever was a time. "If
you'll excuse me, I have a lot to do." Her back to him, Amanda
moved off. She didn't want to open old wounds. The past was over.
It would be better forgotten.

"YOU'RE STILL HERE," Ethan said to Amanda hours later, not sure
whether he felt happy about that or not. As attracted as he still was
to Amanda, he was not sure he trusted her. The tête-à-tête she'd
had with his father, for instance. He was sure there had been more
going on there than she had revealed, yet she'd evaded his question, possibly even lied to him about it. Why? Did she still think so
little of him, even after they'd cleared up the misunderstanding
they'd had years ago? Or was she just not the type to really trust
or confide in any man? One thing was certain, though, he would
never get involved with a woman who wouldn't open her heart and
soul to him. He'd had a sham of a marriage before. He didn't want
another one. Any relationship he had with a woman would have to
be full and complete. Only then would he know she loved him with
all her heart.

Pausing only to send a "Yes, I'm still here—unfortunately"
glance at him, Amanda stood at the back door, watching as the
caterers loaded their last truck. It was nearly 2:00 a.m. Seconds
later, to her demonstrated relief, the uniformed workers finished,
and slammed and locked the back cargo doors.

Sighing, she turned to Ethan. Her skin was pale beneath the
smattering of freckles across her cheeks. It didn't take a genius to
see she was shaky with fatigue.

"Well, I guess I can get out of your way now," she said, duck-
ing her head away from his assessing glance and looking for a second like she felt very unwelcome.

Ethan felt a pang of guilt for that, followed swiftly by increasing dismay. Her movements were fatigued and uncertain. "Are you

okay?" he asked anxiously, thinking she looked like she was about to faint.

Embarrassment lit her features. "Yes, Ethan, I'm fine," Amanda reassured him as she smoothly extricated herself from his light grasp. "Really. It's nothing a jolt of sugar and caffeine couldn't cure."

Or a solid eight to ten hours' sleep and a good meal, he thought. However, that wasn't what she'd asked for, or in his realm to give. It wasn't any of his business how long or how hard she worked, even if it was, like now, to the point of sheer trembling exhaustion.

"Maybe if I could borrow a can of cola or something—" she continued wearily, pushing a wave of her strawberry-blond curls from her eyes.

He looked away from her pale ivory skin dusted with golden freckles, trying not to notice that they went all the way down her neck now, disappearing into the bodice of her form-fitting evening dress. "All we have in the pantry is caffeine-free diet, nothing with sugar in it. But..." Striding purposefully to the freezer, he pulled out a carton of chocolate chocolate chip ice cream. Yep, this was loaded with caffeine and sugar. It would wake her up in a hurry and get her out of here in a hurry. He tossed it to her reflexively. "How about this?"

She caught it with a wide receiver's ease. She smiled as she read the label. Too late, he remembered that particular flavor had been a favorite of hers years ago, his too. They'd had it every time they visited the ice cream shop near their high school. But if she remembered that, too, her face gave no clue as she murmured appreciatively, "It's fine, Ethan, thanks."

He liked the way she said his name, so soft and easy. But he couldn't think about that now. Just about getting her out of here. Feeling hungry himself now that he thought about it, he got out spoons and dishes, then sat down with her at the table. As in years past, he noted her appetite was still dainty, his of truck-driver strength. Nevertheless, between the two of them, they just about emptied the pint of Haagen Dazs. "God, this is good," Amanda said, sighing after her third mouthful of the sinfully rich dessert. "I haven't had it in a long time."

"Watching your weight?" he chided, without thinking.

"And my cholesterol. I guess you're not?"

He shrugged. "Haven't had to, yet." With relief, he noted the color was coming back into her cheeks, some of her shakiness fading. She'd been right, caffeine and sugar did do the trick. He continued to watch her curiously and asked, "Do you always work this hard?"

She lifted her chin and looked at him with open defiance, as if daring him to comment further. "I've worked harder."

He lifted both palms in a gesture of self-defense. "Hey, I didn't mean to insult you."

She stared at him bluntly, still looking, despite his apology, as if he'd slapped her. "Didn't you?" she retorted coolly, lowering her gaze once again.

Hurt now himself, he said in a baffled voice, "No."

Still looking as if she didn't quite believe him, she stood and carried her empty dish to the sink, rinsed it and slid it into the dishwasher. "I've got to go. Thanks for the ice cream."

To his surprise, he realized he didn't want her leaving this way. Maybe because there'd been too much unnecessary animosity between them in the past. It was time they had peace. "About what you did for Tim this evening," he said, remembering with gratitude how gentle she'd been, how swift to react, how she'd done the right thing, "taking his father off that way—"

She waited, her whole body tense.

"It was kind of you," Ethan continued awkwardly, genuinely grateful for her quick thinking and even quicker action. He finished bluntly, "It saved us all a hell of an embarrassing scene."

Without warning, a challenging light came into Amanda's clear blue eyes. "Your father would've preferred there was a scene, that Heather see what kind of family she was marrying into."

Ethan had already guessed that much. It didn't help, feeling Amanda's searing disapproval about Harrison's attitude, though. "She already knows what kind of family she is marrying into," Ethan prophesized darkly, not bothering to hide his feelings on this. There was no point—Amanda already knew. "It would be impossible to be around Phil Summerfield at any time and not know, but she doesn't care." At least for now. He wondered if it would be different, once she was married, legally joined to that flashy, disreputable clan.

Amanda continued looking at him with frankness. "Is it their lack of class or their shady reputation that gets to you?"

"Both," he said flatly, not bothering to mince words. And he knew, whether she would admit it or not, if the situation were reversed, if it were her daughter involved with the Summerfields, she would feel the same. But right now she was comparing this situation to the past, sitting judgment on him. Nevertheless, he still owed her one for saving the moment earlier. If Tim and his father, or even Phil Summerfield and his father, had gotten into it, there would have been a real brawl.

At a loss for words, they regarded each other in wary silence. But as he watched her now, something else seemed to be weighing on her mind. Something that had to do with him. Again, his curiosity got the better of him. He wanted to know what she was holding back. "Why did you help Summerfield?"

She shrugged inconsequentially. "I felt sorry for him, okay? He's clearly out of his league socially here and—" abruptly she stopped and bit her lip, as if censoring her thoughts in front of him "—well, that can't feel good. His wife told me he rarely drinks, and never to excess, but tonight he was so nervous about coming here he couldn't help it. Then, once his liquid courage hit his empty stomach... well, you saw the results."

He studied her, picking up on all she wasn't saying. "You're angry with me for disapproving of his actions, aren't you?"

She lifted her chin in silent challenge. "I think you could be more compassionate, yes."

He didn't like the way she was judging him. "How would you feel if it were your daughter about to be publicly humiliated?" he asked, unable to keep the defensive undertone out of his voice.

She sighed. "I hadn't thought of it that way. I guess I would've been angry, too. But I would've also tried to look past that to figure out why he'd done what he did."

Silence fell like an unbridgeable chasm between them. "Tim assured me he had a talk with his father and it won't happen again," Ethan said finally, for lack of anything better to say.

She studied his reaction, again seeing more than he would've liked about what he was feeling, thinking. "You don't believe him, do you?" she baited tartly.

The knowledge that she apparently thought him to be every bit the blue-blooded snob his father was rankled him. Exerting the legendary Holbrook control over his emotions, he turned his gaze away from her steady blue eyes. "I think Tim wants to believe that.

Whether or not his opinion will bear out . . . I guess we'll just have to wait and see," he said as he moved to show her out. They both would.

In the meantime, he'd have to try and keep his distance from Amanda. His life was complicated enough right now. He didn't need to add her patent disapproval and the lingering unease generated from their badly ended teenage romance to the stack of problems he confronted daily.

"I CAN'T BELIEVE IT!" Babe said, dancing round and round the kitchen Monday evening. "I actually have a date to the Winter Fling, and not with just anyone, but with Billy Ferguson."

"Who's Billy Ferguson?" Amanda asked, getting the ingredients for dinner out of the refrigerator.

"He's this basketball player in my class." Babe took a stalk of celery from the crisper and bit down on it.

"So he's tall, then," Amanda ascertained fondly, glad to see her daughter in such an unexpectedly happy mood.

"Well, no . . . he's not really. He's only five-ten. He's a point guard, Mom. You know, the guy who brings the ball up the court. You don't have to be tall for that."

"Oh." Amanda knew next to nothing about basketball. Apparently her daughter was learning about it now.

"In fact," Babe continued, reaching over to get a carrot to munch on, "sometimes it's better to be a little shorter if you are a guard. And Billy's glad of that because he doesn't think he's going to get any taller." Finished, Babe's lips twisted into a frown. She lapsed into silence.

Amanda regarded her daughter affectionately. Clearly something was on her mind. What, precisely, she didn't know—yet, but she would. "Does it bother you he's shorter than you?" she asked casually. Given Babe's height, most of the boys in her school were shorter than she was.

"No, not really. Although I doubt he'll ask me to slow dance with him because of that." Babe's latent unhappiness increased.

"Well, maybe you can fast dance together," Amanda suggested as she slid several pieces of cooked chicken into the food processor and set it on chop.

"I doubt it, Mom. I don't think Billy knows how to fast dance. He's . . . well . . . he's never gone to the school dances before."

Amanda absorbed this information silently as she gave the noodles simmering on the stove a stir. It wouldn't be much fun to go to a dance and not dance. On the other hand, going with a date—even a nondancing one—was better than sitting home alone. "How do you know Billy?" she asked, opening a can of cream of chicken soup and adding that to her chopped celery and onion.

"He's in my honors geometry class. He's pretty smart, too. Sometimes we help each other with our homework."

"He sounds nice. I'm looking forward to meeting him." Amanda drained the cooked noodles and began stirring in the chicken and vegetables. "So, what do you wear to the Winter Fling?"

"A semiformal."

"Hmm. Guess that means a shopping expedition is in order."

Babe brightened up at the thought of a new dress. "Thanks, Mom. When can we go?"

"How about tomorrow afternoon, after school?" Amanda slid the finished casserole into the oven, then wiped her hands on her apron. "We can go to the mall and then stop by your grandparents' house on the way home, show them what you've bought."

"Okay. Sounds great."

As Amanda expected, the shopping expedition with her daughter the next day was fun but exhausting. They visited every store in the mall at least twice and tried on scores of dresses before finally deciding on a burgundy taffeta dress with a fitted bodice and full skirt. They purchased satin shoes and a matching evening bag, which would be dyed to match her dress, then finished off their trip by eating dinner at the mall's cafeteria. "Will Billy be getting you a corsage?" Amanda asked.

"I don't know. I hope so." Babe grinned enthusiastically.

"Well, then, you better let Billy know what color your dress is. You know, just mention it in passing tomorrow in class. And you might find out what he's wearing. You might want to get him a boutonniere."

"Okay." Babe grinned again, almost beside herself with excitement. "This is so much fun, Mom!"

"I know, for me, too," Amanda replied affectionately. Times like this she wondered where the time went. It seemed just yesterday Babe was an infant, and now here she was, going to her first formal dance. As expected, Amanda's mother was just as excited as she had been over Babe's big date. "Darling, the dress is lovely!" Amanda's mother said when Babe took it out of the box. "You've got to try it on for me!"

Although more than willing to oblige, Babe looked back at Amanda. "Is it okay, Mom? I know you've got that early meeting with Ethan Holbrook tomorrow, but—"

At the mention of Ethan's name, Amanda's father did a double take. Her mother was almost as shocked. Babe picked up on the unease among the adults immediately and lapsed into silence.

Amanda swore silently to herself. This was something she would rather they not have known. Not that she could blame Babe. She hadn't told her daughter not to say anything about it, because then she would've had to explain why she didn't want them to know she was working for Ethan.

"What's going on?" Babe asked, confused. "Did I say something?"

"No, honey," Amanda's mother said, still staring at her daughter with distress. Deciding evidently to let her husband handle it, she turned back to her granddaughter with a fixed smile that was not to be refused. "Now, let's go upstairs and see that dress." She touched Babe's shoulder, directing her toward the front hall.

"Amanda, can I talk to you in my study?" her father said.

She knew that look. His request may have been issued in the form of a question, but it was an order, nonetheless. "Sure." Feeling like a disobedient schoolgirl, she followed him into the tiny room at the front of the house. It was a cluttered, messy room smelling faintly of tobacco smoke. Her father's computer and books were stored there. She turned around to face him, and in an effort to get the upper hand in this conversation, made sure she was the first one to speak. "Before you get all bent out of shape, Dad, just let me talk. My reason for seeing Ethan Holbrook tomorrow is strictly business. I'm handling his daughter's wedding."

That didn't seem to reassure him much. "I see," her father responded icily after a moment. He stared at her with thinly veiled disapproval, a flush creeping up over his face, then shook his head silently, as if he couldn't believe how stupid and foolish she had been, in accepting a job with his enemy. "And how does his father feel about that?"

His smooth tone was no indication of calm, rather the reverse. "I don't see that it matters," Amanda retorted, her own adrenaline level beginning to rise. Her father was acting like she had robbed a bank!

"Then you don't know Harrison Holbrook," her father countered sarcastically, his eyes blazing with anger.

Watching him pace the room agitatedly, the hot color creeping up past his temples, she felt she was being sucked back into a miserable past there was no need to resurrect. She also knew it took two to fight, and there was something to be said for the ability to turn the other cheek. Especially if it meant preventing another resurgence of this old misguided personal war. She sighed impatiently. "Dad, this ridiculous feud between the two of you has gone on long enough."

Her father disagreed. His voice lowering to a steely rumble, he said, "The man hates me, Amanda, hates me! And," he continued sourly, "I admit I don't have much use for him, either." Compressing his lips tightly, he said autocratically, with an expression of absolute right, "I want you to stay away from him. The rest of the Holbrooks, too."

She stared at him, wishing she could understand the rigidness of his attitude about this. "I don't understand this, Dad." It wasn't like her father to carry a grudge. Raking a hand through her hair, she spoke in the calmest tone she could manage, "People have acted unkindly toward you before. You've always been able to forgive and forget. Always. Except with Harrison Holbrook. Why?"

Her father folded his arms against his chest. He clenched his teeth and shook his head, looking as if he hardly knew where to begin, there were so many ill feelings stored up inside him.

"It wasn't just a single incident that formed my feelings about this man, but years of working for him, struggling, seeing him cut others to the bone without a flicker of conscience or regret. Harrison Holbrook is a ruthless, single-minded man who doesn't give a damn about anyone but himself. The only thing he cares about is getting richer, Amanda, and he's never cared whose back he had to step on to get there."

Suddenly she found her heart was pounding. All her life, she had hated conflict of any kind, and the talk of this feud, seeing her father—such a steady, unshakable, genuinely nice man—so visibly upset, made her feel physically ill. A combination of stress and nerves assaulted her. And yet there was still so much more that she had to know, wanted to know. "Why did he fire you, Dad?" she demanded, her voice harsh and low.

Her father's scowl deepened. He straightened autocratically. "Because I refused to be a ruthless bastard, too. He ordered me to lay off half the men who worked for me. I couldn't do it. These were decent human beings with families to support, not numbers in some overearnest accountant's ledger. But to him that's all they were. Numbers. Disposable commodities. When I refused to do as he wanted, he fired me." Lloyd snapped his fingers. "Just like that."

She remembered the struggle that had ensued—the days when the family had lived on a steady diet of cereal and peanut butter, because that was all they could afford. "I remember how rough it was for us then." How they'd had to sell off their possessions, one by one, to make ends meet. The Christmas without presents...the day the bank had come to repossess the family car...

Her father nodded grimly, reminding her in a voice laced with pain. "We almost lost everything, Amanda."

Amanda gave a sigh of relief, remembering, "But you pulled through." And with her mother's help and the whole family's cooperation, they'd managed to hang on to their house.

Lloyd's face and body were as inflexible as any piece of furniture in the room. "Yes, I did," he agreed, an edge of righteousness creeping into his voice. "And when I got my own contract programming business off the ground, I made sure everyone else he had fired had a place to go, too," he continued proudly. "But they weren't the only ones who came to work for me, Amanda. There were others, top technical people who saw the way HCI treated its employees. They jumped ship, too. Harrison Holbrook blames me for that. And I'm telling you he will never forgive me. He's also a man who always pays his debts, one way or another."

"You think he'd hurt me to get back at you?"

"I think he'd hurt you because you are a Webster, yes," her father said firmly.

Feeling stunned and shaken, she digested all he had told her. She was able to see now why the two businessmen would never get along. But as for the rest of it, surely her father was just being paranoid. "What happened between you and Harrison has nothing to do with Ethan and me," she protested vehemently, knowing she was right.

Again, her father disagreed. With a great deal of dislike, he said, "Ethan is very influenced by what his father thinks. He always has been. If Harrison were to decide you should be fired, I have no doubt that's what Ethan would do."

Uneasiness sifted through Amanda. She had seen the way Harrison had looked at her the night of Heather's engagement party. She remembered what he'd said. She didn't doubt for a second he wanted Ethan to fire her now, this moment. But Ethan hadn't done so. Yet.

Didn't that prove something? Or did it? Knowing she and her father weren't likely to ever agree on this, she didn't bother to argue. "Dad, please. Can't you let the past be just that?" She knew she wanted it to be over, finished.

He shook his head. "I wish I could, honey, but the bottom line is I don't trust Harrison Holbrook or his only son. And neither should you."

Chapter Five

Amanda and Ethan's next meeting was held at Ethan's office, during his lunch hour. Heather drove over from school, and the three of them had sandwiches and coffee while they worked on pulling the details together. Unfortunately it didn't take them long to hit a snag—due to the absence of Heather's mother. Not wanting them to panic, Amanda was quick to soothe, "In cases like this, there are several things we can do. For instance, the duties of the mother of the bride can go to a grandmother—" Amanda looked at Ethan, wondering if that would be possible.

He explained both were deceased, so that wasn't an option.

She continued doggedly, "Or an aunt—"

He shook his head regretfully, his mood as gloomy as the overcast sky that could be seen out his corner office windows. "I'm an only child. So was Iris."

Trying hard not to notice how silver his eyes looked in the muted gray daylight, Amanda said, "Sometimes a close friend of the family can step in. Perhaps someone you've been dating—" She looked at Ethan inquiringly, wondering if he had any really close women friends, or if he was as aloof with them as he was with her, especially since the night of the engagement party at his home.

Heather shook her head, letting Amanda know unequivocally that wasn't an option, either. "Daddy doesn't date seriously. He hasn't since Mama died."

Did that mean he wasn't over Iris's death yet, after nearly a decade? Amanda wondered. Or simply that he, like herself, had little time for establishing a romantic life, when trying to work full-time and raise a daughter alone? Whatever the truth, there was no clue in his closed expression.

"What exactly does the mother of the bride have to do?" Ethan asked, helping himself to one of the large chocolate chip cookies the delicatessen had sent over.

Amanda waved off his silent offer of a piece of cheesecake and recited the duties from memory. "She has to greet guests prior to the ceremony."

Ethan shrugged unconcernedly. "I can do that."

"And she has to help arrange all the details of the wedding, like the flowers."

His expression became less certain. Nevertheless, he announced softly but firmly, "With help, I can do that." His eyes pinned hers. "You can help me on that, can't you, Amanda?"

She nodded. "That's what you're paying me for." The longer she stared into his eyes, the harder it became to keep track of what they were talking about. She swallowed hard and dropped her gaze back to the list in her hand. It took her only a second to find her place and go on in a deliberate, casual tone. "Usually, she pays for and helps choose the bride's trousseau—"

"Daddy, I can do that," Heather interrupted. She got up to take the piece of cheesecake Ethan had offered earlier. Resting a hip on the corner of his desk, she cut into the rich dessert with a fork. "In fact, I'd prefer to do that." She cast her dad a determined look over her shoulder.

"Okay," Ethan agreed.

Amanda made a note to herself about what had been decided, and then continued with relief, glad their work was almost over. "And last but not least, the mother of the bride hosts the bridesmaid's luncheon and attends any showers given for the bride."

Ethan looked less happy about that.

Heather put her unfinished plate of cheesecake aside. "Daddy, I don't need anyone there for those things," Heather said, after a moment, seeing how uncomfortable he was about being the only man at a female gathering. "You can pass on them. Really you can."

Ethan frowned, obviously not feeling that was an option. He pushed away from his desk and got restlessly to his feet. "Honey, I don't want you to be alone."

Heather shrugged. "Well, we could ask Charlene. She's always been like an aunt to me, and she was Mama's best friend."

"I guess we could at that," Ethan said.

Heather turned to Amanda, explaining, "She doesn't have any kids of her own or a job or anything, so I'm pretty sure she could do it."

"I know she'd want to," Ethan murmured, no emotion readily discernible on his handsome face. He looked at Heather. "Why don't you let me talk to Charlene first, and then if she's amenable, the two of you can get together?"

Heather circled his desk and threw herself into her father's arms. "You're really wonderful, you know that?" she asked in a thick voice.

He hugged her back, hard, and teased, oblivious to Amanda's presence in the room, "Keep telling me that."

"I will," Heather promised emotionally. Without warning, she had tears in her eyes. Ethan looked as worried as Amanda felt.

He regarded his daughter gently. "Are you okay?"

I hope so, Amanda thought. She'd hate to have the whole wedding fall through now. Especially when they were off to such a good start, planning-wise.

Heather nodded, swallowing with visible difficulty. "It's just…I miss Mama. I wish she could be here for this. She would've loved helping me get ready to get married."

Amanda's heart went out to the lovely young woman, as did her father's. "I know," he said softly, holding his daughter tenderly in his arms.

Amanda waited for Ethan to say he missed his deceased wife, too, but the moment passed and he did not. If Heather noticed what he didn't say, she gave no sign as she struggled to pull herself together.

"But I have you and Grandpa and Tim," she continued determinedly, wiping her eyes. "So I'm not going to feel sorry for myself." Without warning, she glanced at her watch. "Oh my gosh. Look at the time. I've got to fly or I'll miss my economics class." Quickly the three of them concluded the remaining business. Seconds later, she was gone.

"Sorry about the brief histrionics," Ethan said, after his daughter had departed. He turned back to Amanda, adding apologetically, "Like her mother, Heather can be high-strung at times."

Amanda began gathering up her notes and stuffing them into her briefcase. "You don't have to apologize. All prospective brides are overly emotional from time to time. It goes with the territory." Amanda paused, letting him know with her direct gaze she meant what she said. These weren't just polite disclaimers on her part. "She really is lovely, Ethan. You're lucky to have her."

"I know," he said, his deep voice resonating with the affection he felt for his child. He compressed his mouth into a frustrated line. "I have to agree with her, though. It would've been nice if Iris were here to see Heather get married. It would've meant so much to both of them."

She waited politely for him to pick up the conversation, but he didn't. She considered his vaguely brooding expression for a moment, then, her curiosity overriding common sense, not to mention all rules of polite conversation, she threw caution to the wind and asked, "You had a good marriage, didn't you?" He must've, if he hadn't dated anyone seriously in ten years. On the other hand, she'd been divorced for almost that long, too, and she hadn't dated anyone seriously, either.

Ethan looked up in surprise, the candidness leaving his eyes. "Yes. I guess we did, although our life together was far from perfect, as is most people's I suspect," he said slowly. He gave her an odd look, and moved nearer, close enough for her to get a whiff of his cologne. "Why?"

"I don't know. I—" Amanda began to feel flustered. It wasn't like her to get so personal with clients. In fact, never before had she impetuously asked questions that bordered on rude. "I guess I'm just curious because we used to know each other, years ago."

The mention of the past acted like a curtain going down over Ethan's eyes. Their unexpectedly intimate mood broken, his expression swiftly changed to one that was all business. Going back to his desk, he glanced at his calendar and picked up a pen. "So, what's next on the agenda for this wedding?"

Properly chastised and fighting a blush, Amanda went back to her briefcase and got out her own weekly planner. "We need to select and order the flowers. I've already agreed to meet Heather at the wholesaler late tomorrow afternoon, around five."

Ethan frowned and scratched something out on his calendar, and replaced it with a few precisely written words. "I'll be there, too, then."

Amanda nodded. "All right." Realizing she had been dismissed, she paused only long enough to write down the address for him and hand it over. "I'll see you then."

He didn't look up as she exited, merely said, rather tersely, "You can count on it."

I SHOULDN'T HAVE LET Amanda get to me like that, Ethan thought, as he prepared for his one-thirty meeting with his father. But he couldn't help it. Her question about his marriage had prompted a deluge of memories, none of them good. The sobering truth was if Iris had lived, he might very well be divorced from her by now. Certainly the only thing that had held them together that long had been their mutual, encompassing love for the daughter they had shared and their mutually privileged backgrounds.

Heather didn't know that, of course, nor did anyone else suspect the grim reality of their unhappy union. Mainly because he and Iris both had been so good at putting on a happy front for all the world to see. But they hadn't been happy, and he doubted they ever could have been.

But he couldn't dwell on that. And he couldn't worry about what Heather's marriage might or might not bring her, either. Right now he had all he could do to save the family business from going down the drain.

Unfortunately his father didn't view their problems in the same way. He was afraid it was a rift between them that was only going to get worse.

"Ethan, we need some creative geniuses at HCI. And we need them yesterday. If you won't consider trying to buy out Webster's think tank, at least consider hiring back some of our former employees," Harrison said gruffly, from the other side of his desk.

"You mean steal them back, don't you?" Ethan countered dryly.

His father's steely glance narrowed. "I mean offer them contracts they can't refuse."

Ethan struggled to remember his father was ill now, and that any stress would exacerbate his condition. "You know what kind of war that would create?" he asked softly.

His father lifted a trembling hand in an uncaring manner and slowly, painstakingly, lowered it again. "This is business, Ethan. Survival of the fittest."

"Meaning you don't care if you tick Webster—" and his family, Ethan mentally added "—off royally."

His father fumbled on his desk for his glass of water. "He didn't care how 'ticked off' I got when he stole my best men from me years ago."

No one was more aware of how that had hurt their company than Ethan, but that didn't mean he wanted old grievances to cause new problems. Especially with the details of this wedding still to be worked out, with Heather's happiness on the line, too. Dammit, she ought to have the right to get married without World War III erupting around her. In all likelihood, problems would start for her and Tim as soon as their vows were said. Surely they should have a little peace now! Dredging up every bit of patience he had left, he reminded his father, "Dad, I know you think you have every right to steal those employees back, and maybe you do, but if you do that, this feud will start up all over again." The tension would be unbearable.

"I've got a news flash for you, son. The feud never died."

"Maybe it should have," he groused.

His father shook his head in obvious exasperation. "What's gotten into you?" he demanded unhappily. Then more shrewdly yet, he continued in the same emotionally annihilating tone, "It's Webster's daughter, Amanda, isn't it? She's turned your head again—"

"Don't be ridiculous," Ethan said gruffly. "There's nothing between us." Nor could there ever be. Not when she couldn't even bring herself to level with him about a single unpleasant conversation with his father.

And there were other reasons, too, he admitted to himself silently. In the years since they had been apart, she'd changed. Grown colder, more remote, somehow. And if there was anything he didn't want it was a liaison with a woman who deliberately cut herself off from her emotions or shut him out. He'd had that with Iris. He wouldn't suffer through a relationship like that again.

His father continued to study him relentlessly. "We need a think tank of our own, Ethan. One that is comparable to the Webster Group. If we're to survive at all, we've got to develop and implement the new technology in our computers as fast as the foreign competition."

"I'll step up the search for competent technical people," Ethan said.

"You wouldn't have to search if you'd just consider luring some of Webster's key people."

Ethan knew his father would like that, would consider it final justice. But he couldn't, wouldn't, be a part of such underhanded tactics. There'd been too much animosity in the past between the two families. He wouldn't further the feud.

"First of all, I doubt any of Webster's people would jump at an offer from us—"

"Of course they would," his father retorted confidently. "Everyone has their price, it's just a matter of finding it, then making an offer they can't refuse."

Ethan didn't agree with that, but he knew there was no sense arguing with his father; he wouldn't change his mind. His father believed that in business, the ability to make the hard, even unpopular, decisions enabled one to survive. He'd never shied away from them, and never would. Whereas Ethan had always been endowed with his mother's unceasing compassion. He knew what had to be done, and because he was his father's son, he could do it. But he also felt the ramifications of his actions; his father didn't. And that, he sensed, was something that also wouldn't change. "I still plan to look outside the Webster Group for new-hires," he informed his father. Unlike you, I have to live with my conscience.

Harrison made a dissenting sound, then finally gave up. "I don't care where you get them so long as you find some geniuses, and do it soon."

Ethan knew that, too.

"So you see it might be a little awkward if we don't have a woman friend to kind of step in and help out where Heather's mother would've," Ethan explained to Charlene Davenport later the same evening. He had stopped by her University Park home after dinner. Despite frequent invitations, it had been months since he'd been there, and then only briefly to attend a large party in her honor.

"Of course I'd be delighted to help out," Charlene said, looking every bit the pampered heiress and recent divorcée she was, in her short, two-piece white suit and seamed stockings. She went to her desk and picked up a white leather-bound notebook embossed with her initials. "Now, who did you say the consultant firm was?" Her stiletto heels clicked as she crossed the marble floor and sat down beside him on the sofa. Her short silk skirt rose up slightly as she sat down and crossed her legs at the knees, then placed her gold-trimmed notebook on her lap.

Ethan listened to the jangle of Charlene's gold bracelets as she began to write "Notes for Heather's Wedding" with large, beautiful strokes across the top of the page.

"Moonlight and Memories." He waited for her to get that down, before adding, "Amanda Stratton is handling all the details."

Charlene sat back abruptly, and with a well-manicured hand, pushed the fringe of frosted blond hair from her heavily made-up eyes. "Oh, I think I know their work!" she exclaimed with all the bubbly enthusiasm of a proper southern belle. "I attended a wedding last year that I think was done by them. It was wonderful!" She went back to writing on her pad. "How'd you happen to decide on them?" she asked, knowing full well that when he'd been married to Iris, Iris had handled all the details of their social engagements.

Ethan regarded the woman beside him with amusement. It was clear from her overly tolerant look that Charlene didn't credit him with enough brains or experience to be able to hire someone decent on his own. "Heather had heard the firm did wonderful work and wanted to try them. I said okay. So far, it's worked out fine."

Charlene paused. "You like this Amanda Stratton then?"

"Yes."

"Hmm." Charlene made a teasing moue, then batted her eyelashes flirtatiously at him. "Well, my next question is obvious. Is she pretty?"

Knowing the only thing that would shut Charlene up was an answer to her question, Ethan said, "Yes, as a matter of fact, she is." Very. But beauty wasn't everything, as he had learned long ago.

"Single, too, I suppose?"

"Yes."

"How old?"

His exasperation growing, Ethan sighed and did some rapid calculating. Amanda was three years younger than he, which would make her... "Thirty-nine, I think. Why all the questions?"

Charlene smiled and shrugged. "Just satisfying my womanly curiosity about this consultant you've hired, that's all. I might want to use her services some day, or recommend them to a friend, although I am curious. How do you know precisely how old she is? I mean, that isn't a fact that is usually divulged to an employer."

Ignoring the hint of snobbery in her voice for Heather's sake, Ethan said bluntly, "We went to high school together."

"That's strange. I don't believe I know her, and I thought I knew all of your and Iris's friends."

Amanda hadn't been Iris's friend, nor was it likely they would've been even now, Ethan thought.

"Is Amanda's family still in Dallas?" Charlene continued, ignoring Ethan's silence.

"I'm not sure, to tell you the truth. I think her folks live in Richardson now, although she and her daughter have a condo just north of here."

Charlene retained her cordial tone. "She's not a part of the old guard then?" She doesn't live in Highland or University Park?

"No."

"That's too bad."

Again, Ethan detected the faint hint of snobbery behind the barrage of questions and ignored it. It wasn't Charlene's fault she thought that way. Like Iris, she had been reared to mingle only with people of a similar background. She never ventured outside her sphere, except to shop. The upper middle class was foreign to her. Thank God his father, knowing Ethan would one day have to run HCI from factory to boardroom, had possessed the sense to send him to a public high school rather than the insulated private institutions Charlene and Iris had attended. His background there allowed him to blend into the mainstream, and enabled him to meet Amanda. Beautiful Amanda.

Her mind on the task again now that her curiosity had been satisfied, Charlene went back to writing in her notebook. "So when do you want me to get started?"

"Why don't you give Heather a call tomorrow, let her know you're going to help out? Then we'll go from there." Ethan knew they didn't need much help from Charlene, only her presence at the all-girl gatherings like the bridal luncheon and the barrage of wedding showers Heather's friends were planning to give her.

"Will do. And Ethan," Charlene said, as she walked him to the door, after her attempts to entice him to stay later had failed. "Do call me if you need anything—anything at all."

Was it his imagination or was there more in that invitation than had been customary in the past? he wondered. Figuring it had to be a misreading on his part, he shook off the suspicion she was interested in him now in an entirely different way than she had been in the past. They'd been family friends far too long to think about anything beyond the platonic. "Thanks, Charlene. I will." Cordially she showed him out.

Ethan returned home to finish going over the help wanted ad they were planning to run in all the national computer magazines. He had it placed by noon the next day and was already sifting through a stack of resumes Compu-Job-Search had sent over. By four, he'd set up several interviews.

"It's a start," his father said when informed of Ethan's actions. "But it'd be a hell of a lot faster to go over and raid the Webster Group's talent."

Ethan fought back a retort. Would nothing ever change?

"READY TO LOOK at flowers?" Amanda asked the following day.

He nodded, looking less than thrilled. "Sure."

"Do I detect a note of reservation in your voice?" Amanda teased, not really surprised by his reluctance, although she loved the florist's warehouse. Spacious and cool year-round, it was filled with every variety imaginable of blossoms and greenery. The air was redolent with the delicate scent of new blossoms.

"I just don't know how much help I'm going to be," Ethan said, looking even more masculine than usual in the feminine surroundings. "To me, one bunch of flowers is the same as the next. Not so to my daughter—which probably means this little chore will take forever."

"You can skip it if you like," Amanda offered, although personally she'd hate to see him duck out on it. To truly appreciate the wedding, as well as understand the costs, he needed to be in on the planning of it every step of the way. Or at least someone from his family did.

"No. Heather needs me," he said firmly. "So I'll stay here."

Exactly what her response would've been had she been the father and Babe the bride-to-be, Amanda thought, pleased to see his devotion to his daughter.

Fortunately Heather arrived soon after, sparing them any further awkward attempts at conversation. "Daddy, hi!" Heather said.

"Hello, Ethan," the expertly coiffed society matron beside Heather chimed in. "Heather invited me to tag along." She stepped toward Amanda, bejeweled hand extended. "I don't believe we've met." Introductions were made cursorily. "Ethan tells me the two of you went to high school together," Charlene Davenport continued.

Amanda fought her uneasiness; she had the funny feeling this sophisticate was staking out her territory where Ethan was concerned. "Uh, yes, we did."

"Daddy, you didn't tell me that!" Heather exclaimed, beginning to look very excited. "Were the two of you in the same class?"

Amanda blushed at the thought of what might come out if this conversation were to continue unabated. "No, we were several years apart," Ethan answered her.

Anticipating Heather's next question, Amanda added, "We had a fine arts class together. It was pretty mundane, actually."

Heather looked from Ethan to Amanda and back again, not buying the "mundane" remark for one moment, while beside her, Charlene continued to look very intrigued about their past relationship as well. "Did the two of you ever go out?" Heather asked.

Looking as if he felt as uncomfortable as she, Ethan avoided the question altogether and said, "I thought we were here to pick out flowers, not take a trip down memory lane."

"You did date then, didn't you?" Heather continued, looking at Amanda, then back to Ethan. Despite her father's impatient glare, she was not the least bit daunted. "How sweet. What happened?"

"I went away to college," Ethan said tersely.

"And we lost touch," Amanda put in pleasantly. "There's really nothing more to it than that." *That we want to divulge, anyway.* "And there won't be any flowers, either, if we don't get cracking and get something decided. Now, Heather, what sort of arrangements did you have in mind for the church? Long-stemmed tulips are always pretty, as are roses—"

"No, no, no," Charlene interrupted, taking charge of the conversation once again. "I'm sure Heather doesn't want anything as pedestrian as that, Amanda. We want something elegant... sophisticated.''

The inference that only someone of Charlene's wealth and breeding could make an appropriate selection stung Amanda. Although in her personal life, she might have taken the speaker to task for a remark like that, in her professional life, she had no recourse but to simply ignore the other woman's insinuation and go on. ''In that case, you might think of lilies of the valley, orchids, freesias or stephanotis. We have lots to look at, so let's look around first before we even try to decide. Also, you may want to consider the symbolic significance of each flower—''

''I didn't know flowers had meanings!'' Heather said.

Amanda smiled, beginning to relax as she concentrated on her work. ''Oh, yes. For instance, the gardenia stands for joy, the forget-me-not true love, the orange blossom purity, the white daisy innocence, the red chrysanthemum sharing.''

''So... I could be sending a message to Tim with what flowers I select to be in my bouquet?'' Heather asked, delighted.

Amanda nodded and got out her notebook. ''Maybe we should go over all the meanings, before you decide what will work with the color scheme you've selected for your wedding.''

''I'd like that,'' Heather said. She turned to her father and Charlene. ''Isn't this interesting? I can't believe how much Amanda knows!''

Nor, apparently, could Charlene, Amanda thought, judging by the disgruntled look on the other woman's face.

''I still think we ought to think first about elegance,'' Charlene insisted, a little too petulantly for Ethan's taste.

''I'm sure Amanda can help us find plenty of elegant flowers, Charlene,'' Ethan said, giving her a pointed look, ''that also have appropriate significance.''

To Amanda's relief, Charlene got the message and fell silent. She was glad he had defended her, but she was sorry it had been necessary. As much as she had come up in the world since they had known one another, as sophisticated as she had seemed there was still such a chasm between them socially. It was large enough to let her know it would never be closed.

Pushing the depressing knowledge aside, she forced herself to concentrate on her work. Not Ethan, not Charlene. It took a little over three hours, but finally they figured out precisely what flowers to order for the wedding. As the other two women departed, Ethan looked as glad as Amanda that it was over. "Sorry about that," he said to her, as soon as Charlene and Heather had left.

"There's nothing to apologize for," she said, giving a final check to her prodigious volume of notes.

He reached over and shut the cover on her notebook. "I think there is," he said softly but firmly, commanding her full attention. "I don't want anyone being rude to you."

The slightly pitying way he looked at her made her feel even worse. She gulped around the tension in her throat, but held his gaze unflinchingly as she placed her notebook in her bag. "Unfortunately it's happened before and I'm sure it'll happen again," she said crisply. "I'll handle it."

"You shouldn't have to." She started to walk in the direction of the front office at the warehouse and he fell into step beside her. As they walked, he shook his head, recollected ruefully, "I've known Charlene forever, and I've never seen her act that way. Usually she's polite enough to be Miss Manners herself. The only explanation I can see is that Charlene feels protective of Heather."

Was he really that naive? In this instance, apparently so, she thought with barely leashed irritation. It would have been obvious to even the most uninvolved bystander that Charlene was interested in him. But knowing she couldn't tell him that without sounding as jealous and vaguely threatened as she felt, Amanda remained silent. So Charlene didn't want her catering Heather's wedding. Charlene hadn't hired her. Ethan had, she reminded herself firmly. And she had a job to do.

Determinedly she turned her attention to that. "Look, don't worry about Charlene," Amanda soothed as professionally as possible, all the while thinking defiantly, *I'm not going to.* "Planning weddings is a highly emotional activity. It gets to everyone." She forced a cheerful smile. "Believe me, I'm used to dealing with all sorts of personalities and reactions."

He still looked skeptical, concerned. Finding his searching glance disconcerting, Amanda glanced down at her notes and kept studying them until she found her place and got her thoughts back on the business at hand. "If you'll hang on a minute, I'll get a rough estimate of the cost of the flowers."

He waited while she went up to the front office.

"It looks fine," Ethan said, after reviewing it. He glanced over at her. "You're sure the selections are appropriate?"

Amanda nodded. Heather had done a super job.

"Is there anything at all you'd like to see added?" he grinned.

Amanda grinned and unable to help herself, said tartly, "You mean besides long-stemmed tulips and roses?"

He grinned, well aware she'd just brought up the two flowers Charlene had vetoed because they were so pedestrian. "Besides that," he said dryly.

She was glad to see he hadn't lost his sense of humor. She ducked her head, feeling suddenly shy as a renewed sense of intimacy fell over them. "Not really."

"Whatever you think it needs," he said in a soft, serious voice, "don't hesitate to add."

He was generous, Amanda thought, almost to a fault. She wondered what it would be like to have so much money to spend that cost was no object, none at all. She'd never had unlimited funds, even when married to her wealthy ex.

She wondered what it would be like to spend time with him again—not on the wedding, or business, but just as friends.

Without warning, Charlene came dashing back into the warehouse, her arm waving wildly, her high heels clicking like a runaway typewriter on the cement floor. "Ethan, I'm glad you're here! I've got trouble with my Ferrari! It won't start!" Breasts heaving in the tight white silk bodice of her fashionably short dress, she halted breathlessly before them. "Would you be a dear and come out and take a look?"

If he was annoyed or perturbed, she thought, he wasn't showing it. "Sure," he said easily. He looked at Amanda. "You coming?"

The idea of a threesome was not at all appealing. "I'll catch up with you later." She didn't miss Charlene's smug look as she walked off with Ethan.

THE LOOSE DISTRIBUTOR CAP hadn't fooled him one bit, Ethan thought. Charlene had just wanted to get him away from Amanda. Maybe Charlene had designs on him. He'd always thought her interest in him was related to her friendship with Iris, and perhaps in the past it had been, but somewhere, at some point, that had changed. Now she wanted him to pay attention to her. He had no interest in Charlene at all. Yet the fact remained he'd already asked her and she'd agreed to help out with Heather's wedding.

That wouldn't be over for another four weeks.

He swore, contemplating the tension ahead—that was, if today had been any indication of the dramas to come. He would have to let Charlene know exactly where she stood with him if she persisted. But he hoped that wouldn't be necessary, at least until after Heather's wedding. In the meantime, maybe he could just avoid her.

His biggest regret was the rude way she had acted toward Amanda. Although Amanda had seemed to take Charlene's snobbish attitude in stride, he knew it had to have hurt her.

In the future, he'd do his best to protect Amanda, too. He owed her that much. Maybe she wasn't the right woman for him . . . but she deserved a hell of a lot more than what Charlene seemed disposed to give her. She deserved to be treated with dignity. And one way or another, he would see that she was.

Chapter Six

"You mean there's more than one type of invitation, too?" Ethan asked in bewilderment the following day.

Amanda had to struggle not to laugh; the depth of his dismay was almost comical. "Afraid so."

"No wonder Heather wanted me to handle this part of the preparations," he moaned, completely overwhelmed, as she began to show him different print styles and colored papers, inks and linings.

"Relax. You're going to manage this just fine, Ethan."

"So you say. I'll probably pick out something she hates."

"Then it's her fault for not being here."

"You think so?"

"She had her choice, to do this or delegate it to you. Obviously it's not that critically important to her or she would have been here herself."

He thought about that for a moment, looking temporarily pacified. But as soon as they got back to the many, many choices in front of him, he was bewildered again. "I knew her getting married during the school year was a mistake," he grumbled, leaning forward, elbows on his knees, raking both hands through his hair, "I knew she wouldn't have time to attend to all these details and manage her classes and schoolwork, too."

"But she was determined to do it," Amanda put in softly, her heart going out to him.

"Right. And knowing that, what could I do?" He met her eyes for confirmation that he hadn't made a mistake in giving in to his only daughter's whims.

"You certainly couldn't let her run off and elope. After all, she's only going to get married once. Her wedding should be special," Amanda continued to soothe.

"Exactly my point," he said, briefly mollified. "But this—" he gestured to the array of samples spread out over the conference table in Amanda's office "—this is ridiculous!"

"If you think it would be easier or more expedient, I could just pick out something appropriate myself."

Although he looked tempted to let her do just that, he finally shook his head no. "I promised her I'd do this."

Amanda wondered if he would be more comfortable with something trendier. "We don't have to go with any of these types of invitations. For instance, one of my clients used a card of Brueghel's wedding scene for her invitations—"

"No, I don't want anything that arty."

"How about letting Tiffany's make the decision, then, assuming I can pull some strings and get them to do a rush job for us? They've been in business for 140 years and have set the standard for social correctness. You can't go wrong hiring them to do your invitations."

Ethan sighed, looking very relieved. "Sounds good."

"You'll still have to look at the different colored inks, paper and lining, though," she warned.

He groaned comically and put his head in his hands, then straightened with a beleaguered sigh she suspected was mostly for show. "All right. How soon do you have to have an answer?"

The corners of her mouth inched up in mirth. "Today. The invitations should have been sent out yesterday. We don't have a moment to spare."

His eyes twinkled as he watched her profile closely. "You're a slave driver, you know that?"

Amanda grinned and ducked her head, pretending to study the myriad of sample invitations spread out over the table in front of them. She didn't feel like a slave driver. She felt like a teenager again...like the years that had passed had drifted away. It was nice being comfortable enough with him to chat and to tease . . . to feel so perfectly in sync . . . even if the reasons for their being together were anything but romantic.

"Amanda?" A familiar feminine voice interrupted her reverie. "Oh, dear! I'm sorry to interrupt. I—I didn't know you had company."

"Mom, hi." Amanda got up so suddenly she bumped into the edge of the table and sent the coffee sloshing over the rims of their cups. "Ethan, you remember my mother—?"

"Actually we never met." Ethan said awkwardly but honestly as he dabbed at the worst of the spills with a napkin, then finished, stood and offered his hand. "It's nice to meet you, Mrs. Webster."

"Yes. Nice to meet you, too," her mother echoed stiffly and unconvincingly. She looked back at Amanda. "Darling, we have to talk."

Amanda knew that voice; it wasn't one she liked. She turned to Ethan. "Why don't you go ahead and look at these samples? I'll be back in a moment."

"Take your time," he said amenably.

Amanda led her mother off down the hall, to the coffee room at the rear of her building. Irritated with her mother's brusqueness toward Ethan, she shut the door firmly behind them. "You could have been nicer, Mom."

"And you could have been less friendly."

"What's that supposed to mean?"

"Ever since your father heard about your being involved with the Holbrooks again he's been a nervous wreck. He's not sleeping at night or eating. Worse, some corporate headhunters approached several of his top scientists about leaving his firm to go work for HCI at double the salary."

Dread filled Amanda. "Did they take it?"

"No, thank goodness, but your father feels it could just be a matter of time before they do, especially if Harrison Holbrook keeps upping the ante."

Amanda knew her mother hadn't come all the way down here just to give her that bit of information. "What are you asking me to do, Mom?" she asked warily.

"To divorce yourself from Ethan and his family entirely, to let another consulting firm handle Heather Holbrook's wedding."

To let her parents talk her out of this would be setting a dangerous precedent, Amanda knew. "No."

Her mother's worry increased. Briefly Amanda was flooded with guilt. She reminded herself her mother always worried and turned away from the mute pleading on her mother's face. "Mom, I've got to get back to Ethan."

"Amanda—"

"We'll talk later, when I have more time." Her tone brooked no argument. Knowing when it was prudent to give up, her mother let her go.

"This isn't the last of this conversation, Amanda," her mother called after her.

How well I know that.

Ethan glanced up when she entered the room. "Everything okay?"

She wondered how he could sit there so calmly when his firm had just tried to steal some of the Webster Group's best men. Briefly she filled him in on what her mother had told her. He looked as shocked as she had first felt, and then very angry and concerned. "I'm sorry, Amanda—" he said and got abruptly to his feet.

Relief filtered through her as they squared off. "Then this wasn't your idea?"

"No, I was strictly against it." He braced a hand on his waist, shoving his suitcoat aside.

But he'd known.

He read her concern and his eyes darkened. "I promise you, it won't happen again." Reaching across her, to the table, he picked up the samples he'd selected for the invitations. He went over them briefly, detailing his selection, as he handed them to her. Finished, he gave her a brief formal smile that didn't begin to reach his eyes. "If you'll excuse me, I've got to go home and talk to my father."

She followed him to the door. "Ethan—" She hesitated when he turned around to face her. "You won't tell your father where you heard this, will you?" She didn't want the feud between the two families firing up again, any more than it already had. Tensions and tempers were running high enough as it was.

He shook his head solemnly. "No, I won't," he reassured her softly. And then his voice hardened. "But I do plan to read him the riot act. HCI has never had to stoop to stealing to succeed. It won't start now."

Seeing the look on his face, she believed him.

AMANDA MET up with Ethan again the following day, this time in the lobby of the Adolphus, for the purpose of working out more wedding details. Although he said nothing about what had happened with his father, she wondered if they'd had an argument, and if Ethan had won. But since nothing was forthcoming on the subject, she didn't feel she had the right to ask.

They needed to concentrate on the reception.

Amanda got out her notebook. She had just opened it when they were interrupted unexpectedly. "Ethan, darling, what are you doing here?" Charlene Davenport said with all the cunning and guile of a waiting crocodile as she crossed the lobby and stopped at his side.

Beside her, she felt Ethan stiffen. Nevertheless, his voice was cordial when he spoke. "Amanda and I are here to check out sites for the reception."

Charlene pouted. "You should have told me. I could have helped."

Ethan forced a sociable grin. "Thanks for offering, Charlene. I appreciate it. But it's not necessary. Amanda has everything well in hand."

Charlene sent Amanda a tight smile, then turned back to Ethan, her low cultured voice oozing charm. "What about later this evening? Are you free? I'm having dinner with friends. You remember Pamela Weston? She and her husband are meeting me here. If you joined us, it'd be a cozy four."

Ignoring the other woman's snub, Amanda touched Ethan's arm and murmured a polite excuse. Not waiting for a response, she turned and crossed the lobby. He joined her again moments later. Blessedly she turned around to see that Charlene was nowhere in sight.

"Sorry about that," he said with a beleaguered sigh.

Amanda glossed over what she preferred not to discuss. "No problem. We were a bit early, anyway. Now, are you ready to see that banquet room?"

He nodded, still looking concerned about her feelings. Amanda was more aware than ever the two of them were from radically different worlds.

After they decided on a banquet room, Amanda spoke to the manager. Half an hour later, a contract had been signed for the evening of February 14, a deposit paid. "Now where?" Ethan asked.

Amanda consulted her list. "To the bakery to help Heather and Tim decide on a cake."

The happy couple had already arrived when Amanda and Ethan walked into the store. "See anything you like?" Amanda asked, unable to help but notice a bit enviously how radiant Heather looked whenever she was with her fiancé. What would it be like to be that young and hopeful again, she wondered, that naively blissful?

Heather pointed to a bride and groom for the top of the cake. "We've got the decorations. Now all we have to do is decide on the flavors of cake and icing."

"That ought to be easy," Ethan said.

Amanda laughed. "You haven't tasted their carrot cake with butter-cream frosting and walnuts. Or their cheesecake with apricot filling."

Minutes later, they'd all sampled the two varieties Amanda had spoken of. "What's this?" Ethan said, as he savored a bite of yet another sample put out for them to try.

"Mmm." Heather tried some, too. "That is good."

Ethan handed Amanda a small bite in a white paper cup. "What do you think, Amanda?"

She took a sip of water to cleanse her palate, and then, very aware Ethan was watching her, took a bite of the proffered sample. It was rich and heavenly. She licked a bit of icing from the corner of her lip, feeling fourteen again and painfully aware of each breath she took, each beat of her foolish young heart. "This is their biggest seller, their hazelnut *génoise* cake, spread with their mocha butter cream and white chocolate." Was he remembering what a chocolate freak she was? Or how he had once been prone to indulge her—bringing her chocolate-covered cherries and chocolate-dipped pecan clusters for no reason other than he wanted her to be happy? His eyes indicated he was.

"I like it," Heather said enthusiastically as she too sampled the bakery's biggest-selling cake. "Don't you, Tim?"

With a great deal of effort, Amanda turned her mind to her work, not her memories. "Are you sure?" she said. "You haven't even tried half of their selections yet. There's pineapple, raspberry, Italian rum...."

Ethan shrugged as he looked at his daughter, then back at Amanda. "I could handle a few more," he decided as he eyed the samples the baker was setting out for them.

He always had possessed a voracious appetite, Amanda remembered reluctantly, for everything. It was disconcerting to find out that this much about him hadn't changed any more than her love of chocolate had changed.

She swallowed around the sudden dryness in her throat. The cake . . . they were here to pick out a cake. "I think that would be wise."

"Okay," Heather said reluctantly to her father. She raised an index finger in the direction of his nose. "But if I gain weight from all this and can't fit into my wedding dress, you know who I'm going to blame!"

The tension between Ethan and Amanda was broken as they all laughed at Heather's joke. Deciding it was the looking at him, the standing so close to Ethan, that was getting her in trouble, she carefully kept her distance, and hence, was able to maintain her professional demeanor. The next few minutes were spent eating and comparing. Tim especially liked the chocolate fudge, with chocolate almond icing. "That would be a perfect groom's cake," Amanda said.

"It's awfully rich," Heather said, frowning. "With the champagne and all that food . . . Daddy, did you taste it?"

Ethan shook his head no.

"Well, you've got to!" Heather said.

Because she was closest to the tray the bakery had set out for them, Amanda reached over and got a sample for him. She handed the flimsy paper cup to him, then forgetting for a moment her resolve not to look at him directly, watched as he let the flavor of the cake melt in his mouth. "I see what you mean," he said, smiling, and licking a bit of icing from his thumb, "it is rich. But good, very good."

His eyes met Amanda's, held. She tried but couldn't hold back her answering smile.

"What do you think?"

Feeling as if she would drown in the unrelenting intimacy of his eyes if she looked at him any longer, she drew in a quick breath and turned her glance away. "I think it's up to Tim."

He still wants me, he's making that very clear. She could handle that; she couldn't handle wanting him, too.

"I say go with it," Tim said.

"Okay, then, it's settled," Heather said. "The groom's cake in chocolate almond, the wedding cake in hazelnut *génoise.*"

"You sure are easy to please," Amanda said, as they wound up the paperwork for that in short order.

"That's because I'm so happy!" Heather said, linking arms with Tim.

"Have you decided on where you are going to honeymoon?" she asked the happy couple as, the deposit for the cakes paid, Ethan joined them once again.

"I meant to speak to the two of you about that," Ethan said. "The honeymoon is going to be my treat. Two weeks' paid vacation, wherever you want to go. So how about it? What'd you have in mind? Mexico's really nice this time of year—"

For the first time that day, Tim looked tense. "Not Mexico," he said, quick to dismiss that idea. Then, as if realizing how ungrateful that must have sounded, he amended nervously, "Not that it isn't a great idea, Mr. Holbrook, your, uh, giving us a honeymoon and all, but . . . I just think somewhere else would be better, that's all."

Heather faced him curiously, as surprised as Amanda that Tim was being difficult about such a lavish gift. To date, he hadn't objected to any specific item in the often-overwhelming wedding plans. In fact, he'd been quite content to let his bride-to-be run everything. "Why not Mexico?" Heather demanded, her voice both challenging and hurt. "I love Acapulco! And you know that, too!"

"I know, and I didn't mean to insult you, Heather. Or you, either, Mr. Holbrook. It's just . . . we've both been there already," Tim continued, embarrassed.

Heather regarded him in stony silence.

Tim was quiet, too. For a moment, he avoided Ethan's and Amanda's gaze. Amanda felt for him, realizing he wouldn't want either of the two older people to witness his argument with Heather. Seeming to struggle with some inner turmoil, he glanced away before returning his eyes to Heather's. "How about Hawaii?" Tim asked persuasively.

"We've both been to Hawaii, too. In fact, given our backgrounds, I doubt there's a place worth going to we haven't already been."

Tim's face turned blotchy with red-and-white patches. Without warning, his voice grew as stubborn and petulantly demanding as Heather's. "I know that, but I want to do something different. It seems like everyone we know goes to Mexico to honeymoon." She shot him an angry glance. Tim continued, no less stubbornly, "If you want to go somewhere warm, how about the Caribbean?"

Heather blinked, still not understanding his sudden emotion any more than Amanda did. "The Caribbean would be okay," she said finally, still looking mystified, but understanding, as did Amanda, for whatever reason, Tim wasn't going to back down on this.

"I'll send some travel brochures over then," Amanda interjected, smoothing the way back to group harmony, "if that's okay with all of you."

"Fine," everyone murmured in unison, a little dazed.

"So what next?" Heather asked.

This time Amanda didn't have to consult her list. "William Noble's. We've got to pick out gifts for the attendants."

"Okay, we'll meet you two over there," Heather said.

Ethan and Amanda walked to her car. She slid behind the wheel as he got in on the passenger side. "Was it my imagination or did Tim get unusually nervous back there?" Ethan said.

"He was nervous—but that happens to a lot of prospective grooms. Maybe it's just prewedding nerves. Maybe he feels Heather's making too many of the decisions about the marriage."

"He hasn't seemed to mind thus far," Ethan commented with a shrug of his broad shoulders.

"No, he hasn't. Then again, maybe many of the other details—like where to hold the reception, for instance—aren't that important to him. I can see why he'd want to have a say-so in the decision about where to honeymoon."

"Not just a say-so, but the ultimate say," Ethan stressed, buckling his seat belt.

Amanda reached for her shoulder harness, as well. "It bothers you he was so adamant?" she said as she strapped it tightly over her body and started her car.

"It bothers me he was holding something back," Ethan said, moving around until his large body was adjusted comfortably in the front seat of her small sedan. He rested an elbow on the door frame, next to the window, propped his chin on his upraised fist. "I'm not sure what he wasn't telling us," he murmured, still staring distractedly at the passing Highland Park business district, "but I know he wasn't telling us everything. And what's more, Heather knew so, too. I've never seen her look so hurt where he was concerned."

Amanda hadn't, either, but she also felt Ethan was overreacting here, too, in his desire to protect his only daughter. "Look, Ethan, their argument was private," she said, braking hard as they came up on a swiftly changing traffic light. "Or at least it should have been," she continued as they settled back against their seats. "That's probably why Tim was so flustered, why he felt he couldn't say everything that was on his mind." Still keeping one eye on the traffic light, she slanted him a quelling glance. "You are intimidating, you know."

"Me?" He palmed his chest with both hands. "How?"

The light changed and Amanda drove on. She kept her eyes on the traffic while she talked. "Well, you're supersuccessful, very prominent socially and businesswise. From what Heather's told me of Tim, his family has only come into wealth in the last fifteen years or so." She turned to look at him again as they paused at yet another light. "He still remembers what it felt like, before the oil boom, when his dad was struggling to keep his construction business in the black. These days, his family has arrived...and yet they haven't, because unlike the rest of the old guard of Dallas, they weren't born with silver spoons in their mouths."

Briefly Ethan looked taken aback. "Is that how you see me?" he asked, hurt.

It wasn't how she used to see him, Amanda thought, as the light changed and she urged her car forward once again. She used to see him just as the boy that she loved. Now...it was different. She saw him in his world and knew she could never be a part of it, that no matter how nostalgic or sentimental the idea, they could never go back in time, to the innocence of their youths. It just wasn't a practical option, and she was nothing if not supremely practical.

Seeing her turn up ahead, she wordlessly guided her car into the lot. Sidestepping what she couldn't answer honestly without offending him, or what might lead them into an even more intimate discussion of themselves, she said briskly as she shut off her car engine, "Right now, I see you as a client, who needs very much to get to William Noble jewelers."

Heather and Tim had arrived and were being helped by an obsequious salesperson when they entered the store. Thankful to have something to concentrate on besides the handsome man at her side, Amanda threw herself into her job wholeheartedly. And not until a few hours later, did they finish up. Fortunately, during that time, Ethan pretty much let her be and concentrated on the task at hand. While Amanda advised Heather and Tim on what would be appropriate gifts for their attendants—bracelets for the women, cufflinks for the men—Ethan quibbled with the jewelers over prices and the quality of the jewels. Eventually, when he got precisely what he wanted for the price he wanted, he praised the service they received. Yet she had the feeling from the occasional inquiring glance he gave her that the discussion they'd started wasn't over yet, and wouldn't be until he'd had his say.

She kept her distance from him while Heather and Tim picked out their wedding rings and the jewelry Heather would wear on her wedding day. Finally the job was completed.

Still in awe of the staggering amount of money that had been spent on the wedding gifts, Amanda drove Ethan back to her office, where he'd left his car earlier. The parking lot was deserted, except for his car. Because she didn't need to go into the office again, she left the motor running.

Confident, he smiled over at her. "Well I guess this is where I take my silver spoon and get out," he said, stretching lazily.

Amanda blanched at the provoking comment and swore inwardly. She should have known better than to make a remark like that to him. She should have known how he would feel. Worse, he was a client! And whether she meant it or not, she had insulted him.

"Ethan, I'm sorry. I shouldn't have said that," she apologized self-consciously, the heat of a blush coming to her face in the dwindling twilight. "I was just trying to explain how Tim must feel when confronted with everything he has to confront these days."

Ethan unfastened his seat belt and turned toward her, the rich, beguiling scent of his after-shave wafting over her as he drew nearer.

"It's always going to be there between us, isn't it?" he said softly, his eyes sad.

"What?"

"Money, the issue of it. How much I have, how much you don't."

What could she say in response to that? It was true. She looked down at her hands numbly as they tightened over the steering wheel ineffectually. Realizing it was going to be a very long conversation if they were to resolve anything or salvage their client/consultant relationship, she switched off her car. The silence fell like a deafening cloak around them. "Okay," she sighed heavily, still looking straight ahead, "let me have it with both barrels."

He put a hand under her chin and turned her face to his. "I don't want to yell at you. I don't want to fight," he said, overenunciating each and every word.

She glared at him and withdrew from his gentle grasp. "Then what do you want?" Without warning her voice was tense, breathless.

He shrugged. Apparently that was not so easy for him to put into words. "Maybe for you to understand me," he said quietly. "Or at least try—the way you would've years ago—before everything got in the way of us being together."

His frank comment flooded her with renewed guilt. Since he'd come back into her life, she'd spent so much time thinking about *her* feelings about him, his money, that she hadn't given more than a passing thought to his. And that wasn't fair, to either of them.

Although her initial instinct was to turn away from that searing, searching gaze, she forced herself to hold his glance and confront the issues between them. "All right. I'm listening."

His mouth twisted wryly. After a thoughtful moment, he spoke in a soft, reflective tone. "It's funny, in one sense I guess you were right in what you implied about me. I do have 'everything.'"

"Yes, you do." More than she would ever have, or could ever dream of having.

"But I still feel like so much is lacking in my life."

As he spoke, she was very aware of the intensity of his gaze.

"There's a lot I don't have."

"Such as?"

"A wife, a lover, a friend."

The breath she'd been withholding came out in a rush and she volleyed back wryly, "I've seen the way women look at you,

Ethan." *Charlene, for instance.* "You could be married if you wanted to be."

"Maybe. But I don't want to be married to just anyone," he disagreed simply. "Do you?"

"No." She took a deep, halting breath, aware how her heart was pounding. "But then . . . I don't really want to be married, period."

"Why not?"

"Because. Because I like my life the way it is. Because I know what to expect. Because marriage only complicates matters, and my life is complicated enough as it is."

"Maybe so, but is it full enough?"

Now he was talking about something else—his own dissatisfaction with his life. Was it possible he was lonely, too? She knew in some ways he was as cynical and disillusioned as she had become over the years.

"I've got plenty of business to keep me busy." So much so that when combined with her devoted parenting of Babe, she didn't have time to think, never mind worry, about the obvious deficiencies in her personal life.

"Yes, I know," he murmured unhappily. "I can see how you've gone after money and power."

His pragmatic analysis both annoyed and unnerved her. "Providing a stable, financially sound life for myself and my child is not the same as pursuing a career with ruthless ambition," she countered stiffly.

"Maybe not," he agreed softly, "but the treadmill you find yourself on when you're doing it is one and the same."

"You're wrong."

"I hope so, Amanda, for your sake, because money and power won't give you happiness. It just brings a whole new set of problems with it."

She could see he was trying to help her, but he was going about it all wrong. Her emotions flaring out of control, she retorted passionately, "At least you don't have to worry about being thrown out of your house because your father's boss fired him." She stopped in surprise and bit her lip. She didn't know where that had come from, either, yet this seemed to be her night for putting her foot in her mouth and impulsively saying the unpardonable.

"No, I don't," he agreed tightly, picking up the gauntlet she'd thrown down. "I have to worry about keeping a business that used to be on the cutting edge of technology afloat. I have to worry about the thousands of people HCI employs. I have to find a way to get HCI back on track or know that if it fails, that if all those thousands of people are out of jobs, that it was my fault, Amanda. Mine. I have to live with the constant burden of that. Not to mention my father's expectations or my daughter's or even yours."

His words packed a powerful punch and brought on an avalanche of guilt. She had judged him harshly. "I'm sorry." Her voice sounded as small as she felt.

He sighed heavily and raked a hand through his straight white-blond hair. "This wasn't what I wanted to say to you."

No, she thought, but maybe it was good it had been said. They'd needed to clear the air.

He looked at her directly. "You're probably not going to like it, but I'm going to lay it on the line with you, anyway. There are a lot of holes in my life right now, a lot of deficiencies. Heather getting married makes them all the more glaring."

She had an idea where this was going. Complications of this nature she didn't need. "I don't think I want to hear this." She reached for the door handle.

He caught her other hand before she could push the door open, and held her beside him. "I may have been born with a silver spoon in my life, but I am far from content," he said, anger and frustration battling with the honesty in his low voice. "I want more than I've got now, Amanda. Much more. And frankly," he said, his fingers releasing hers slowly, "I would think if you were honest with yourself, that you would want a helluva lot more in your life, too."

Was he suggesting they pick up where they left off, have an affair? What? She didn't know and she didn't care. Feeling angry and frustrated now herself, she decided to go into the building, anyway—if only to get away from him and this unexpected truth-telling session—and got out of the car. "That's the trouble with you, Ethan," she said coldly, enraged he could think things were so simple or so easy. She regarded him icily over the roof of the BMW as he got out of the car and stood on the other side of it, facing her. "You always have wanted too much. You've always felt entitled to have everything." She slammed the door, not knowing where the wellspring of pent-up emotion was coming from only knowing she couldn't have stopped the venting of it if she'd tried. "Whereas I never have. I'm one of those people who have to make do with what they have." Her heels clicking on the sidewalk, she stalked toward the front of the building.

He caught up with her at the portal.

Looking into his face, she saw that he was disappointed in her again, that he had never really forgiven her for thinking the worst about him years ago, for letting it end the way it had, any more than she had forgiven him for thinking the worst about her. Her shoulders slumped forward with the weight of the despair she felt. She should've known this would catch up with them sooner or later, that they would have to square off and try to deal with these residual feelings.

"Maybe you shouldn't...just make do," Ethan said softly, touching her arm lightly, persuasively. His hand dropped. He remained motionless. "Maybe you should want more." And then softer still, "Maybe if you did, you would get it."

"Maybe," Amanda countered, dismayed that he should be turning this conversation onto such an intimate level. She couldn't help it, she was still afraid to hope for rainbows—when she knew there were only storm clouds up ahead if she chose to pursue this course. "And maybe I'd only end up disappointed."

And that she couldn't risk, because when it came to Ethan...she knew she couldn't handle loving him again. She just couldn't. Not when she knew how his family operated, feeling it was okay to do and say anything as long as they were protecting their own. So for the time being, she would continue to play it safe, to avoid his probing gazes and intimate questions and the light of desire she sometimes saw in his eyes. It was the only way she knew to protect herself from being hurt again. The only way.

Chapter Seven

"Well, here they are. All two hundred and fifty of the invitations for your half of the guest list," Amanda told Ethan early Thursday evening when he met her at his front door.

He relieved her of the large cardboard box, his matter-of-fact attitude at odds with the unrelenting intimacy he'd evoked the last time they'd been together. She told herself she was glad he had taken the hint and backed off, accepted the fact that whatever they had shared long ago was history, never to be repeated. Nevertheless, she knew a tiny moment's regret when he looked at her with all the welcome the average citizen had for the IRS.

He set the large box down onto the living room floor, beside a glass-topped mahogany coffee table, and sank down on the braid-trimmed white moire sofa beside it. "What about the rest of them?"

She took one of the graceful *bergère* chairs to his right. "I delivered them to the Summerfields this morning. I have someone from my office helping to address them."

"Oh, good." He glanced down at the large box of engraved invitations. He frowned reluctantly, remarking, "It looks like a lot more than two hundred and fifty."

"I know, but it'll go quickly, I promise."

"I hope so." He looked at the stack dubiously.

Amanda glanced around. Although there was no reason for her to be uneasy being alone with him, his large home seemed exceptionally quiet. "Where's Heather?" She'd left a message for the bride at her sorority house to meet them there.

"She has a government test tomorrow. She's back at her sorority house studying."

Amanda tried to contain her disappointment. She'd hoped just to show the two of them what to do and then leave as swiftly as possible. She hadn't planned on staying herself. "So she won't be helping you?"

Ethan shook his head regretfully. "No. And I won't ask Charlene, so you can forget that," he warned.

At that, Amanda tried not to grin. The man-hungry woman's pursuit of him was almost comical. Or it would have been if Charlene hadn't been so intent on slighting Amanda simultaneously. Reluctantly her thoughts returned to the chore ahead of them, and it was all she could do not to bite her lip in frustration. "If we'd had more time I could've hired a calligrapher to help out with this. But everyone I know is already busy. And those invitations have to go out tomorrow afternoon, at the very latest."

Ethan regarded the large box of invitations. "I'm sure I can handle this," he said cavalierly.

He didn't look sure. "Would you like me to stay around and help?" She knew she couldn't do it alone, either.

He regarded her silently, then, seeing how easygoing her attitude, heaved a sigh of relief. "Would you? I don't know the first thing about this."

"Sure." Amanda shrugged out of her coat and pushed up the sleeves of her cashmere dress.

Unlike her, he'd had time to change after leaving the office and was dressed for comfort and warmth in soft dove-gray cords, loafers and a white crew-neck sweater. It was disconcerting, seeing him so casually attired—maybe because it reminded her of times past, when he hadn't always worn a suit and tie.

Pushing away the fond memories that threatened to surface, she concentrated on her instructions. "The first thing you have to know is how to put one of these together. A small reception card must be enclosed with each engraved invitation. And also a response card, so we'll know how many will actually be attending."

Ethan watched as she put the invitation together in the proper way, then followed suit, albeit a little clumsily. "Well, that was easy," he said with a self-satisfied grin when he'd finished.

"Now we only have to do it two hundred and forty-eight more times." She laughed as he groaned in mock trepidation.

For the next hour they worked companionably side by side, speaking only occasionally about the most mundane details of their chore, until all the invitations had been assembled. "How's your handwriting?" she asked, as they finished.

"Fair. Why?" he asked curiously.

She rummaged around for the box of black pens she'd brought, aware that the tension she'd felt upon arriving at his home had gradually faded, allowing them to be friends again. "All the addresses must be handwritten in black ink. It helps if they're legible."

"I imagine so," he said wryly, his hand brushing hers briefly as he took the proffered pen.

She glanced over at him, appreciating the relaxed atmosphere between them. But that shouldn't have surprised her. When it came right down to it, they had always worked well together. She remembered the two of them decorating the school gymnasium, in preparation for the prom. He'd stood on a ladder, tacking up the long rainbow-colored strands of crepe paper she'd handed him. They'd had so much fun, talking and laughing while they worked together. Only later, after she'd been summoned to his father's office, had everything fallen apart.

But she didn't want to remember the past.

Pushing away the unhappy memories, Amanda took a copy of the guest list and tore it in half, handing him the *A* to *L*'s. "I'll start with the *M*'s."

"I don't know about you, but I need a coffee break," Ethan said an hour and a half later, stretching.

"Coffee would be great," Amanda said. She followed him into the kitchen. "Where is everyone tonight?"

"I don't have full-time help anymore, not since Heather left. I have a housekeeper who comes in during the day, to clean and cook for me when need be, but otherwise I'm on my own."

"What happens when you entertain?"

"I hire a caterer." He regarded her curiously. "What about you? Do you have help?"

"No. Babe and I do all our own housework."

"Do you want a maid?"

"Not really. I think one would just get underfoot."

"I know what you mean. That's precisely why I don't have live-in help. I like my privacy in the evenings."

The coffee had stopped brewing. He looked in the pantry and came out with a box of chocolate-covered marshmallow cookies. "Remember these?"

How could she not? They'd shared them every day for lunch, during the spring they had dated, but she told herself his bringing those particular cookies out now meant nothing except that he was hungry. She nodded, and in an effort to break the new, very different, wellspring of tension she felt, she teased, "You could never get enough pinwheel cookies."

"Still can't."

He opened the package and offered it to her. Mindful of her waistline, she took only one, then watched as he downed three. "Ever wish we could go back in time?" he asked whimsically.

"Sometimes," she admitted as he poured them both a steaming mug. "The funny thing is, I don't feel much older now than I did then, and yet almost twenty-five years have passed." She compressed her lips ruefully, wondering where the time had gone. "We're both firmly into middle age."

His glance was understanding. "I know. The outside changes. But what's in here—" he palmed the region over his heart "—stays the same."

Did it? Amanda wondered as she took her first sip of the strong black coffee. Was she still the same girl who had fallen head over heels in love with him? Or had she changed? Was she no longer capable of such impetuous emotion? Part of her was afraid to know. Part of her was afraid of being seduced into finding out.

She glanced at her watch. Nearly ten. "We better get back to work," she said, already rising.

Briefly sorrow rimmed his eyes. "Sure."

They were down to the last fifty invitations when the muscles in Ethan's shoulder began to cramp. He didn't say anything about it, but she could tell by the look on his face and the sudden way he dropped his pen that he was in pain. "What is it?" She was on her feet before she could think.

His look of embarrassment deepened. "I hurt my right shoulder and arm a couple years ago in a fall. I was out jogging and slipped on some wet pavement, landed on my shoulder. It still bothers me from time to time." He winced again and with his left hand, massaged his right shoulder.

"Let me help." She was already moving toward him.

He blushed, reluctant. "No. This is silly. I can—"

"Come on, Ethan, where does it hurt?"

He sighed, then acknowledged, "Between my spine and shoulder blade. Yeah." He arched his back slightly as she found the spot, then closed his eyes and briefly bit his lip. "And on down my arm—"

She could feel the knotted muscles and knew as tense and tight as they were, they had to hurt. Using all of her strength, she massaged the tightness out of his arm and shoulder, not stopping until his cramping muscles had relaxed once again. Satisfied at last that he was okay, she let her hands drop and stepped back.

Ethan sighed and opened his eyes. "God, that felt good," he said softly, his look one of open admiration. "You really have a magic touch."

She shrugged off his compliment and went back to the small stack of invitations she had left. It was more important than ever that she finished these and got out of there. "Thanks."

He continued watching her for another half a minute. When he spoke again, his voice was low and gentle, and laced with gratitude. "You know, you've done so much," he said, putting a staying hand on her wrist. "You could go home now. I could finish these."

It was an easy out, but one she knew—on a professional level—she couldn't take. Aware that he was still holding her wrist lightly, and that his palm was warm and strong and faintly calloused, she queried practically, "What if your arm cramps up again?" He had no answer for that. "I'll stay until the job is done," she continued firmly, giving him no chance to argue with her. "It won't take us long to finish."

"Okay," he said, releasing her slowly. "Thanks."

Half an hour later, the job was complete. Together, they stacked envelopes, securing bundles of fifty or so with large rubber bands. "These need to go out tomorrow," she said. "If you like, I can take them to the post office myself."

"Actually that'd probably be best," Ethan said. "I've got interviews scheduled all day. And my secretary's already swamped."

"No problem." Amanda reached for her coat.

Ethan picked up the box of addressed invitations. "I'll carry these out for you."

"Thanks." She looked at him gratefully. She knew it was silly, but she hated going out alone after dark to an empty car.

She led the way to her car, and after unlocking it, opened the back seat on the driver's side. He slid the box in, then stepped back away from the car while she shut the door.

Amanda glanced up at him. The way he was looking at her made her think he wanted to kiss her. But the moment passed, and he did not so much as move toward her. Telling herself she was glad he hadn't made a pass at her, she ducked her head and slipped behind the wheel. "Good night, Ethan."

He watched as she put on her seat belt and started the engine, and then bid her adieu with a casual lift of his hand, his deep voice echoing in the night, "Good night."

"WHAT KIND of bridal showers do you want, Heather, and how many?" Amanda asked late the following morning.

"I don't know. I haven't even thought about it, to tell you the truth. What kind are there?" Heather asked. Her dreaded government exam over, she was relaxed and happy.

Briefly Amanda covered the various types. "Well, I want my friends from the sorority house to give me a lingerie or personal shower," Heather said. "And Charlene can give me a recreation-for-two shower. All my mother's old friends will probably want to go to that."

"What about Tim's family? Is Mrs. Summerfield going to want to give you a shower?"

Heather's anticipation faded with lightning swiftness. "Probably."

Amanda put down her pen. "Is something bothering you, Heather?" If there was a problem that pertained to the wedding plans, she needed to know about it.

Heather toyed with the ends of her long, silky blond hair. "This is probably going to sound horrible of me but—" she lifted troubled eyes to Amanda's "—I'm not comfortable around Tim's family yet."

Was that all! "Those things take time," Amanda soothed.

"I know." Heather wrung both hands together nervously. "The problem is I'm not sure I'll ever be comfortable around them. Our families are so different. Our values are so different."

Amanda knew that was true. But she'd also seen how much affection Tim and Heather had for each other. "Do you love Tim?" she asked gently.

"With all my heart," Heather confessed.

"Then it'll work out."

Heather sighed, her worry still evident. "I hope so."

Amanda hoped so, too. She'd hate to see any outside pressure lessen the young couple's love for each other.

"So did you and Heather decide about the showers today?" Ethan asked Amanda late that afternoon, when he arrived at her office.

"Yes. Everything's all set." Remembering the near kiss of the night before, or what she had imagined to be a near kiss, Amanda busily sorted through her notes. She thumped them together against the polished surface of her teak desk and gave him a purposeful smile, the same as she'd give any client. "Are you ready to look at the videotapes of musicians?" she asked formally.

Nodding, he took off his jacket and loosened his tie. Lines of weariness edged his mouth. She gathered he hadn't had a good day. Absently she wondered if it had anything to do with the interviews he'd said he had this afternoon, and if any of those interviews were the people from her father's company—people he had promised HCI would not try and steal.

He sat on the couch, looking as if his collar was choking him, and unbuttoned the first two buttons of his starched white shirt. "Has Heather decided who she wants to play for the actual ceremony?" he asked with the brusqueness of one who'd already put in a full day, and then some.

"Yes. We've already hired a flute-and-harp duo to play while the guests are being seated. And your church organist is going to play the wedding march. All you have to do is decide who should play for the reception at the Adolphus. Heather mentioned she wanted a jazz band, but she didn't have time to view all the tapes and decide which one."

Ethan rubbed at the back of his neck. "So her old Dad is elected, hmm"

He didn't look old to her. But knowing it would sound as if she were being overly familiar if she said that to a client, she kept silent. She and Ethan were on far too intimate terms as it was. She had to keep her distance if she were to get out of this emotionally unscathed.

Fortunately Ethan spotted a jazz band he liked almost immediately. "I like this band," Ethan said, after viewing the third tape.

"Let's call and see if they're available," Amanda said. Minutes later, disappointed, she hung up with a sigh. "They're booked for Valentine's Day."

Ethan groaned and reached for another videotape. "I guess we keep looking then."

Unfortunately they kept running in to the same situation. Either Ethan didn't like the band or the band was already booked. "How many jazz bands do you know of in the Dallas-Fort Worth area?" Ethan asked, obviously frustrated after the third failed attempt to book a band for the reception.

"Over one hundred, not counting the ones formed by students at UT, SMU and UNT. But my guess is, with your blue-blooded guest list, you're going to want to go with a group that's a little more professional than a student group."

"You're probably right," Ethan said, reaching for yet another videotape.

Worried because this was taking much longer than she had figured, Amanda glanced at her watch. Ethan frowned as recognition lit his eyes. "I keep forgetting you have a daughter at home. Do you need to get there?"

Yes, Amanda did. But she also needed to get this done, too. She knew she wouldn't be able to rest until Ethan had hired a band and all that was settled. "It's no problem. Just let me call her."

Babe answered on the third ring. "Hi, Mom. Where are you? We were supposed to go over to Grandma's for dinner tonight. We're supposed to be there by seven-thirty."

"I know, honey, but I can't. I'm working late with a client."

"The Holbrook wedding again?" Babe asked.

"Yes. Listen, would you do me a favor and call Grandma and tell her I can't make it? Explain to her why. And about your dinner—"

"It's no problem, Mom. Really. I'll just heat up one of the TV dinners in the freezer."

As Amanda talked, out of the corner of her eye, she saw Ethan shrug out of his jacket and kick off his shoes, as if settling in for a long, long night. "You're sure?"

"I'm fifteen, Mom. I think I can handle this."

Aware Ethan was watching her, Amanda blushed slightly and took the droll hint the way it was intended. "Okay," she said, chastened. "I'll be home as soon as I can, but . . . the way it's going now—" she glanced at her watch and saw it was already six-thirty "—it'll probably be late."

She hung up to find Ethan still watching her. "Too overprotective, 'Mom'?" he teased, silver eyes sparkling.

She cleared her throat and admitted wryly, "So Babe tells me."

"Heather tells me the same thing."

They exchanged looks. She had the feeling at that moment—as parents, anyway—they were perfectly in sync. "It's hard not to worry, isn't it?"

"Very, but it gets easier the older they get."

"I hope so," Amanda said. Right now, she couldn't imagine ever being able to let go.

"Back to business," Ethan said, sliding another tape into the VCR.

It took another two hours, but finally they located a band Ethan liked that was also free for the fourteenth. Amanda hammered out the terms of the gig, as per Ethan's specifications. She was just putting down the phone when her father walked in to her office, unannounced.

He took one look at Ethan, who was lounging on the brocade sofa, the first couple of buttons of his shirt undone, his tie loosened, his shoes and jacket off, and an angry red flush covered his face. Amanda knew at once, despite the fact she was perfectly attired and seated on the edge of her desk across the room, that her father had the wrong idea about what had been going on. He thought they'd been, if not physically intimate, then emotionally intimate, and remembering how easily she and Ethan had just been talking, Amanda knew he wasn't far from the truth. Nor was he a fool. Remembering how angry and unforgiving he'd been when he'd talked about the Holbrook clan the other day, it was all she could do not to gulp. She didn't want a scene here. And saving the moment was not going to be easy.

"Dad, hi," Amanda said finally, breaking the uneasy silence that had fallen between the three of them with the smoothest, most cordial tone she could manage. "What are you doing here?" Feeling unaccountably nervous and incredibly culpable, she got to her feet. Why hadn't she anticipated this happening? Why hadn't she kept whom she was meeting with secret?

Her father looked at her, his deep disapproval in her evident. She knew without him saying a word that he felt betrayed by her in the worst possible way, because she hadn't listened to his advice about staying as far away from the Holbrooks as possible. Looking back at him, she felt guilty and embarrassed. She had done nothing wrong, but she doubted her dad would ever believe that now. Damn, she thought on a burst of inner frustration. Why did life have to be so complicated?

Sighing loudly, her father said, "Your mother was worried about you." He lifted the wicker hamper in his hands slightly. "She sent you some dinner."

Lloyd's doublespeak fooled no one. Amanda knew he had come to check up on her.

Angry at having been treated like a child, Amanda raised her brow in silent remonstration and looked at her father. Their glances clashed in silent battle. Her job required her to work late from time to time. They all knew that. Never before had her mother been prompted to send her dinner before. Which meant only one thing. They had surmised, from their talk with Babe, that she was here with Ethan.

Not wanting Ethan to know this was anything irregular—she could see he was embarrassed enough already, too—Amanda took the hamper from her dad. "Thanks," she said in a clipped tone of voice, her effort to be polite not quite succeeding. "Tell Mom I appreciate it—as always."

Her father pretended to cough, then, steadfastly ignoring Ethan, looked at her in a way that commanded, rather than asked, "Amanda, may I see you alone?"

Taking the not-so-subtle hint, Ethan reached around for his shoes and coat. "I was about to go, anyway, Amanda. I'd like to see copies of those contracts with the band once they're signed."

She thanked the heavens his tone was strictly business. She flashed him a look of silent apology for her father's rudeness and was heartened to see it was received in the same cooperative spirit that she'd sent it. Smiling, she promised, "I'll messenger them to you tomorrow."

"Thanks." He smiled back at her, his glance radiating concern for her, then turned to her dad. "Sir, nice to see you again."

Although Ethan's tone was sincerely polite, her father barely nodded and completely ignored the hand Ethan proffered. With another silent, telling look at Amanda that seemed to say "I'm sorry you're going to have to deal with this because of me," Ethan dropped his hand. "Well, goodbye all," he said awkwardly.

Amanda shot him a look of gratitude. "Goodbye." Not wanting Ethan to bear witness to any further unpleasantness, Amanda waited until she was sure Ethan was gone before she started in on her father. "How could you do this to me?" she turned toward him angrily. He was treating her like a child!

"Do what?" her father ground out, setting the picnic basket full of dinner down on her desk with a heavy thud.

Amanda stormed around her desk and began straightening up. "Check up on me."

"Your mother and I were worried about you, as I see we had a right to be. Amanda, where is your head? What can you be thinking, entertaining him here like this?"

She dropped the stack of papers she had just picked up and felt her face go white. "Like what?" The words spilled out of her numb lips like shards of glass.

Her dad stared at her in exasperation. "I think you know perfectly well what!"

"Spell it out for me," Amanda retorted angrily. If she was going to be accused of something, she wanted him to be specific.

"Cozying up to him!"

Rage pumping through her veins, Amanda struggled to control her soaring temper. Her jaw set, she stormed back, "Nothing was going on here tonight."

Her father looked her up and down contemptuously, finally accepting the truth in that. His glance narrowed accusingly. "Would you be able to tell me the same thing if I hadn't walked in and interrupted?"

"This is ridiculous," Amanda muttered, refusing to answer. She was not going to be drawn back into this feud. She wasn't.... Nor would she let him make her feel guilty for doing her job, earning a living so she could support herself and her daughter.

Her father stomped nearer, the censure in his voice deepening. "What does he want with you, anyway? Have you stopped to ask yourself that? I know the Holbrooks, honey. And I got to know them the hard way. They never do anything without an ulterior motive.''

Her face awash with color, she turned to face him. She knew his presence here was motivated by concern for her, but instead of helping her, he was being humiliating. If only she could make him see that. In the most conciliatory voice she could muster she asked, ''What kind of ulterior motive could have prompted them to hire me?''

''I don't know, but they must want something from you if they're trying to get on your good side after all these years.'' His lips thinned suspiciously. ''Has Ethan asked you about business? My business?''

''No. He hasn't said a word,'' she admitted truthfully.

''But you know HCI has been after my best men!''

She thought of the interviews Ethan had mentioned and again wondered uneasily just who it was he was considering for hiring. She also remembered his promise to her that it wouldn't happen again—ever. ''That was all a mistake,'' she countered angrily, her voice ringing with conviction. ''Ethan said so. When he found out about it, he straightened the whole thing out.''

Her father raised a brow and countered, just as smoothly, ''Either that, or he concocted another devious way to get what he wants.''

Amanda pressed her hands to her temples, aware of a tremendous tension headache coming on. ''Dad, this is too much!'' she stormed again.

His expression darkened even more. ''You don't know them like I do,'' he countered warningly.

Didn't she? She'd been set up by Harrison Holbrook, but her father didn't know any of that. He didn't know the initial loan that had underwritten his business had come from his dreaded enemy. Nor would he ever find out, if she had anything to do with it.

Tension radiating through her, she dropped her hands to her sides.

''Amanda, please, do us all a favor and get another firm to handle his daughter's wedding,'' her father said, trying to use a more persuasive tact.

Amanda shook her head in regret. ''I can't, Dad. It's too late.'' *And I don't want to.*

He stared at her for a long moment, looking betrayed and frustrated, then shook his head in mute remonstration. "I hope you don't regret this," he said sadly.

Amanda hoped she didn't, either. She knew she was walking a fine line between family and friend. And if push came to shove she might very well have to choose.

Chapter Eight

"Bad morning?" Mimi asked, walking into Amanda's office.

"The worst," Amanda confirmed with a scowl, pouring herself a third cup of coffee from the thermal carafe on her desk.

Mimi held out her own cup and waited while Amanda freshened hers. "Fight with Babe?" she asked, settling down on the sofa across the room.

Amanda walked over to join her. "Worse, a fight with Dad," she confessed wearily. She'd been so upset about it, she'd tossed and turned all night.

Mimi's expression became immediately sympathetic. She, too, had suffered her share of quarrels with their parents. "What was it about?" she asked gently.

Amanda adjusted a throw pillow behind her back and took another sip of coffee. "He wants me to drop the Holbrook wedding."

"Any particular reason why, other than this feud he and Ethan's father have been nursing the past quarter century?"

"He thinks Ethan is using me."

Mimi's eyes widened. "Is he?"

Not her sister, too! "How could he be?" Amanda demanded, exasperated.

Mimi took another careful sip of coffee. "You're saying he hasn't made a pass at you?" Mimi's tone was faintly disbelieving.

"No. Why would you think he had?" Amanda asked, aghast.

Mimi shrugged. "I don't know. Just the way he looks at you sometimes when you're not aware of it, like you're some angel he's suddenly discovered inhabiting these offices."

Heat flooded her cheeks. "Don't make fun of me."

"I wasn't."

Amanda stared at her sister. Realizing what Mimi said was true, she shook her head in mute defeat. As much as her pride demanded it, there was no covering her anguish. She traced the Moonlight and Memories logo on her mug. "I thought I could handle this," she confessed softly, relieved to be able to tell someone how she felt. "I thought I was."

"And?" Mimi prodded gently, with all the understanding an older sister could offer.

Amanda shrugged, feeling tears of despair and futility fill her eyes. "It's still there . . . the attraction between us. I can feel it. I know he does, too."

"But?"

"But it'll never work between us—ever." Thrusting her cup aside, Amanda got up to pace the office, her Donna Karan heels digging into the carpet.

"Why not?"

"Because we're from two different worlds." Worse, all the reasons that had existed before in regard to them not seeing each other still existed.

"Maybe your worlds aren't as different as you think," Mimi offered hopefully, coming over to lace an arm around her shoulders.

"That's what I wanted to believe, but we went over to William Noble the other day to help Heather and Tim pick out gifts for all the attendants. You should see the wedding rings they selected. Mimi, the jewels alone for this wedding cost more than the mortgage on my condo. I've been trying to make light of it, to pretend I'm of the same social class as he is, but I'm not. The truth is, I won't ever be. And his friends—people like Charlene Davenport—they know it, too."

"I'm sorry."

So was she.

"So what are you going to do?" Mimi asked, going back to retrieve her coffee cup as Amanda resumed her restless pacing.

"I don't know." She shrugged helplessly. "Try to avoid spending any time alone with him, I guess."

"You're that attracted to him, that it bothers you to be alone with him?"

Reluctantly Amanda nodded. She had to be honest with herself about at least this much. Seeing him the other night, in cords and a sweater, sharing cookies and coffee, even holed up together looking at videotapes…it was all too intimate. Maybe because the memories evoked were too intimate. "I just can't hack it anymore," she confessed in a broken whisper. "I'm afraid if we do spend time together, alone, something will happen. He'll say something or try to kiss me—" or look at me like he looked at me the other night after he finished carrying the addressed invitations to my car, Amanda added mentally "—and I don't want to make a fool of myself over him again. I don't think I could hack the humiliation." Or the heartache.

Thankfully, Mimi understood and was quick to come to her rescue, as always. "I'll tell you what," she offered persuasively. "Why don't you let me be a go-between for the next few days? I can oversee any work that has to be done that needs his approval."

Relief flooded her. "Would you mind?"

"No, of course not. What's next?"

"Someone has to write the copy for the formal press releases and get his approval."

"No problem." She smiled her encouragement. "And Amanda, cheer up. This wedding'll be over before you know it."

That was precisely what she was afraid of, Amanda thought after her sister left—that it would be over, and that she'd never see Ethan or spend time with him again…. Would she always feel this sense of unfinished business where she and he were concerned? Or would it fade, as it had the last time when she stopped seeing him on a daily basis? All she knew for sure was that she had to try and get him out of her mind, out of her thoughts, out of her heart.

"YOU'VE BEEN AVOIDING me," Ethan said.

Amanda smiled at Heather, who was having her formal bridal portrait taken. The only reason she was here was because Heather had specifically requested her presence, saying she needed Amanda's moral support for the stressful occasion, and Amanda hadn't the heart to turn her down. That didn't mean she felt it was safe to spend time with Ethan, however. She was still wary, fearful of being hurt.

"Don't be ridiculous," she lied through her teeth, her smile frozen on her face. Glad they were out of earshot of the others—Heather especially—she turned her attention to the clipboard in her hand.

He remained where he was, towering over her. Both hands braced on his hips, pushing the edges of his suitcoat back, he countered in a voice not to be denied, "I want to talk to you, Amanda."

Her decision to protect herself first and worry about his feelings second, intact, she countered, "Heather needs me here."

"Heather is doing fine on her own. So is the photographer and his assistant."

Catching the edge of warning in his low tone, Amanda glanced up. "Ethan—"

His steady regard narrowed dangerously. "It's either here where they might overhear, or in the hall outside the studio. Take your pick."

She knew he meant business. One way or another he was going to have his say. Her chin lifted a notch. "Outside."

"I thought you'd see it my way," he muttered with satisfaction.

What choice had he given her? she thought resentfully. She either gave in to his demands or he would make a scene. Some choice. Pasting a bright smile on her face she couldn't begin to feel, Amanda faced his daughter. "Heather, I'll be right back."

"Take your time," Heather called back cheerfully. Looking at Ethan, she dipped into a deep ladylike curtsey. "Don't I look fabulous, Daddy?"

Fatherly pride lit his features. "Beautiful, sweetheart. Just beautiful." Ethan gave her the thumbs-up sign.

"Make it fast," Amanda ordered tersely as they stepped out into the carpeted hallway of the office building, which for the moment, was deserted.

He faced her, bracing one shoulder against the wall, blocking her path back to the studio door. "I want to know why you're avoiding me," he said, folding his arms across his waist. Not sure how to handle this, she was silent. "Does it have anything to do with what your father said?" he prodded.

Surprise had her lifting her chin. "How do you know what my father said?" she asked, aware they were standing very close, close enough for her to breathe in the soap scent of his skin and the scent of Obsession.

"Because he talked to me, too," Ethan confided, his voice dropping another intimate notch. "He told me to leave you alone, that you'd already been hurt enough by me and he didn't want to see it happen again."

For a moment, shock held her motionless. "I'm sorry," Amanda mumbled, keeping her countenance cool and dispassionate with effort. *As long as he doesn't know the depth of my residual feelings for him, he won't be able to hurt me.*

Ethan made a ninety-degree turn, until his back was against the wall. "You had nothing to do with what he said. I know that." He looked down at the floor before turning his glance back to her face. "What bothers me is that you obviously believe it's true, that I would somehow take advantage of our situation to benefit my company or myself."

She knew he would never behave so callously. Unlike his father, Ethan was a man who cared about people and their feelings. "I know that's not true," she retorted, more emotionally than she would've liked.

He gave a dubious shrug and cast her a look of conflict. "If you feel that way, then stop avoiding me, stop letting our fathers' sins be our sins. Their fight has nothing to do with us, Amanda. Or at least it shouldn't. No one should be able to dictate whether or not we can be friends." He uncrossed his arms and took her hand in his. "I've enjoyed being with you again, renewing our friendship." Fitting their palms together, he brought their hands up, between them. "I thought the feeling was mutual."

It was, very much so.

Maybe she had been a fool to think she could disguise her feelings. Ethan had always been able to tell what was on her mind, in her heart, so easily. That was one of the things that had drawn her to him in the first place. Maybe the only way to ever really get over him was to get to know him again, spend time with him. Dismantle and dissolve all these memories and feelings she still carried around inside her. And if she couldn't get rid of them...well, that meant something, too, didn't it?

His hand tightened, until the heat of his skin burned through to her palm. She knew he was waiting for an answer, that she'd done them both a disservice, acting the way she had. "I'm sorry. Run-

ning from you was a cowardly thing to do. It won't happen again."
Love or hate, she would face him with the truth.

"Then you'll let things get back to normal and stop using Mimi
as a shield? As charming as she is, I'd much rather deal with you
directly," he said, grinning and playfully squeezing her hand.

And I, you. "I'll work with you on this wedding," she promised, trying not to notice how unburdened she suddenly felt, how
happy deep inside.

"Good," he sighed, looking greatly relieved, then escorted her
back inside. Thankfully the rest of the portrait-taking session went
smoothly. Heather was delighted to have both Amanda and her
father there, insuring everything was done correctly, and it was only
as she went back to the dressing room to change that Ethan cor-
nered Amanda. "About this weekend," he began, more tenta-
tively than usual. "You've heard the Summerfields are giving a
barbecue for Tim and Heather out at their ranch."

Amanda nodded. That was one of the things Heather was so
worried about. "Yes."

"Heather told me she'd already asked you to be there and that
you planned to go."

Again, Amanda nodded. "I promised I would."

"That being the case, I need a favor."

Maybe my dad is right, maybe he does want something from me.
But as soon as she had the thought, she pushed it away. She was
being ridiculous again. Paranoid. "What?" she queried cheerfully.

Ethan frowned self-derisively and lowered his voice to a confid-
ing whisper, "I don't trust myself to be able to hold my temper with
Tim's father, if he gets drunk again. You were able to handle him
before. I was hoping you might be willing to keep an eye out and
do so again, if it becomes necessary."

Amanda had suffered the same fear and had already planned to
do so. "No problem," she assured him blithely.

He smiled his relief. "It's quite a drive, over an hour and a half
from the city. I'm going to take the HCI helicopter out. You're
welcome to go with me, if you like."

She smiled, realizing she'd be crazy to refuse, considering how
pressed for time she'd been lately. "Actually that would help me
out. I have a lot to do Saturday. Not the least of which is help Babe
get ready for her date to the Winter Fling."

"That's Saturday night?"

"Yes, and I'll need to get back by seven at the latest, because her date is due to pick her up at eight." She paused, seeing the first and only snag in the arrangement. "Will that pose a problem for you?"

"None at all. I had planned merely to put in an appearance around one or two, stay a few hours, and head back to Dallas."

"Great."

He scanned her with approval. "I'll meet you at HCI headquarters around noon then? Just tell the security man at the door who you are. He'll have someone escort you to my office. Then we can go to the helipad together."

Again, she thought how different their worlds were, and how much the same. They had different social roots, true, and different lifestyles that went with that, but they also had daughters they were raising more or less alone, daughters they adored. And that particular similarity in their lives created a powerful bond. "Noon it is then," she said, determined to keep this joint outing in perspective, to view it as the casual convenience that he no doubt viewed it, too.

Nevertheless, no sooner had Amanda made the promise than she was wondering if it was a mistake.

"CHEER UP. It can't be that bad," Amanda said, as the helicopter took off from the roof of the HCI building.

"I look that glum, hmm?" Ethan said. He settled back in his seat and looked at the view of the downtown area beneath them.

"Like you want to go anywhere but to this barbecue," Amanda said. Although he'd dressed appropriately in faded jeans, a chambray shirt, string tie and a corduroy blazer, he didn't have the festive attitude needed to insure a good time at the outdoor activities.

"Sorry. I can't help but wonder what's in store for me—and my daughter," Ethan grumbled.

Amanda adjusted her full skirt and petticoats around her and followed his gaze, watching as the city traffic and tall buildings disappeared from their sight, to be replaced by flat areas populated by suburbs, shopping centers and parking lots. "Look at the bright side. It's a beautiful day without a cloud in the sky. The temperature is in the mid-sixties." Just looking at the outdoors, Amanda felt a case of spring fever rage through her.

"I guess you're right. We couldn't have had better weather." His glance slid over her blue denim western dress with the double-eyelet white petticoat beneath. Like Ethan, Amanda wore western boots—hers were the same deep red as the bandanna she wore around her neck, his a soft brown leather. A corner of his mouth lifted. "You look nice."

He was just being polite. He was not viewing her as a woman he could date, she told herself firmly. "Thanks." Uncomfortable with the compliment, she turned her attention back to the scenery. They lapsed into silence, appreciating the marvelous view.

The barbecue was in full swing when they arrived, with everyone seeming to have a wonderful time. To Amanda's relief, not only was Mr. Summerfield sober, but he was also at his gregarious best and ready to entertain Heather's family and friends again soon.

"You know, I have an idea how much this wedding is costing you," Phil Summerfield told Ethan frankly. "And the wife and I would like to do something to help out. So I was thinking, if you don't have any objection, we'll spring for the rehearsal dinner. Plan it, host it, pay for it, everything. You wouldn't have to worry about a thing. That's often the responsibility of the groom's family anyway."

Ethan looked both stunned and wary of the offer. "That's very kind of you, Phil," he said stiffly, when he finally found his voice. "But I've already made arrangements—"

"Well, shoot, we could still host it and pay for it," Phil said, choosing to overlook Ethan's less-than-enthusiastic response to his generous offer. Phil glanced at Amanda for confirmation. "You could handle a switcheroo like that, couldn't ya, honey?"

Yes, Amanda thought, I could easily send the bill for the party to you, Phil, but if I did that, you'd also have complete creative control over the party; it would only be fair. And that she could see Ethan didn't want. The Summerfields' taste wouldn't suit the Holbrooks. And the last thing Heather and Tim needed was to be embarrassed among friends and family.

Fortunately for Amanda, Ethan recovered before she had a chance to answer Phil.

"Really, I insist," Ethan cut in firmly. "But thank you," he said with obvious difficulty. "I really appreciate the offer."

Phil Summerfield nodded thoughtfully and clamped the fat cigar he held between his teeth once more. Between puffs of smoke, he said, "Don't trust me and the missus to do it up right and not embarrass all your fancy friends, do ya, Eth?"

Ethan's smile remained fixed, cordial, while beside him Amanda agonized. She hoped and prayed this wouldn't turn into a shouting match between the two men. "I just think this would be simpler, that's all," he said graciously.

"Uh-huh. Sure," Phil said, unappeased.

"Ethan, darling, come say hello to Pamela Weston and the rest of the group," Charlene Davenport intervened.

For once, Ethan looked grateful for the woman's attention. He glanced at Amanda.

She let him know with a look it was okay with her. She was perfectly fine where she was; she had no wish to expose herself to Charlene's little snubs. "If you'll excuse me," he said, then walked off with Charlene, leaving Amanda and Phil Summerfield standing there, feeling awkward.

Fortunately she was rescued from having to speak when Ethan's father joined them. "Nice party," Harrison remarked to Phil Summerfield. "Couldn't have done better myself."

Phil wasn't fooled by the flattery; he knew Harrison had little use for him. Harrison was just relieved Phil hadn't embarrassed the Holbrook clan. Phil met the older man's gaze shrewdly and said a grudging, "Thanks."

Fearing these two might pick up where Ethan and Phil had left off, Amanda decided to stay around—just in case.

"I understand Tim's about to graduate, too," Harrison continued, resting his weight on his silver-handled cane.

Again, Harrison's tone was unusually pleasant and gregarious. Amanda wondered at the older gentleman's attempt to be nice. It was so unlike him. Usually Harrison Holbrook ignored or insulted those he considered beneath him, party or no. If Phil was as suspicious as Amanda was of Harrison's unusual kindness, though, he hid it well, Amanda thought.

"Yes, he's getting his MBA from SMU in June," Phil said proudly, smiling as talk turned to his only son.

Harrison adjusted the trembling grip he held on his cane and seemed to search long and hard for something else nice to say. "But he graduated from UT/Austin, right, as an undergrad?"

"That's right," Phil said, ignoring the awkwardness that had fallen over the three of them. "Summa cum laude, too."

"So Heather said." Despite the pale color of his skin, Harrison looked properly impressed. "I heard he was in a fraternity there, too."

Phil frowned, admitting, "For part of his sophomore year, but he didn't like it, so he quit."

"Really? Why? I'd think . . . the social connections alone would have made it worth his while," Harrison said shrewdly.

To Amanda's surprise, Phil looked baffled by his son's actions, too. "I felt that way, too, but there was just too much tomfoolery for Tim's taste, so he got out, and actually, his grades went up after that, so the missus and I had no reason to complain."

"Hmm. Interesting," Harrison said, already seeming bored by the pedestrian exchange between future in-laws.

Satisfied things were on a sociable-enough level to allow her to leave, Amanda excused herself politely and wandered off to check out the buffet tables set up next to the house. Once alone, she visually checked out the entire area, thinking so far, so good.

"Glad to see you could make it," Ethan's father said at her elbow.

Amanda was so startled by his unexpectedly cordial attitude, not just toward her, but toward everyone, she almost dropped the serving spoon into the potato salad. "Hello, sir. It's nice to see you again, too," she answered politely.

Although Harrison had obviously been ill for some time, he looked worse today. His hands were shaking, his gait slow and uneven. Amanda wanted to offer to help him fill a plate for himself, but she knew that would hurt his feelings. So she continued to move slowly down the line, helping herself to sliced brisket, ribs and ranch-style beans.

"Heather looks happy, too," Amanda commented conversationally as she watched Harrison struggle to add a small piece of cornbread to his plate.

"That's what I wanted to talk to you about," Harrison said, indicating a shady place off to one side where picnic tables had been set up. "I've been wanting to do something special for my granddaughter on her wedding day, and since Ethan has already taken care of the wedding and the honeymoon, and the Summerfields are giving them a condo, I thought I'd get them each a car."

"That's very generous of you, sir," Amanda said, confused, "but I'm not sure what any of that has to do with me." Or even why he was telling her this.

Harrison struggled to cut his meat. "I'd like you to sound Heather and Tim out about color and so forth, and then go down to the Mercedes dealership and select the two vehicles. I want to present the cars to them on the day they return from their honeymoon. And I want it to be a big surprise. No one, absolutely no one, must know. Not even Ethan."

Why not? Amanda wanted to ask. Would Ethan object to his father giving the couple so lavish a gift? But she knew to ask that would be rude, and so she remained silent.

"Of course I'll see you're paid a fee for helping locate what I want for them," Harrison continued. He looked her straight in the eye. "I just don't have the energy to see to it myself. And with time already running short...you're the only person I know who could find out what we need to know about their preferences without giving anything away."

He was probably right about that, Amanda thought. And Heather did love surprises. So had Ethan when he was a teenager. "I'd be glad to help you," she said finally, still feeling a little bit uneasy about his newfound pleasantness for one and all. Maybe he was mellowing in his old age. Maybe Ethan had talked to him. Maybe Heather had. It was clear to her, in the way he looked at them, that Harrison loved both his son and his granddaughter dearly. Maybe he was making an effort to adjust to the marriage of Tim and Heather for their sakes. Certainly he was bright enough to have figured out that he wasn't going to stop the wedding or even delay it, any more than Ethan was. One way or another, Heather and Tim were going to be married....

"Having a good time?" Ethan asked an hour later, as the country-and-western band struck up a lively tune.

"Yes, I am."

"What were you talking to my father about?"

Amanda shrugged, then remembering her pledge to secrecy where the cars were concerned, said evasively, "Nothing special. The details of the wedding. How nice this all is today."

Although she'd trained her gaze away from his while she told the necessary fibs, he kept his eyes firmly on her face. "You're sure? I don't want him hassling you like he has in the past."

"He didn't." Which was another surprise. The last time she'd seen Harrison, he had issued a hands-off warning in regard to his only son. This time, he hadn't mentioned it. Maybe because he knew there was nothing for him to worry about, she thought, depression swamping her anew. Certainly if something substantial was going to develop between her and Ethan, it would've already begun. Instead, after an initial pass—made out of a mixture of ego and curiosity on his part, she supposed—Ethan was keeping her at arm's length, and she was wisely doing the same.

So why couldn't she feel better about it?

The rest of the afternoon passed swiftly. Mr. and Mrs. Summerfield were perfect hosts. The party was still going strong when Ethan and Amanda boarded the helicopter shortly after five, and it looked as if it might go on all night.

"I hate to say it, but maybe I was wrong about Tim's family," Ethan said when they were airborne once again.

"Their ranch is beautiful," Amanda agreed. Clearly they were doing their best to welcome Heather into their family, and if Heather wasn't completely comfortable with them yet, Amanda knew she would be one day, so long as everyone kept making the same concerted effort to be tolerant and graciously accepting of one another. "His family seemed more self-assured when on their own turf, too."

Ethan frowned. "I just hope Tim's father doesn't blow it again and drink too much at the wedding."

"I'll do my best to see he doesn't, although if what we saw there today was any indication, I don't think we have anything to worry about on that score. He's trying too hard to make Tim happy."

UNFORTUNATELY THINGS WEREN'T all roses back at Amanda's home. She knew at once from her daughter's swollen, red eyes that something had gone terribly wrong. "What do you mean your date stood you up?" she said, incensed, when Babe's story tumbled out.

"Just that," Babe sobbed. "He had one of his friends c-c-call and tell me he wouldn't be able to make it after all."

Amanda couldn't begin to understand how or why anyone could be that heartless. "Did he tell you why he couldn't go tonight?" she asked gently. Maybe there was a plausible explanation. Maybe Babe had just misunderstood.

"He s-said everyone was making fun of him for asking me out. They already call me Amazon Woman behind my back, but then the other guys started calling him Tiny Man in the locker room. He just couldn't take it."

"Oh, honey, I'm sorry." Fury at the boy's callousness flowed through her like a red mist as Amanda took her sobbing daughter into her arms and hugged her tightly. "I wish there was something I could do."

In the background, the phone rang. Hoping it might be her date with a change of heart, Amanda went to get it. Ethan was on the line. "I can't talk now. I'm in the middle of a crisis," she said, before he could get a word in edgewise.

"What happened?" he asked anxiously. "Is Babe all right?"

Briefly Amanda explained while her daughter continued to sob as if her heart would break. "The bastard," Ethan said grimly when she'd finished her rapid, but careful, explanation. "How could he do this to her?"

"I don't know, but I've got to go. I'll call you later, when things cool off. Okay?" Not waiting for him to answer, she hung up the phone.

While Amanda held her, Babe cried until there were no more tears left. Finally she took a deep hiccuping breath and dried her eyes with the soggy tissue she held in her hands. "I'm s-sorry, Mom. I didn't meant to ruin your day."

"All I care about right now is you," Amanda said, smoothing the tousled hair from her daughter's face. She handed her a dry tissue and studied Babe's red-rimmed eyes. "I think you need some ice for that."

"What does it matter if my eyes are swollen? I'm not going anywhere anyway," Babe said disconsolately.

The doorbell rang.

"This seems to be our day for interruptions," Amanda said, getting up to answer it. When she opened the door, Ethan was standing on the threshold, a beautiful bouquet of red and white roses in his hands. "These are for Babe."

For a second, Amanda was speechless. She moved aside to let him in. "That's very sweet. I'll go get her. Babe," she called, rounding the corner between the entryway and the kitchen.

"I don't want to talk to anyone," Babe murmured grumpily.

"Mr. Holbrook has something for you. Why don't you come on out and say hello?"

"Mom, I'm a mess!"

"He knows and he doesn't care. Please, honey." Amanda wanted Babe to realize not all males devalued her worth.

"Hi," Babe said sheepishly when she saw Ethan.

He handed her the roses. "The guy's a louse, sweetheart. I know you don't feel this way now, but you're better off losing him."

"Easy for you to say," she sniffed. "Now I don't have a date tonight."

"I'm sure there are others who don't have a date tonight, too," he retorted. "Well, aren't there?" he demanded goodnaturedly.

"Yes," Babe said reluctantly.

"Any of them your friends?" Ethan continued to prod.

Babe gave him a weird look, as did Amanda. "Yes," she said, "Why?"

"Maybe they'd like to go out tonight, too. With the three of us," he inclined his head toward Amanda. "Some place fun."

Babe seemed to like the idea. "Why don't you call them?" Ethan continued persuasively. "See if they're free for dinner?"

Amanda could almost see the wheels turning in her daughter's head. "You mean it?" she demanded excitedly.

He shrugged and slid his hands in his pockets. "The more the merrier."

Babe looked at her mother. Still stunned by his announcement, Amanda didn't know what to say. "All right, I will!" Babe said, racing off up the stairs.

"You don't have to do this," Amanda murmured, leading him into the living room once the coast was clear.

"I want to," he said, as if it were just that simple.

She couldn't deny Babe needed a diversion. Or that he was being a true friend, the kind he had been to her in high school. "Okay," she said finally. "I owe you for this one. And I'll pay—"

"The heck you will!" he countered, incensed. "It's my invitation, I'll pick up the check."

"I can't be in debt to you like that!"

"Then pay me back some other way, say with a home-cooked meal or something."

"You're serious, aren't you?" She regarded him silently.

He nodded and said, softer yet, "I want to get to know you again."

They were interrupted by footsteps thundering down the stairs. "Sally, Heather and Rachel can all go!" Babe reported jubilantly. "So where are we going and when do we pick them up?"

Ethan laughed. "How about dinner and a movie—some place casual, like Chili's? We can figure out what flick we want to see while we eat dinner. And we can go as soon as everyone can be ready."

"Half an hour?" Babe asked, looking at Amanda to see if it was okay.

Amanda nodded. Anything to make her daughter happy. Anything to make her forget the trauma of being stood up for a date.

"THANKS FOR A WONDERFUL evening," she told Ethan hours later when they'd returned to her home. They'd had a terrific time. She'd never seen the girls so animated. He'd been the perfect escort. And now as they lingered on her threshold, she realized she, too, hated for the evening to end.

He smiled and took her hand in his, the gesture casual, friendly. "Thanks for letting me do that. I haven't had so much fun in ages."

She tipped her face up to his, resting the back of her head against the door frame. "You used to do that for Heather?"

He smiled and nodded, the happiness he felt reflected in his eyes as he admitted openly, "When she was younger. Once she started driving . . . well, it all became different," he said, lifting a shoulder. "They didn't need a chauffeur anymore, so I was relegated to the status of chief financier, and that's about it." As he finished, sorrow radiated in his low voice.

Her heart went out to him; she had an idea what he was going through. "You miss it, don't you, being a full-time father?"

He nodded, looking suddenly sentimental. He swallowed and his hand tightened over hers, squeezing hard. "Yes, I do, and I have a feeling it'll only get worse as she gets older. I sometimes think I don't want her to get married, because I don't want to lose her," he finished on a husky, honest note.

She had an idea what it had cost him to tell her that, to admit that he had some sort of character flaw. "You're supposed to think about gaining a son, not losing a daughter," she chided gently.

He released his grip on her hand and stepped back, thrusting both hands in his pockets. "Is that what you're going to do?"

She chuckled softly, all too aware of the moonlit sky above them, the lateness of the hour, the cold air coming in the open door. "I doubt it," she retorted. "But you have my permission to say the same thing to me then." That is, if they were still in touch with each other then. She knew they might not be. The thought saddened her, and not wanting him to see, she ducked her head.

"Amanda—" He touched her cheek.

She lifted her face to his. They stared at each other, both of them fighting the attraction . . . both of them feeling a confused mixture of emotion, until whatever he'd been about to say was lost in the moment, the sense of togetherness, the sense of continuing, perhaps inevitable separation.

He dropped his hand, did the prudent thing, and stepped back. "Good night," he said softly.

So soon? she thought, disappointed, although she knew he was right to end it now. They both were. Her breath filtered out slowly. "Good night."

Chapter Nine

"How's Babe doing this morning?" Ethan asked Sunday, shortly after noon.

Amanda cradled the telephone receiver between her shoulder and her ear as she finished up the last of the lunch dishes. "She seems okay, although I don't know how she'll do tomorrow when she has to go back to school and face all her friends."

"That probably will be rough," he sympathized.

Yes, it would be. And she had a lot to thank him for. "You were great with her last night," Amanda said. He'd known exactly what to say and do to get Babe's mind off her troubles.

"I was glad to help out. Listen, as to the reason I called. Heather told me the proofs for her formal wedding portrait had come in."

Amanda scrubbed at a spot of mustard on the countertop, then whisked the soapy cloth over it until it gleamed. "Yes, I had them sent over to her Friday," she said, pausing to move the phone to her other ear. "Has she decided on which one she wants to use? I need to notify the photographer's studio tomorrow morning."

"That's the problem. She can't decide. And frankly, neither can I. I was hoping you might have selected one you liked best," he said hopefully.

"No, actually I haven't had time to study them myself."

They fell silent, both mulling over the possible ways to solve the dilemma. What was good for her business, unfortunately, wasn't always the best for her family, and right now, her family took precedence over anything work-related. "Normally it wouldn't be a problem. I'd be glad to drive over to your place or meet you at the office, but I really don't want to leave Babe alone today."

"I understand." He paused reflectively. "Do you think she'd mind coming over here with you?"

Amanda hesitated. She knew that Babe wouldn't mind being with Ethan again after the good time she'd had with him last night. Under the circumstances, what choice did she have? The work had to be done.

"I think that would be all right," she said finally. "For today." *And today only, she stressed to herself. She wouldn't let things get out of hand, the way she almost had last night.*

"I'll see you shortly, then?" Ethan asked.

"In about an hour," Amanda affirmed.

As she had predicted, Babe was delighted to go see Ethan and his daughter Heather. "Is Heather pretty?" Babe wanted to know during the drive over.

"Very pretty," Amanda acknowledged. She shot Babe a curious look when they'd halted at the next stoplight. "Why do you ask?"

"I don't know. I just…I wish I looked better, that's all," Babe said unhappily, glancing down at her long lanky form.

"I know how you feel," Amanda empathized. "I'm insecure about my looks, too."

"You?" Babe sat up straighter, not bothering to mask her surprise.

"Sure. And I'll bet you, ten to one, that Heather is insecure about her looks, as well. I think everyone is, honey."

"I can't believe that," Babe mumbled, sinking as far down into her seat as her seat belt would allow. "I bet Christie Brinkley doesn't worry about her looks."

Amanda smiled and guided her car into traffic once again. "Bet she does. Bet she studies her mirror and agonizes over every tiny line like you and I. And imagine if she gets a blemish! Why, it's a true disaster!"

At Amanda's comical tone, Babe began to laugh. "I guess you're right, Mom. Maybe I don't have it so bad after all."

Nevertheless, Babe tensed visibly when they walked up to ring Ethan's bell. It didn't help when she saw how beautiful Heather was, even in jeans with a hole in the knee and an SMU sweatshirt. Happily Heather and Ethan both went out of their way to make Babe feel at home. They even invited her to look at the photos with them and to offer her opinion. Babe shyly agreed, and soon, caught up in the process, was as relaxed as everyone else in the group.

It took almost an hour, but finally they were all in agreement over which photo should be used in the press releases. "Thank God that's over with!" Ethan said, as Heather dashed off to show Babe some of her trousseau.

"All these details beginning to weigh on you?" Amanda asked sympathetically, knowing she should be in a hurry to get out of there now that their business was done, but wasn't.

Ethan nodded. "Between my problems at work and this wedding, I haven't had any time for myself at all."

"I know what you mean. I'm feeling the same."

"I guess you would be." He sighed, and then, as he looked at her, his silver eyes began to twinkle. "Well, you know what they say," he drawled in an exaggerated Rebel accent, stretching his long limbs lazily. "There's no time like the present for a little R and R."

She laughed and sat up straighter. This was the old Ethan, devilishly attractive, flirtatious—one she had a hard time fighting, or wanting to fight. "I've never heard anyone say that," she said, a shade too breathlessly.

The corners of his mouth quirked up in good humor. "Yeah, well, I just made it up. How about it? Will you and Babe spend the rest of the afternoon with us?"

Put that way... it wasn't a date... wasn't really anything except a get-together between mutual friends. With children who were nearly the same age. Children who seemed—at the moment, anyway—to have an awful lot in common. It would be a shame to break that feminine camaraderie up, she thought pragmatically. And the older-sister-like attention Babe was getting from Heather was helping to bolster her spirits. Reluctantly she relented. "That would be very nice, thanks. If you're sure this is what you want, that is." She really didn't want to impose.

His eyes met hers, held another significant moment. "It is." His friendly smile deepened. "Up for a game of tennis on the court out back?"

She needed an activity to work off this incredible physical tension she was suddenly feeling. Amanda smiled, rising to the challenge she saw in his eyes. "Why not?"

"You didn't let me win!" Amanda complained when they had finished their third set.

"Of course not," Ethan said. "That wouldn't have been fair."

She faced him, hands splayed on her hips, aware that it wasn't just the cooling winter breeze or the fifty-two degree afternoon temperature or winter sunshine putting color into her cheeks. "Oh, so it was fair to pulverize me on the court?" she prodded merrily.

He gave her an indulgent look and retorted drolly. "I didn't pulverize you, Amanda. You only lost by two sets."

"Meaning what?" she asked sweetly. "It could have been worse?"

"Meaning," he said, grabbing her around the waist and reeling her in until her hips and torso lightly brushed his, "I play to win."

Suddenly Amanda was breathless from more than the workout. "Ethan—" She splayed her arms across his chest, wedging distance between them.

"You haven't changed, you know that?" he murmured appreciatively. "You're still the same incredibly complicated and awesomely beautiful girl I fell in love with all those years ago."

"You're wrong," she said, trying to ignore the thundering of her heart. "I have changed."

"Yes, I know," he amended wryly. "You're even more difficult to get to know than you were then."

Amanda stiffened, hating the way he was making light of something so important. "For good reason—"

"For all the wrong reasons," he corrected her gently. "You've put up a wall around your heart, thinking that if you have enough money and power to become completely self-sufficient, in debt to no one—emotional or otherwise, that you'll never be hurt again."

"It's true," she whispered, distressed, hating the open disapproval she saw on his handsome face.

"Is it?" he murmured in open challenge.

"Yes," Amanda retorted, secure in her knowledge of this much. If people couldn't get to you, couldn't tell what you were thinking and feeling, they couldn't hurt you. It was a lesson she had learned very well during her years with Ethan, during her marriage. "And you'll never convince me of anything else. You see, I'm older now. Wiser." Not the same stupid little freshman he used to know.

Frustrated with her steely resolve, Ethan shook his head in mute remonstration.

"Stop trying to change me!" Worse than his insistence on arguing with her about this was his constant, veiled disapproval of the way she lived her life.

He shrugged. "I can't help it. I know what you need, Amanda." When she was about to protest, he cupped her face with both hands, and his thumbs traced her lips, evoking a trembling sensation. "Because I need, too, Amanda," he whispered tenderly. "I need you. I need this. I have since the first day we met."

His lips touched hers, and in that instant, all the years that had passed faded away. She was fifteen again, he was eighteen. And all that existed were the myriad of powerful feelings swirling around inside them. Love, desire, passion, and yes, he was right, even need. But needing Ethan Holbrook was a dangerous route to take. Hadn't she proven that to herself before?

Breathless, she broke away. "No. Ethan, no."

His hold on her relaxed, but he didn't remove the arms that encircled her waist. Nor did he apologize for the kiss. He merely studied her, dark gray eyes burning into her face, telling her without words all that was still in his heart and would be for the rest of their lives, as well as how much she would have to change and trust if there were a prayer a relationship between them could work.

"How do I look?" Babe asked as they began the drive home. "Can you tell I'm wearing makeup?"

"Not really." Heather had done a good job, showing Babe how to apply blush and mascara and a hint of translucent lip gloss.

"What about my hair? Do you like it better curly?"

"It looks very feminine," Amanda admitted, trying without much success to forget the passionate yet tender kiss Ethan had given her, and the equally powerful way she had responded.

No, she wouldn't think about that.

"Maybe I should get a perm." Babe flipped the sun visor down and looked into the mirror attached to the other side of it. She made a face at her reflection. "Heather thinks that would help."

"I'm sure it would," Amanda agreed dryly, remembering she herself had suggested the same thing several times to her daughter, and been rejected every time. But maybe that was the norm. Maybe Babe just needed to hear these suggestions from a peer, a new friend . . . someone she could look up to.

In silence, Amanda parked the car in the condo garage and led the way into their home. "Is everything okay with you?" Babe asked finally, still close on her heels.

Distracted, Amanda turned around and nearly bumped noses with her daughter. "What?"

"You seem awfully quiet, Mom. Usually you have a lot more to say. A whole lot more."

Shaken was the word for it, Amanda thought. *Shaken to her very soul.* "I'm fine." It's just that Ethan kissed me. And I didn't expect it, didn't want it. Can't get over it now.

"How about Dominoes pizza for dinner?" Babe asked.

"Fine, whatever you want."

Babe went to call in their order, then returned to sit with Amanda in the living room. Ignoring the report about the stealth bomber on *Sixty Minutes,* Babe said, "So you knew Ethan in high school, huh? Is he in your old yearbook?" Babe asked. "What'd he look like then? Never mind. I'll go get it and find out. What a hoot! Imagine, you guys being our age!"

Amanda buried her face in her hands. What had she gotten herself into, letting those two get acquainted!

"He was cute, Mom!" Babe said minutes later as she cuddled next to Amanda on the sofa and turned to the page bearing Ethan's senior class picture. "A real jock!"

Yes, and he still was, Amanda thought, studying his handsome boy-next-door visage, deeply tanned skin and white-blond hair. "Did you have a crush on him?"

God, yes. One she hadn't gotten over, to this day. "Why does all this matter to you?" Amanda asked curiously, sidestepping the question as she reached out to ruffle her daughter's strawberry-blond hair.

Babe chose her words carefully. "Because the way you look at him sometimes . . . I think . . . I don't know, that there's something there."

"I think you've been reading too many romantic novels!" Amanda said, getting up to pace the room restlessly. "Is that the pizza man?" She moved to the window to look out.

"I didn't hear anything," Babe murmured. She watched her mother carefully, then ducked her head back in the old yearbook, to study the pictures carefully. "Amazing," she said. "Some of the clothes you wore then are like the ones we wear now. . . ."

Everything runs in cycles, Amanda thought. Even love?

"So, YOU HAD QUITE a weekend," Mimi said the next day at the office.

News traveled fast. "Where'd you hear that?"

"Babe. I called to talk to you last night, but she said you were taking a bubble bath and she didn't think you were *ever* coming out. You only do that when you're upset or extremely tense. So what gives? It can't be trouble with Ethan—Babe said you had a good time together yesterday."

To her mortification, Amanda—who until recently hadn't had any trouble keeping her emotions under wrap—felt herself blushing scarlet. "Mimi, leave this alone."

"I would," Mimi countered softly in her protective big-sister voice. "Except I'm worried about you, Amanda. I don't want to see you get hurt, and this trip down memory lane with him, well...I know you had reservations about dealing with him earlier and I think you were right. I just can't see a liaison with him leading you anywhere you want to go."

Her sister's assessment was disturbingly close to the feelings Amanda had been trying to bury for the better part of twenty-four hours. Irritated, she sighed and said, a bit more curtly than necessary, "The job will be over soon. I just have three more weeks."

"All the reason you should be keeping your distance from your old beau," Mimi pointed out casually.

She knew that, too. The problem was it wasn't so easy to stay away from him. There were all the details of the wedding still to be resolved, for instance. And then there was Ethan himself. He was a powerful, magnetic man, who was very sure of himself and the goals he wanted to achieve. In the face of his formidable will and easygoing charm, she sometimes felt like a daisy in the path of a man on a steamroller. It was either be plucked or crushed.

Not in the mood for any lectures from her big sister on this topic, Amanda said irritably, "Look, what we had was over years ago."

"Are you sure? I have to agree with Babe. Whenever I see the two of you together... there are some definite sparks."

Amanda knew that, too. And although the hopelessly foolish, sentimental part of her wanted desperately to jump-start their old romance, the sensible part of her said to just let the past be over.

It wasn't realistic of her to think any lasting liaison was really possible, was it?

"Delivery for Ms. Amanda Stratton," a young man in suit and tie said from the door.

He had a small, gift-wrapped box in his hand. Amanda went to sign for the package. "Who's it from?" Mimi asked, watching curiously and taking a seat on the edge of Amanda's desk.

"I don't know." But the receipt said William Noble jewelers. Knowing how expensive anything that came from that shop had to be, that she couldn't possibly reciprocate or even come close, made Amanda feel sick inside.

Her hands were shaking as she opened the card. "I owe you so much," it said. It was signed simply "Ethan."

"Go on. Open it." Mimi said, apparently knowing better than to ask her what the card said.

It took her the better part of two minutes to wrestle the silver paper and ribbon from the box, but finally Amanda got the jewelry case open. Inside was a beautiful diamond-and-sapphire bracelet. Beside her, Mimi gasped in stunned amazement. There was no doubt the jewels were real. "Holbrook," she breathed in awe. Stunned, she cast Amanda an admiring glance. "It must've been some family outing you had yesterday."

It had been, Amanda thought sadly. And the knowledge Ethan felt he somehow needed to pay her for her company was unsettling and seemed to highlight the main differences between them. "I can't accept this," she said, closing the box with a snap, feeling tears of mortification and anger come to her eyes.

"What?" Mimi said, shocked.

But Amanda was past the point of caring what anyone thought, even her loving family. "Hold the fort down for me," Amanda said, already heading for the door. "I've got to get something settled." The sooner, the better.

"YOU GOT THE BRACELET," Ethan said when she met with him in his private office at HCI.

"Yes, and I'm returning it." She thrust it at him.

"Why?" He looked hurt. "I saw you admiring it the other day when we were at William Noble with Heather and Tim."

"That's not the point," she said, exasperated, running a hand through her strawberry-blond curls.

"Then what is the point?" he asked, mimicking her terse tone.

"I can't accept this . . . it's way too expensive. And it's inappropriate." Surely he must know that.

But he apparently didn't. "Why? Because we just started dating?"

"What we had yesterday wasn't a date, not really."

"The next one will be," he stated emphatically.

"There won't be a next one," she vowed, just as firmly.

He stepped closer. "Why not?"

She folded her arms at her waist. "For all the reasons that existed before." His stormy countenance matched her own. She dug her heels into the plushly carpeted floor even further. She didn't want to be arguing with him, didn't want to have this conversation at all. "Ethan, please, we've been through this," she pleaded softly, trying to make him see reason. "You know we're from two different worlds." Maybe she'd forgotten that yesterday, but the bracelet had brought it all home again.

"And you know I don't care about that," he countered gruffly.

"You should. Otherwise, you're going to get hurt. We're both going to get hurt."

He came nearer, toe-to-toe. With his hand under her chin, he tipped her face up to his. "Are you telling me you didn't feel something when I kissed you yesterday?"

She couldn't deny it, even if she wanted to, not when he already knew the truth. "I'm saying I don't want to become your lover, Ethan. I don't want a casual, physical affair."

"And you think that's all I'm offering you?" he asked incredulously, dropping his hand.

"Besides the jewelry, yes. Realistically, Ethan, what else could there be?"

It was his turn to look shocked. "I guess I was wrong about a lot of things," he muttered, putting the box aside. "I'm sorry if I offended you," he said finally. "I just wanted to do something that showed I cared."

"Ethan, I've been this route before. I've had gifts lavished on me. Gifts I couldn't possibly reciprocate. I ended up being called a gold digger by my ex-husband's family. They thought I married their son for the money he stood to inherit one day. They never let me forget it. It was a miserable experience. I can't go through that again, and I certainly can't put Babe through it, even inadvertently."

"I wouldn't do that to you," he swore, understanding softening the lines of his face.

"Your father would."

His face reddened. He didn't dispute what they both knew to be true. "If you want to talk about that...your father hates me, too, Amanda," he said gently.

"Precisely my point," she said turning away and massaging her temples where a raging headache was starting. "We have no future together, Ethan." Straightening, she looked out the window at the Dallas skyline. "We're kidding ourselves if we ever think it might be so."

He moved closer and spoke in a soft, lulling voice. "You won't fight to be with me?"

She ducked her head and studied the painted steel window sill. "We tried that once. It didn't work."

He reached out and gently touched a lock of her hair. "We're older now."

"But apparently no wiser." She turned to face him, leaning one shoulder against the glass. "I'm sorry, Ethan. This just isn't going to work."

He stared at her, finally beginning to believe she might be right. Feeling like her heart was breaking, Amanda turned, "I've got to go."

He reached out and caught her wrist in a light, staying grasp. "That's it? You reduce our feelings to dollar signs and then leave?"

Maybe she had said it callously. Maybe in the final analysis that was best. Yesterday, playing tennis with him, she'd been able to pretend for a while that nothing else mattered. But today she knew it wasn't true. Before, when she'd been involved with him, she'd been hopelessly young and naive. She hadn't known what she was letting herself in for. Now, having dealt with people like Charlene Davenport, she knew what she would be getting into if she got involved with him. And she knew she couldn't take it. And even if she could, there was no way in hell she'd put her daughter through it. Just imagining what a barracuda like Charlene Davenport would do to someone with Babe's fragile self-image made her go cold inside. "It's the way it has to be," she said sadly, facing him, and feeling her heart breaking.

"You're wrong, Amanda. Furthermore, your attitude is demeaning to both of us."

Maybe it was. But that didn't change anything. "I'm not going to change my mind," she said softly.

For that, finally, he had no reply.

Chapter Ten

"Have you heard a word I said?" Amanda asked Ethan at noon the following day. Although he'd been perfectly cordial upon greeting her, his subdued silence since was a little unnerving, especially as she had expected him to have more input on the details of Heather's wedding.

Ethan glanced over at her, seeming more distracted and vaguely upset than ever. Feeling responsible for his mood, Amanda took a deep breath. "I know I was really emotional yesterday. I—shouldn't have been so ungracious when I returned your gift." When she'd had time to think about it, she had realized he hadn't meant anything by it, one way or another. He had just been giving her a gift—on Highland Park scale.

His look darkened at the memory she evoked. "No, you shouldn't have," he agreed in a tone that let her know he was still stinging over the rejection.

"But it still had to go back," she reminded him gently, unable to help but notice how good he looked in his charcoal wool suit, or how the fabric brought out the gray in his eyes.

He sighed heavily. "Maybe it did at that," he agreed.

A silence fell between them, so intense and complete she could hear the varying meter of their breaths—hers, rapid and shallow, his, deep and even. "Ethan, I still want to be friends," she said softly, putting her notes aside for a moment and walking over to his side. "Is that possible?"

For a moment, he didn't answer, merely pushing his swivel chair away from his desk. "It's possible." His eyes met hers as he absently straightened his blue-and-charcoal paisley tie. He pushed away from his desk and got up to walk around the room restively. "And I'm sorry I've been inattentive," he said, offering his back to her as he stared out his office window. "I had a shock earlier today," he continued in the same distracted tone. He sighed and dragged a hand through his hair. "I'm still not sure how to handle it."

Relief filtered through her at the knowledge she wasn't responsible for his mood, to be replaced swiftly by worry. "What happened?"

He turned to face her. "I was in my father's office and I saw a report from a private detective agency on his desk." The grooves on either side of his mouth deepened. "He's having Tim investigated."

Shock held her briefly motionless. "Why?" Amanda asked.

"He doesn't approve of the wedding."

Neither had Ethan initially, but he'd grown to accept it as inevitable for his daughter's sake. "And he expects to find something on Tim, something that might stop the wedding?" she asked, aghast at the news, but not really surprised. This sounded like something Harrison would do.

Ethan shrugged his broad shoulders listlessly and folded one arm on top of the other in front of his chest. "You know Phil Summerfield. His father does not have the best reputation in town, either personally or in business. My dad thinks like father, like son."

"And you don't?"

"No, I don't. I'm not like my father. Why should Tim be a carbon copy of his?" He turned back to the window, stood looking out at the downtown area.

Seeing how much he needed comforting, her heart went out to him. Unable to do otherwise, she moved to his side and gently touched his arm. "Ethan, I'm sorry. I can see how much this is upsetting you. If you'd rather I come back tomorrow, to finish up the details of the wedding, I can." They weren't getting much done, anyway.

"No, we need to get this done. And I need to talk to someone who understands." He paused and his eyes lit with sudden inspiration. "Do you feel like going for a ride?"

It was easy to see how hemmed-in he felt. Easier still to understand the instinctive need to roam free of all emotional and physical constraints. "Where?" she asked curiously, glad he wanted her company. In his current mood, she didn't think he should have to be alone. She doubted his other friends like Charlene Davenport would understand his concern over his father's actions. Most likely, Charlene would applaud Harrison for what he'd done.

"Lake Ray Hubbard. The helicopter's on the roof. We could be there in fifteen minutes."

She knew she owed him, for helping her out with Babe in her daughter's hour of need. She spread her hands wide in a gesture of conciliation. What were they waiting for? "Let's go."

When the helicopter landed short minutes later, the lakefront was deserted save for an occasional fisherman in the distance. The Texas sky above was gray and cloudy. As they began to walk along the shore, a fine mist of rain began to fall. "Sorry," Ethan said.

Amanda put up the hood on her coat. Having always loved the outdoors and the change of seasons, she didn't mind the brisk way the wind was picking up or the moisture in the air. "It's all right," she soothed, touching the sleeve of his overcoat with her gloved hand. "Just talk. Start from the beginning and tell me what's on your mind." She sensed a lot more was going on between father and son than what he'd let on so far.

Ethan turned up the collar on his overcoat until it reached the midpoint of his ears. He had no hat with him, and the wind tossed the layers of his white-blond hair. "It isn't just finding out about the detectives," he admitted, tucking his chin down into his collar for warmth. He sighed heavily. "It's a lot more than that, Amanda. I've known since I was a kid that HCI would someday be mine. I've been groomed to take it over. And I wanted that. What I couldn't hack was working with my father. He's got a hard edge to him that is really tough for me to take. Like what happened to your dad, for instance. I never would've asked him to fire those men."

He shrugged, not bothering to mask his disappointment in his father, and then continued, disheartened. "My dad thinks that's a weakness in me, and he's never been shy about pointing that out. That's why I worked in Atlanta for so many years. I didn't want to be here, fighting him."

"But you're back now," she pointed out quietly.

"Yes. And I'll be honest, it's where I want to be. I want to take over the company in June. I want to run HCI my way."

"But you think your father won't approve?"

"I know he won't. And that's where the problem comes in. Dad's not supposed to be under any stress. It'll worsen his illness. I don't want to do anything that will aggravate his condition. And yet I have to do things my own way. So I end up walking this fine line between love and resentment, and it's eating me up inside."

They paused atop a rocky ledge overlooking the lake and stood together, watching the water lap at the shore in choppy gray waves some six feet below. "Did you tell him you know about the private investigator?"

"Yes. He thinks he's doing the right thing."

Amanda turned so the wind whipped the hair away from her face, rather than into her eyes. The fish and algae smell of the lake assaulted her nostrils. "Has the detective uncovered anything about Tim or his family that would prevent the wedding?"

Ethan shook his head no, relieved. "No, thank goodness." Withdrawing a hand from his pocket, he touched her elbow, guiding her away, to the tree-covered shoreline to the west. "Heather's heart would be broken if the wedding were called off now."

"So what are you going to do?" Amanda asked, lengthening her strides slightly to match his impatient ones.

"There's nothing I can do," he muttered in frustration. He balled his gloved hands into fists and thrust them into his pockets. "I told my dad to call off the hound dogs."

"Do you think he will?" Amanda asked.

"Honestly? No."

"Are you going to tell Heather?"

"God, no. It'd break her heart. She thinks the world of her grandfather, and if truth be told, I'd just as soon she not learn about his frailties at this late date."

Amanda glanced over at him thoughtfully, aware the misting rain had dampened the strands of his hair until they were a dark gold. Ethan's ears were red from the cold where they rose unprotected above his collar. She bet they stung as much as her face. They couldn't afford to stay out here much longer, especially with the temperature constantly dropping. "So what next?" she asked, suppressing a shiver with effort.

"I don't know." Ethan shook his head, the troubled lines around his eyes deepening. "I guess I get through it, day by day."

Like they all did. Feeling the need to comfort him as she would any friend, she reached over and briefly touched his shoulder. "I'm sorry you've been having such a tough time."

"I'm grateful you could take the time to listen." He halted his steps and reached over to squeeze her hand, his gesture as strictly platonic as hers had been. "Damn, but it's cold," he said, not bothering to suppress a shiver.

Amanda laughed. "I thought you'd never notice," she teased.

"What do you say we find a restaurant somewhere and warm up with some hot chocolate, and go over those wedding plans we were working on?"

Amanda smiled, glad everything had returned back to normal. "Sounds good to me."

ONCE ETHAN HAD TALKED his problems out, they were able to get the necessary business done without further delay. Unfortunately Amanda's dealings with his father later the same evening were not quite as painless. "Were you able to get the cars I wanted for my granddaughter?" Harrison Holbrook asked the moment she walked into the library of his Highland Park home.

Amanda opened her briefcase to show him the brochures and price lists she'd picked up for him. "I'm still working on it. The color Heather prefers is not in stock at the Highland Park Mercedes dealership, but they're checking with other dealers around the state, and if they can get one here in time, then they will."

"And if not?" Harrison asked, frowning.

"I guess we could look into getting another car, but it's a little premature to be thinking about that. The dealer seems to think he can work something out, given a week or so."

"I heard you and my son took the chopper out to the lake this afternoon," he continued, watching her shrewdly.

Amanda purposefully kept from showing any emotion. "Sir," she said in the polite but firm tone she always used with rude clients, "I don't think—"

"That it's any of my business?" Harrison interrupted. He gripped his cane until the knuckles on his trembling hand turned white. "It is if you talked about me, and Ethan told you about the private detective I hired."

Unwilling to betray the confidences they'd shared, Amanda said nothing. Not that it mattered to his father.

"You don't have to answer," Harrison continued autocratically. "I can see by your reaction he did talk to you."

Since he'd brought the question up, Amanda was unable to resist the opportunity given her. Wanting to find out more about what the devious Harrison was up to now, for Ethan's sake, as well as her own, she threw caution to the wind and asked, a trifle ingenuously, "Why did you hire someone to investigate Tim and at the same time have me work on buying him and Heather such lavish wedding gifts?" His actions didn't make sense to her. That was, if he was doing everything above board.

"I believe in covering all my bases," Harrison replied succinctly, his gray eyes gleaming mysteriously. His cagey smile broadened, momentarily making his face lose its customary pallor. "Thus, whatever happens, I'll be prepared," he finished smugly.

Yet he would be just as happy if the wedding were called off, Amanda thought, disturbed by the older man's unapologetic duplicity. Poor Ethan. He had to deal with this incorrigible man every day.

"At any rate, I don't want the cars actually purchased until the day after the wedding takes place," the old man continued, lifting a small tumbler of what looked to be bourbon and branch water to his lips.

"Fine." Amanda knew whatever way he chose to do this would be fine with the dealer. The Holbrook name and money worked miracles all over Dallas.

Harrison withdrew the pocket watch he had chained to his vest, checked the time, and replaced it. "I hope you're keeping track of the hours you're spending looking for my gift."

She nodded acquiescently, wishing all the while the interview with him were already over. If only she could have refused this job without offending him. But fool that she was, she had taken it, and as a businesswoman who valued her word, would have to follow through with it. "A very strict accounting, sir." She didn't want him to accuse her of cheating him later, and made sure everything was very well documented.

He nodded, looking inordinately pleased about that much. "Very good. I'll settle up with you after the wedding, also."

"That would be fine." Amanda smiled with a cordiality she couldn't begin to feel. Ethan's father or not, she really detested this man. And she didn't trust him, either. "Now if you'll excuse me, I really have to go," she said politely.

He made no comment, merely nodded his dismissal, but continued watching her as she left. A shiver crept down her spine as she wondered what Ethan's father would do next.

THE FOLLOWING DAY was a busy one for Amanda, and although she didn't hear from Ethan directly, she thought of him often as she dealt with the florists, the minister, the musicians and the caterers for Heather's wedding. Around four, Babe called to ask if she might go to a friend's home for dinner and an evening of studying. Amanda gave her permission, then exhausted, headed home herself.

For once, there was no rock music blaring when she opened the door. Kicking off her shoes where she stood, she sorted through the mail in the front hall, then went upstairs to change into a thick canary-yellow jogging suit. No sooner had she gotten her dinner started than the front doorbell rang.

The bouquet of yellow roses was the first thing Amanda saw when she opened her condo door. Her glance traveled up to Ethan's face. The apology in his eyes was as gentle as his low voice. "I gather my father grilled you about our trek to the lake."

"How did you know?" Did that mean his father had told him about hiring her to purchase the cars, too?

"He mentioned it in passing, said he ran into you unexpectedly yesterday evening."

So he hadn't told Ethan about hiring her.

"I'm sorry. He didn't tell me the gory details but I can't imagine your conversation with him could have been very pleasant," he said nervously.

Nor was it as bad as Ethan suspected. Not sure what to say, for fear she'd give away something she had promised not to—namely Harrison's surprise wedding gift to his granddaughter and her prospective groom—Amanda said nothing in response. She took the bouquet he handed her, drinking in their fragrant depths, the petals like silk against her face.

Realizing he was still worried about her reaction to his father's meddling, she lifted her eyes to his. "It's not your fault, Ethan. I know you can't control your father any more than I can control mine. And leaving the way we did, when we did . . . it would have been hard for him not to find out about it."

As her next thought occurred, she felt a tinge of uneasiness. Was that why Ethan had taken off with her? Because he'd wanted to irritate his father? No, she wouldn't accept that. Even subconsciously, he wouldn't use her that way.

"I just wanted you to know I've been thinking about you." Still wearing his business suit, Ethan loosened his tie.

I've been thinking about you.

"It meant a lot to me to be able to talk to you yesterday." He lifted a shoulder in a careless gesture. "Then I felt guilty for unloading on you like that. I know you have enough problems of your own."

That was true. Nevertheless, he was a friend, and she had owed him. "I was glad to help. You were a friend to me when Babe was so down the other night and I didn't know what to do. I wanted to return the favor."

"It was appreciated." His eyes held hers for a moment. He looked past her, toward the interior of her condo, as if suddenly noticing something missing. "It's awfully quiet around here."

Abruptly she realized they'd been standing on the doorstep the whole time, the cool winter air flooding her condo. "Come on in while I put these in water." Her back to him, she self-consciously led the way to the kitchen, stopping briefly in the laundry room to get a glass vase from the storage cabinet. "Babe is at a friend's house, studying for a geometry test," she explained.

"Something smells good."

"Meat loaf. I didn't know I was going to be alone for supper when I prepared it this morning."

He bent his knees slightly, and looked into the oven. "Scalloped potatoes, too."

"And green beans and tossed salad." She almost laughed at his wistful expression. Remembering he'd once tried to teasingly barter for a home-cooked meal from her, she asked, half in jest, "Do you want to stay?"

His eyes held hers again, testing, asking. "Do you really want me to?"

Yes. Her response was quick and honest. But fearing how that would sound and not wanting him to know how attracted she still was to him, she kept her voice level and said only, "If it's what you want. A lot of people don't like meat loaf—"

"I do. Maybe because I never had it growing up."

Another difference between them. He had lobster and prime rib whenever he wanted, while she got by by fixing ground beef or chicken a hundred different ways.

Not wanting to dwell on the differences between them, Amanda checked the green beans simmering on the stove and peeked into the oven. Now that she'd invited him, and he'd accepted, she felt awkward and ill at ease. When would she stop reacting so impulsively, letting her emotions drive her? Just because he looked like he needed a friend didn't mean she had to let him into her life again. Especially when it meant she might very well end up being hurt... again.

Nevertheless, he was here, and having invited him to stay, she would have to do her best to make him feel as welcome as possible. She turned back to Ethan, a smile fixed on her face. "It won't be ready for another half an hour."

"That's fine."

She wished he wouldn't look so agreeable, or so eager to partake in the homey atmosphere of her condo. She would've thought the small but stylish abode would've stifled him after his roomy mansion, but he looked as if he were in seventh heaven as he followed her back into the living room.

He spied their old high school yearbook still out on the coffee table, from when Babe had been thumbing through it Sunday evening. He grinned. "I had mine out too the other night, glancing through it." He picked it up and sat down beside her on the couch. Opening it up, he held it between them, so they could both look through it simultaneously. The first picture was one taken in the gym during an autumn pep rally. The football team was standing next to the coaching staff. "There you are," she said, pointing to him in his jersey.

"It seems like just yesterday, and yet it's a lifetime ago."

"I know what you mean," she said as he turned another page and found a picture of her with the French Club. "Having Babe in high school has brought so much back to me. Watching her go through all the ups and downs of high school makes me remember what it was like to do the same. And I find myself recalling things I'd completely forgotten, things I haven't thought about for fifteen years."

He glanced at her, bemused. "Like what?" he asked in a soft voice.

She shrugged, aware her cheeks were turning shades of red. "Like how it felt to wait for the phone to ring."

And how it felt now, waiting and wondering when she would see him again. Never knowing. Almost afraid to hope.

"Yeah? You think that was hard? Well, try dialing the phone when your fingers were so slick with sweat they could barely stay inside the dial. It was humiliating to get turned down for a date."

"C'mon, you got turned down for a date?" She arched her brow disbelievingly. She remembered all too well how immensely popular he'd been. Any girl would have given her eyeteeth to go out with him.

"Well, yeah," he admitted, surprised she was shocked. "Once."

"Once!" she repeated drolly. He acted as if a single disappointment was too much to be borne. When she thought of all she had fought against to get where she was, it was all she could do not to berate him for his lack of forebearance.

"Don't make light of it," he said, accurately reading her disparaging thoughts. "It was awful. I never felt so humiliated in my life."

It was humanizing, somehow, discovering this about him. Discovering he had feelings that were easily hurt, too. Turning slightly toward him, she rested her elbow on the top of the sofa and propped her chin on her upraised fist. "Just out of curiosity, Ethan...was this before or after you were a big star on campus?"

He reached around to loosen his tie a bit more, dragging the knot down to midsternum, before undoing the first button on his starched blue-and-white striped shirt. "When I was a freshman."

She grinned, more curious now than ever. "Who was it?"

He dropped his attention to the yearbook and turned another page. "Never mind."

"C'mon, give. What does it matter now, anyway?"

"I don't even remember her name," he lied as he kept his eyes firmly on the nostalgia-invoking pictures in front of him.

"The truth, Holbrook!" Amanda demanded.

"Okay. She was...older."

Amanda didn't know what to say. She would have expected him to always play it safe. Maybe she didn't know as much about him as she thought. "You asked out an older woman?"

He shrugged and said "I was a freshman," as if that said it all. Amanda waited patiently for more details.

Seeing she wasn't about to give up now, he finally admitted with a sigh, "I called one of the JV cheerleaders."

"And then?" Amanda asked, dying to hear the rest of this tale.

"What do you think?" Evidently his feelings were still hurt over the abrupt dismissal he had received. "She all but laughed in my face."

"And then what?" Amanda asked, amazed to know everything hadn't been easy for him. He may have been born with a silver spoon in his mouth, but he was as fallible and human as the rest of them.

"And then I learned my lesson. I never stalked older women again."

She studied his chagrined expression. The Ethan she knew in her high school days had dared anything he damned well pleased, including the sly dating of her. But maybe that had been as much a coverup on his part then as her deliberately perpetuated air of self-sufficiency now. Maybe he had had times when he felt vulnerable, and still did.

"Never?" she teased.

He thought about that for a moment, then said finally in a grumbling voice, "Well . . . these days it's hard to tell. You don't exactly ask to see someone's driver's license to ask them out. Besides, once you reach adulthood, and experience more of life, the differences that come from being different ages melt away."

"I guess so." She was surprised, though. She never would have figured anyone as handsome and smart and charismatic as Ethan would've been turned down by anyone. It humanized him somehow, knowing that he had been, and was willing—if reluctantly—to admit it.

"What about you? Did any guy ever not call that you wanted to?"

Besides you? She remembered, without wanting to, how long she had waited for that phone to ring after he'd stood her up for the prom, how hurt she had been. But that was water under the bridge. There was no reason she should be dwelling on it now.

Too late, he realized what he had asked. What he'd inadvertently brought up. His gentle expression faded, to be replaced by embarrassment as he recalled what she did. "Amanda, I'm sorry."

"It's okay." But was it? What would happen if he ever treated her that way again? If she let herself start to care for him and he let her down?

Pushing the traitorous thoughts aside, she uncurled her legs from the sofa cushions and got lithely to her feet. He moved after her. Catching her lightly by the arm, he swung her around to face him. "Don't," he urged hoarsely, pain reflected in his eyes. "Don't go back to the past. What happened then is over."

Was it? Without warning, tears clouded her eyes. She blinked them away. "Sometimes I don't think it'll ever be over, Ethan. Not when every time I see you or am with you I'm reminded of all the animosity between our two families. Maybe we were right to let our friendship end years ago."

"No. Don't say that," he urged, his other hand coming up to her elbow. "I know it's difficult, our seeing each other as friends even now, but the camaraderie we're beginning to discover again is worth it." He saw she wasn't convinced of the wisdom of his advice. He frowned, and his voice dropped another compelling notch as he persuaded, "Finding you again has meant a lot."

To her, too, if she were perfectly honest. But she couldn't let what she wanted cloud what was. She shook her head, confused and depressed. "We're living in a fantasy world to ever think that— that even a sustained friendship would be possible between us."

He set his jaw firmly. "No one dictates to me whom I can or can't see."

She knew he thought that, and he was wrong. "But the pressure is there...the emotional pressure from our families," she countered resolutely, knowing it to be true.

He dropped his grasp on her, his frustration evident. "Well then, dammit, ignore it!"

If only it were just that easy. But they both knew it wasn't, even if he wouldn't admit it to himself. "I can't do that," she retorted in an anguished voice. "Not when every time I look at my father or look at yours I see the disapproval in their eyes. The worry. The pain. I don't want to carry the weight of all those old resentments on my shoulders. And I especially don't want Babe or Heather to feel it, either."

He remained stubbornly naive. "Why should they?"

She let out an exasperated breath and stalked away from him. "Ethan, you know as well as I do how these things work. No one means to be unkind or unfair. Things just work out that way. My life is too complicated right now as it is. I can't deal with the pressure of arguing with our families, too."

Abruptly his expression changed and became one of understanding and regret. "You're right," he admitted sadly, the grooves on either side of his mouth deepening. "I am asking a lot. Maybe...maybe too much. Now isn't the time for us to try and recapture what we once had."

She could see from the look on his face, he wasn't giving up, was simply changing course. She remembered, without wanting to, how he hated to be told no. Was that what she had become to him? Another mountain to climb? A challenge to meet? She didn't want to become yet another extension of his continual battle of wills with his father.

She swallowed around the grittiness of her throat. In the kitchen, the buzzer sounded. Head tucked down to avoid his frankly assessing gaze, she headed for the kitchen, her sweatsock-clad feet soundless as they moved from carpet to linoleum floor.

She glanced in the oven and tested the potatoes with a fork. They were tender but not yet browned on top. The green beans on top of the stove looked like they could stand a bit more cooking, too. "Five more minutes." She replaced the lid on the saucepan and set down the fork.

The next thing she knew she was in his arms, captive against his strength. "Amanda, I'm sorry," he whispered, resting his chin on her temple. "I didn't mean to bring up anything unpleasant."

"Oh, Ethan," she sighed, feeling emotionally overwhelmed, yet cosseted against his warmth. "Don't you think I know that?" she asked, as she tilted her head back to better see his face. "Neither of us wants to remember that horribly unpleasant time."

"Then let's not," he pleaded harshly.

"We can't help it. Like it or not, it keeps coming up."

"Maybe now," he said, tracing her cheek with the pad of his thumb, "but eventually that will fade."

"To be replaced by what?" She pushed away from his chest, knowing tenderness would be her undoing. "New heartache? Ethan, I don't want to be hurt!"

He put his hands on her shoulders. The pressure of his hands increased as he felt her resistance, and resolutely, he guided her around to face him once again. Hands still on her shoulders, he bent his knees slightly and lowered his face so she had no choice but to look into his eyes. "Don't you think I know that?" he whispered emotionally, for a moment looking just as torn up inside as she felt whenever this topic came up. "Don't you think I'd do anything to rewrite history so our breakup wouldn't have happened the way it did?"

The tears she'd been holding back spilled over her cheeks. Mortified, she bit her lip.

He wiped the salty trails on either side of her face with the pads of his thumbs. The light pressure of his fingertips beneath her jaw brought her face up to his. "God, Amanda, I can't bear the thought of losing touch with you once again," he whispered passionately.

She looked up at him, and his mouth closed over hers. She felt the anger in his kiss, the betrayal, the need. Her knees gave way and she sagged against him. Looping her arms around his neck, she held on for dear life. She had wanted this for so long . . . no matter what she tried to tell herself or how she tried to keep her defenses in place.

When at last they broke apart, they were trembling and the oven buzzer was sounding once again. Amanda had no idea how long it had been ringing, nor did Ethan if the stunned look on his face was any indication.

She pressed the back of her hand to her damp mouth, trying to get hold of her spiraling emotions, to quench the desire she felt. A desire evoked by no other man. No other time. "I better get that." She stepped past Ethan and scooped up two hot pads from the counter. Aware he had turned and was watching her, while still allowing her plenty of room to work, she removed the hot casseroles from the oven.

"Amanda—"

"Ethan, I've had about all I can take for one night."

Silence. "I know. Me, too," he admitted then added with just a hint of humor. "So what do you think? Can I still stay and eat dinner? That smells awfully good."

She turned to him, and knew, as soon as she saw his face, that she was going to let him stay, if for no other reason than to let him know she no longer fell apart or swooned from just one kiss. She was a grown woman now. She could handle him. She nodded cordially. "All right. Might as well not let this food go to waste."

"Thanks."

He stepped forward to pick up the cutlery, plates, napkins and glasses she'd stacked at the counter. "Want to eat in here?" he asked.

She nodded and switched on the portable television for the evening news. Anything... anything to diffuse the tension between them.

"MAYBE THERE IS A SOLUTION to this," Ethan said, as Tom Brokaw signed off for the evening.

Amanda got up to switch off the set. "Ethan, please—" She was tired of wishing for what wouldn't happen.

He moved toward her, anyway, taking her into his arms. She remained stiff and unrelenting in his arms.

His hand moved in soothing circular motions on her spine. She nudged away from his touch, only to find her breasts cushioned against his chest. She moved back, to the relative safety of his massaging palm.

"Maybe it's time the feud between our two families ended," he proposed thoughtfully.

He might just as well have been wishing for a trip to the moon, for all the likelihood that would occur. "That'll never happen," she predicted on a long drawn-out sigh, trying not to inhale the subtle lingering scent of after-shave and soap on his skin.

"It would if they wanted it to." His touch grew stronger, more powerful.

"And how would that happen?"

"If we went to them and asked them to let it end."

She glanced up at him, realizing she had the same wishes as he if not the same belief they could actually come true. "Your father would never go for that," she said sadly.

"I have to agree with you on that," he said, "but your father has always struck me as being a sensible guy, where my father isn't concerned. Maybe if we went to him... told him we wanted to be friends again, were going to be friends whether they liked it or not, he'd put his bad feelings for my father aside. Maybe not right at first," he continued when she was about to interrupt, "but...eventually."

She still felt he was wishing for the impossible. Although maybe he had a point. Maybe her father could eventually be persuaded to be reasonable about Ethan, if not his devious father. "Unfortunately we'd still have a problem" she pointed out dryly. "Your father would still disapprove of me."

"Not for long," Ethan said optimistically. His eyes darkened affectionately as they scanned her face with loving reverence. "I think given time you could win anyone over. And besides, it takes two to fight. If your father puts the past aside and stops carrying a grudge against my father, then peace will eventually come about whether my father works for it actively or not."

She had to admit, his logic was beginning to make sense to her. But there were still an awful lot of "if's." "You're putting an awful lot of the burden for this truce on my father," she pointed out calmly, aware how well they fit together, how right it felt to be held in his arms once again.

"Only at the start," Ethan pointed out in a voice that was as soothing as his massaging hands. "Once he caves in, the pressure will be on my father."

Tingles were rippling through her body, lending a lassitude to her limbs, making it difficult to think. "I don't know," she said, not sure she could distinguish between what she wanted and what was in her current frame of mind.

"Please, Amanda." Using the leverage of his thumbs beneath her chin, he tilted her face up to his.

"Hey!" Babe's voice came from the doorway. "Hey..." she said again, a wealth of knowledge and romance in the single syllable. "You two..."

Amanda felt her face burn at the implications she heard in her daughter's voice. Ethan dropped his hold on her and stepped back slightly.

"Are you—?" Babe pointed from one to the other.

"We're just friends," Amanda corrected her daughter, feeling more embarrassed than she ever had in her life. Except perhaps when Ethan had kissed her repeatedly during the acting exercise in front of their theatre arts class.

"Mmm-hmm." Babe obviously didn't believe her for a minute. She grabbed an apple from the bowl on the counter and disappeared around the corner. "I just wanted to let you know I'm home. And I'm going upstairs to talk on the phone. Don't worry," she called, her voice growing fainter as she got farther away from them. "I won't interrupt again," she continued on a burst of muffled laughter.

Color washing her face, Amanda glared at Ethan. Deep inside, she wasn't half as upset as she pretended to be. "Now see what you've started?" she demanded, hands on her hips.

The color of his eyes deepened. He not only knew, he liked it. "So how about it?" he asked laconically. "There's no time like the present."

Try as she might, she couldn't stay mad at him. "For what?" she asked.

His mouth curved up determinedly. "To go talk to your father."

"YOU'RE OUT OF YOUR MIND coming here," Amanda's father said an hour later, after Ethan had finished his short but compelling request for peace between the two families. "And if you think I want you—of all people—seeing *my* daughter you've got another thing coming!"

"Dad!" Amanda chastened him, turning ever redder.

Her father turned back to her incredulously. "Didn't you learn anything at all the last time this guy led you around by the nose?"

"Sir, I take exception to that," Ethan interrupted.

"You can take exception all you want," her father continued bluntly, waving an index finger angrily at Ethan's face. "It doesn't change the facts. You hurt my daughter, and I won't have her hurt or humiliated again."

With effort, Amanda remained calm. She and Ethan had known this would be hard and had braced themselves for it. "Dad, I can take care of myself."

"That's not what you said at the time of your divorce," her father countered without mercy. "You know what a miserable experience that was, Amanda, being shunned by Alex's family and social circle. Do you really want to go through that humiliation again? Do you want to put Babe through it?"

"I wouldn't do that to her!" Ethan countered, beginning to lose his hold on his own formidable temper.

But Charlene Davenport would, Amanda thought.

"Oh no?" her father continued. "And I suppose you wouldn't try to steal the Webster Group's best technical people, either—hire them out from under my nose!"

"I didn't do that! My father did!"

Her dad crossed his arms against his chest. "That further supports my case." He turned to her pleadingly. "Amanda, think! Realize what you're about to get into here!"

Unable to take any more of this unbearable tension, Amanda rested her face in her hands.

Ethan stared at her father for a long moment. Finally he realized what she had known all along, that talking to him on the subject of Harrison Holbrook or HCI was futile. "I guess this was a mistake," he said sadly.

"You guess right," her father responded curtly. "Now get the hell out of my house."

Ethan looked at Amanda, a muscle working in his jaw. "Let's go."

"Not so fast, Amanda," her father interjected. "I want a word with you. Alone."

She'd known this was coming, too.

Ethan looked at Amanda, waiting. She knew he wanted her to leave with him—now, but she couldn't do that. Knowing her father would insist on having his say later, anyway, she might as well get it over with now, before his anger had a chance to build any further. "I'll be along in a moment," she said quietly. "That is, if you won't mind waiting for me." They'd driven over in his car.

Ethan looked even more unhappy. "I'll wait." The muscles in his jaw clenched tight, he turned on his heel and headed for the door.

"You're making a mistake, getting involved with him," her father warned, the second Ethan was outside.

"We're just friends," she countered defensively.

"For how long?"

A heartbeat passed and then another and still Amanda couldn't answer. This wasn't something she was prepared to think about, never mind discuss in detail with her father. Damn Ethan for talking her into this peacemaking foray, anyway.

"Amanda, for once where this man and his family is concerned, use your head. He wants something from you . . . from us. The Holbrooks always do," her father finished heavily with a look of utter exasperation.

"You talk as if you know them intimately!" she stormed right back. And he didn't know Ethan at all!

Her father's face flushed. "I do. I learned about them the hard way and—" he shook his head in bitter remonstration "—I guess you're going to have to do so, too. Judging by the stubborn look on your face, the first time Ethan Holbrook crucified you wasn't education enough. You have to go through the whole miserable, degrading experience again."

"Stop it!" Unable to listen to any more, she put her hands over her ears.

Ignoring her anguish, her father continued harshly, "If you think it's painful hearing about it now, imagine how it will feel when he dumps you again, and he will, Amanda, as soon as he gets whatever the hell it is he wants."

She dropped her hands and stalked away from him. Goaded to the point where she could no longer control her own soaring temper, she shouted back, "You're awful. As awful as Ethan's father."

"So," her father surmised heavily, ignoring the insult she had just shouted out, "Harrison has been harassing you, too!"

Feeling backed into a corner, Amanda said nothing. Her father continued, a wealth of resentment in his tone, "I knew your involvement with them was bound to bring you nothing but misery."

Although she had never walked out on him in mid-conversation, she was sorely tempted to do so now. Wearily she picked up her purse and her coat and cradled them in front of her like a shield. She didn't want to be rude, so she would at least say goodbye on a halfway civil note. "I'm leaving now, Dad." Her look told him she couldn't take any more.

His impassive look faded. "Be careful, Amanda." Her father's voice softened tenderly without warning. There was real remorse in his eyes. "I don't want you to get hurt."

"I know that," she said wearily, resigned.

"Then think!" he urged emotionally, his voice rising in despair once again. "Realize that a liaison with the Holbrooks—any Holbrook—can only bring you pain."

Amanda regarded her father wordlessly, feeling just as world-weary and twice-burned as he looked right now. "And what do you call this, Dad?" she asked softly, bitterly. "Do you think your attitude is wounding me any less?"

ETHAN PARKED IN HER DRIVEWAY and cut the motor. The porch light spread a yellow triangle of light toward the car, illuminating Amanda's features in soft shadow. She looked vulnerable and sad, and not quite ready to go in yet and face her daughter.

Her hands were folded listlessly in her lap. He reached out and covered them with one of his. "I'm sorry," he said, knowing the words were an inadequate expression of all he was feeling and not likely to make her feel any better. "You were right. We shouldn't have gone over there."

"Yes, we should have." Amanda's voice was thick with the pain of her disappointment. She closed her eyes briefly, her thick strawberry-gold lashes resting against her cheek. "Because now we know for sure what I expected all along, that there is no ending this feud between our families, not ever." Moisture beaded on her lashes and trailed languidly down her cheek.

Abruptly recovering, Amanda lifted the back of her hand to wipe at her cheeks. She sniffed and reached for the door handle. Not willing to let her go just yet, Ethan kept his hand closed on the hand in her lap.

"I wish things were different," he started softly, uncomfortably aware of how much that scene with her father had cost her.

It had cost him, too, but not nearly as much. Hardened by years of his father's impossible expectations, the lack of forbearance in his family, he had learned early to shut out the disapproval of others and go his own way. Amanda had no such defenses. She was as vulnerable as a child in this sense.

"But they're not," her voice was muffled. She started to open the door and the overhead light came on.

He gripped her left hand tighter. "Look at me," he commanded when she kept her head down. Finally she complied. "It doesn't matter what they think or feel about us. We can still be friends.''

Her breath left her lips in a long sigh. She stared listlessly ahead. ''I wish that were true.'' Her jaw took on a familiar stubborn tilt. ''But it's not.'' Determinedly she withdrew her hand from his. ''I can't talk about this any more.'' She pushed from the car.

Not about to let the evening end on this note, after all they'd started to share again, Ethan went after her. He caught up with her just as she reached the front steps. ''Amanda—'' He shook her slightly as he turned her around.

''Don't,'' she was crying again, her voice jagged with pain. ''Ethan, don't—''

Ignoring her request to be left alone, he folded her into his arms. She kept her arms down at her sides, but he felt the resistance in her fade slightly as she rested her face on his shoulder.

He held her that way for a minute, maybe more, saying nothing. Finally she started to straighten. When she did, he threaded his hands through the hair at the nape of her neck and guided her face beneath his. He inclined his head slightly to the right, to avoid bumping noses, then touched his mouth to hers. He tasted the salt of her tears on her lips and felt the desperation. Desire welled up inside him—pulsing, strong, real. They needed each other. And he didn't intend to stop kissing her until she knew it and admitted it— if only to herself.

Her hands moving to his chest, she splayed her fingertips across his chest as if to hold him at bay while her mouth moved under his, shyly at first, reluctantly, then as she relaxed, gave in, with increasing ardor. And still he wanted, needed more from her, from both of them. His own passion a hot, driving force within him, he held her tighter and increased the pressure of the kiss, increased it until at last he felt her surrender everything to him—her heart, her will, her resistance. Knowing the embrace could easily get out of hand if they let it, and that they couldn't afford for that to happen—he ended it. His heart pounding, he reluctantly let go. Calling on the last of his control, he finally drew his mouth from hers.

Tears were still sparkling on her lashes. She still looked incredibly depressed. But she was thinking now, too, realizing how much they already had, how much they could have. Wanting to be with him as much as he wanted to be with her.

Don't believe what they say about us, he wanted to warn her. *Don't let them break us apart again, not when we're just beginning to find each other again.* But fearing what new arguments he might conjure up, he said nothing at all.

She looked at him again, then reached inside her purse, retrieved her key, unlocked the door, and with a last mournful look at him, slipped inside her house.

Chapter Eleven

"I thought you might want to see this," Harrison Holbrook said, handing over a plain manila folder. With the use of his cane, he eased into a chair in front of Ethan's desk.

Ethan opened the file. Seeing what was inside—a copy of a marriage license issued in Matamoros, Mexico, dated March 14, eight years ago, and bearing his future son-in-law's name—he swore long and harshly. "Where did you get this?" he asked his father angrily. Maybe it was chicken-hearted of him, but this was exactly the kind of sordid information he didn't want to know and had feared an in-depth background check on Tim Summerfield might turn up.

His father regarded him smugly. "My private detective uncovered it."

Ethan fought to contain his resentment. His father's actions were all too reminiscent of his treatment of Ethan in the past. "Does Heather know about this?" he asked in a curt voice.

"I doubt it, since there's no evidence Tim ever even tried to obtain a divorce. If he told her about it, he'd also have to tell her he couldn't possibly marry her, because if he did, he'd be committing bigamy."

Great. Ethan swore again. What a mess. "You didn't tell her yet?"

"No, you're her father. I thought you should do that."

Thank God for small miracles, Ethan thought on a sigh of relief. Not that it was any surprise his father would leave the dirty work where Heather was concerned to him. He wanted to be a hero in his granddaughter's eyes, and given the nature of the information and Heather's headstrong, emotional nature, there was every reason to believe she'd want to shoot the messenger who brought her such awful news.

Harrison paused, then added, "There's no way she can marry him, son. Not when he's already married. You're going to have to get them to call the wedding off."

Ethan stared at the paper, and at a copy of a Matamoros hotel registration for the same day, signed Mr. and Mrs. Tim Summerfield. If these documents were real—and they looked as if they were—then his father had been right to have Tim investigated. He'd been a fool to avoid it.

Normally a very good judge of character, he couldn't believe he could have been that far wrong about Tim. Not caring it would sound naive, he said, "There must be some mistake here, Dad. Another Tim Summerfield or—"

His father shook his head. "The only mistake was letting your daughter get involved with someone from the Summerfield family."

Thinking about what this would do to his daughter, Ethan felt sick inside. He rubbed at the tension-knotted muscles at the base of his neck.

"There's no mistake, but feel free to check it out yourself if you like." Using his cane, his father pushed clumsily to his feet and shuffled to the door. "I'll be in my office if you need me."

As advised, Ethan spent the morning on the phone, tracking down the facts long-distance. Hours later, he had to conclude his father had been right. Tim did have a wife in Mexico and there was no record of any divorce.

Dreading what was coming next, Ethan canceled his appointments for the rest of the day and went over to the campus to see his daughter. "Let's drive home for lunch, okay?"

She looked at him curiously. "Okay," she said slowly.

Once there, as gently as possible, he filled her in on what he'd learned. Heather looked as shocked and disbelieving as he'd initially felt, while he felt guilty as hell for having to break her heart this way. "I don't understand," Heather cried, the tears streaming down her face. "He never said anything to me about this! Nothing at all! We weren't supposed to have any secrets from each other, ever. Dad, he promised! He said he loved me. He said—" Unable to go on, Heather broke down completely and sobbed as if her heart would break. His own eyes stinging, Ethan held her in his arms as fury engulfed him. Damn Tim Summerfield anyway, for doing this to his daughter, for being such a lying cheat.

"I've got to call him, talk to him," Heather said, pushing away at last.

Ethan handed her a box of tissues and watched her dry her eyes and blow her nose. "I think that's a good idea. Do you want me to stay?"

She shook her head defiantly. "No. I think this is something better handled alone. Do you understand?"

After a moment, Ethan nodded reluctantly. As a father, he wanted to be there to protect his only child. But he also knew much of what they would have to say would be only for the two of them. "You'll call me when it's over?"

"Yes. Where are you going to be?"

At that moment, there was only one person Ethan wanted to see or talk to, only one person who would understand what he was going through. "I'll be with Amanda, over at her office."

Heather caught his arm before he left. "Don't cancel the wedding yet. He—he might have some sort of explanation for all this."

"I hope so, honey," Ethan said, taking her into his arms for one last fierce, paternal hug. "I really hope so."

"MAYBE HEATHER'S RIGHT. Maybe there is some logical explanation for all this," Amanda said after Ethan had finished explaining to her what had been going on. It had been a surprise, having him walk in during the middle of the day. Recalling what had happened the last time they'd been together, how she had responded to his kisses, and then later broke down and cried when her father stubbornly refused to end the feud between the two families, made her have second thoughts about seeing him. But once she'd seen his face, she knew something even more upsetting was going on in his life, and so she'd welcomed him in with an open heart.

"I hope that's so," Ethan murmured, a look of anguish on his face. He reached up and loosened the knot on his tie, undid the button at his neck. "Because if he can't . . ." he swore again, virulently this time, and raked a hand through his blond hair. ". . . What a mess . . ."

"Would you like some coffee or something cold to drink?" Amanda asked.

Still distracted, he didn't reply. "Have you eaten at all today?" she said, knowing she had to say something—however mundane—to help him feel better.

"Uh...yeah, I had some breakfast," he mumbled at length. His hand crept over to cover hers. His fingers tightened around her hand and she could feel the need pouring out of him.

He gave her hand a tug and looked at her. She knew what he wanted, knew it would be foolish to give it to him under the circumstances. But she couldn't deny him the feel of human comfort, not when he was suffering so. She slid over, so she was settled in the crook of his arm, her head resting on his shoulder. His arm tightened over the length of hers in a warm possessive arc. "When did life get so complicated?" he sighed.

She smiled ruefully, thinking of all the ups and downs of her own life, and then answered dryly, "About the time of Adam and Eve, I think."

On her desk, the buzzer sounded. Amanda got up reluctantly to answer the phone, or at least she tried. Ethan held on to her until the last moment. "Yes," she said, putting the receiver to her ear.

"I know you said you didn't want to be interrupted, but Heather Holbrook is here to see you."

"Send her in." Amanda depressed the button and remained where she was, one hip braced on the edge of her desk, her short skirt riding up above her knees. "Heather's here."

Ethan barely had time to straighten before Heather walked in the door.

She seemed calm to Amanda. Too calm. "Are you okay?" Ethan asked anxiously, seeming to remain on the sofa with a great deal of effort.

Heather nodded and her spine stiffened even more. For a moment, she looked very much like her grandfather. Unforgiving, aloof. "I'm fine, Daddy. Amanda, the wedding is off. I'm sorry."

Amanda felt the hope leave her body in one quick rush. Her body had the consistency of Silly Putty. "Oh, Heather honey, I'm sorry."

"It's okay," Heather continued, imposing the same iron will on her self control. "You're the one who's going to lose the commission."

Ethan sat forward slightly, both forearms braced on his thighs. He glanced up at his daughter, concerned. "Then Tim is married?" he queried, his unhappiness with the situation evident.

"Yes," Heather said coolly, her anger at him showing plainly. "Although he *claims* he was also divorced."

"Did he explain why he never told you about it?" Amanda asked, surprised Heather could be so together at a time like this, yet not trusting her poise for an instant. This betrayal had to hurt badly. Maybe it just hadn't sunk in yet. Maybe she wouldn't let it sink in.

Heather shrugged listlessly. "He said he didn't think it mattered. It was a fraternity prank, played on him when he was a sophomore. His fraternity had gone down to Mexico for spring break. He was still a virg—" she stopped, realized she was talking to her father, and blushed. "Uh, inexperienced, and so his buddies got him drunk, 'cause that was the only way he could get up enough nerve to visit a hooker. Only the 'initiation rite' backfired 'cause he got so drunk on tequila he could hardly stand up, never mind...uh, learn anything—" Heather blushed brighter. "So they decided to marry him off instead, as a fraternity prank. He woke up in a really sleazy hotel room the next day with a marriage certificate in one hand, an empty wallet in another. All his cash, his credit cards, his watch, everything of value he had on him, had been stolen."

"And the hook, uh, woman?" Ethan asked, slanting a brief apologetic look at Amanda.

Heather shrugged and looked even more disgruntled as she reported, "Tim said he never saw her again. He called home and told his parents he'd been robbed but was okay. They wired him some cash. He got a quickie divorce—or at least thought he did—and hightailed it back to the States. He told me that's why he dropped out of the fraternity when he was a sophomore at UT, because he was so mad at what they'd done to him."

Amanda could understand that, too. And it probably explained why he had been willing to go anywhere but Mexico for his honeymoon with Heather.

"Does he have the paperwork to prove he got his divorce?" Ethan asked.

"He went home to look for it, but he had no idea where it was, so whether or not he'll be able to find it, I don't know," Heather reported indifferently, her lower lip beginning to tremble.

"So why is the wedding still off?" Amanda said, her heart aching for the young bride-to-be.

Heather crossed her arms in front of her defiantly. "Because he lied to me, even if it was by omission."

"But if it wasn't a real marriage—" Amanda protested, hating to see any couple who was truly in love break up.

"It was a real lie!" Heather stormed back, beginning to cry again.

Amanda and Ethan exchanged a worried look. Ethan turned back to his daughter, his tone reasonable as he watched her dash her tears away. "Sweetheart, let's not be rash here. You love Tim—"

"Did love him. I don't anymore," she retorted stubbornly. Silence fell on the group as Amanda and Ethan both realized, and confirmed with a look to each other, there would be no reasoning with his daughter now.

"Maybe we all need time to recoup," Amanda suggested calmly, giving Ethan another telling look. He got her hint to play it safe and didn't push his daughter further.

He cleared his throat and went over to put his arm around her shoulder. "Amanda's right. I think we all need a little time—"

"I don't. I've already made up my mind," Heather retorted briskly. She turned to Amanda. "I trust you'll take care of everything for me, all the cancellations?"

Only because she saw no other way to pacify the hysterical girl did Amanda nod and caution, "Although I don't think I can get to most of it until next week."

"It'll take that long?" Heather said.

Amanda noticed Heather hadn't yet taken off her engagement ring. A positive sign. Maybe, unlike her grandfather, she could forgive and forget. "It took almost four weeks to plan this much, it'll take another week to undo it."

"Okay."

"In the meantime, until we have some sort of official announcement drafted and printed, do me a favor and don't say anything to anyone?" Amanda pushed. This way, if Heather changed her mind again and decided the wedding was on, then there wouldn't be quite so much chaos.

"Fine. If that's the way it has to be," she pouted.

Amanda looked at Ethan and knew instantly they were in agreement on this; they wouldn't do anything until Heather had had a chance to calm down.

Heather slung her shoulder bag over her arm. Car keys in hand, she said, "I've got to go back to school. I've got class this afternoon."

"You sure you feel up to it?" Ethan asked.

"My engagement ended, not the world," Heather retorted baldly, her chin jutting out stubbornly. Her eyes glinting with anger, she tossed her head. "I'm fine, Daddy."

After she left Amanda and Ethan exchanged yet another look, this one laced with mutual parental sympathy. "Well, she's handling it okay, don't you think?" Ethan asked drolly, with a look that went skyward.

The two of them considered all that had just happened, and then burst out laughing simultaneously. Amanda shook her head ruefully and picked up a paperweight on her desk, juggling it from hand to hand. "Is Tim ever going to have his hands full!"

"And vice versa." He smiled, glad they'd come to the same conclusion. He ambled over to join her and sat down beside her, resting his hips against the edge of her desk. "You think she's going to marry him, anyway, don't you?"

Amanda nodded. "Yes, I do, although it may take her a little while to come to that decision herself." She hesitated, knowing how protective he felt of his child. "How do you feel about that?" It probably annoyed him to find out what Tim had done. Made him trust his future son-in-law a little less.

Ethan was silent, mulling that over. Finally he shrugged. "It's funny. I didn't think I liked him that much. I mean as a young guy, he was okay. Certainly very different from his family, but...as for a potential husband for my daughter, I wasn't sure he was quite good enough. Until I got that report this morning. Then I realized how much I didn't want this previous marriage business to be true... and that told me maybe Tim was a better guy than I'd let myself acknowledge."

As Amanda turned toward Ethan to better see his face, her thigh nudged his. "You don't hold this prank against him?"

Ethan hooked an arm about her waist and pulled her around to face him, so she was standing between his spread thighs. "He was nineteen. We're all foolish at that age. He did the right thing getting out of that fraternity at UT."

His hands were hooked loosely around her waist. Wherever they touched, warmth radiated. "I think so, too," Amanda murmured.

"Although he should have told Heather about it," Ethan continued solemnly.

"Yes, he should have," Amanda agreed wholeheartedly.

"But again, I can see why he wouldn't have wanted to risk it. Our family was so wary of him to begin with, because of his father's reputation for being on the shady side."

Amanda sighed. She looked at the half-finished plans on her desk for Heather's wedding. "So what now?"

"Keep going on with the wedding plans," Ethan said firmly. "Unless I miss my bet, that daughter of mine will come around."

"HI, AMANDA. HEATHER HERE. Listen, our sorority is having a 'little sister' weekend, and since I don't have any siblings, I thought I'd ask Babe if she wanted to go as my guest, kind of hang out with me all weekend over at SMU."

"I'm sure she'd love it," Amanda said, surprised, "but are you sure you're up to it?" Heather had been through a lot the past few days, and according to Ethan, she and Tim hadn't reconciled. Yet.

"I'm fine, and it helps to keep busy. Now, about this weekend..." Heather said with a kind of forced cheerfulness that hinted at the strong woman she was inside. Feeling Heather needed the distraction as much as Babe needed the sisterly attention, Amanda agreed it was a great idea and called Babe down to find out what she thought. Minutes later, it was all settled. Babe had agreed to go, and Heather would pick her up Friday after school and return her home early Sunday evening.

"I HEAR YOU'RE at loose ends this weekend," Ethan said, stopping by her office Friday evening.

Having no reason to go home, Amanda had decided to work late. She put down her pencil and studied his face. Unlike earlier in the week, he looked relaxed and happy. Like he'd found a magic cure-all for his life, the kind she wished she could find for her own.

"There's always work to be done here," Amanda said casually. And for once she could spend the weekend sorting out her files without feeling guilty about neglecting her daughter.

"True, but you deserve a break, too. So, what are you going to do?"

"When?" She faced him self-consciously and put down her pen. He circled around and took a seat on the corner of her desk. "Tonight."

"I don't know." Amanda leaned back until her spine touched the back of her swivel chair. She meshed glances with him. "Probably rent a movie, pick up some Chinese and go to bed early."

He winced comically at her uninspired recitation. "Dull."

"Hmm." Finding his flirtatious mood contagious, she picked up her pen again and worried it between her teeth, all the while eyeing him with mirrorlike abandon. "What are you going to do?" she asked coquettishly.

He grinned, looking like a schoolboy about to commit a prank. "If I have my way?" He slipped both of his hands into his pockets. His eyes gleamed devilishly. "Chase you."

The way he said it made her draw in her breath. *If I go home with him tonight,* she thought, *we'll end up making love. Or coming close to it.* Deciding everything was happening too fast for her comfort, she pushed back her chair and circled around the opposite end of the desk, putting as much space between them as quickly as she could. "Ethan—"

He circled around the opposite way and met up with her in the center of the room. "It's my hope you'll let yourself get caught."

She bypassed him affably and headed for her coat. With him in an openly amorous mood, it was definitely time to leave. "Not a chance," she said with a cool hauteur she couldn't begin to feel.

Despite her hands-off attitude, he followed her anyway, reaching around to help her put on her coat. "Not even for a meal?" he asked persuasively. "I'm alone this weekend, too."

"Call Charlene," Amanda advised dryly. "I'm sure she'd be glad to keep a lonely man company."

"You are too cruel," he chided, his hands lingering possessively on her shoulders. His voice dropped another husky, compelling notch. "And you know it."

She turned to face him and drew in a shaky breath. He was right, she did know how he felt about Charlene, that he wasn't the slightest bit interested. But maybe it would've been better for them both if he had been. Certainly the two of them had more in common than she and he did. Amanda sighed, the argument, brief as it was, already exhausting her. "You know all the reasons we can't get involved yet," she retorted with a weary kind of resignation.

"I know all the reasons you *think* we can't get involved," he corrected her with an edge of impatience lacing his low voice. He dropped his hands and stepped back a pace. "And for a few days, I was tempted to agree with you, but then I thought about it, really thought about it. Amanda, we're too old to have our parents dictating our lives."

She flushed, embarrassed. He made her sound childish, when she was trying to be adult about this. "It's a little more complicated than that, and you know it," she reprimanded him firmly.

"Is it?" His eyes followed her around the room as she nervously straightened things here and there. "I think it's pretty simple. I want to be with you. You want to be with me."

At that, her mouth opened in surprise. She hadn't expected him to be so blunt or sound so possessive about her. She stared at him, perplexed. The last time he'd seen her, the day Heather had broken her engagement, he hadn't pushed her at all, hadn't tried to kiss her. Nothing. They touched in mutual comfort, one parent, one friend, to another, but that was all. She narrowed her glance suspiciously. "What's gotten into you?"

Looking as restless as she felt, Ethan walked over to her desk and picked up a paperweight, stood tossing it idly from hand to hand while it made a dull thumping noise against his palm. "I don't know," he confessed honestly after a moment. His eyes met hers in an agony of self-revelation. "Maybe it's Heather getting married or not getting married. Or watching her blow everything she's built with Tim because of one past mistake on his part, because his family and hers don't see the world in the same blue-blooded way. All I know is, I've wasted a lot of years trying to make my father happy, trying to be the perfect son he wanted, and the perfect husband my wife wanted and a perfect father for Heather. And none of it has brought me the happiness I've wanted or felt we all deserve."

She wanted to be happy, too, and like him, had never found true contentment in every sense. Oh, she had a job she enjoyed and a daughter she loved more than life, but she didn't have a lasting personal relationship with a man, and she felt that void acutely. More than ever since he'd reentered her life so unexpectedly. But not wanting to dwell on that or the reasons still keeping them apart, she focused on what else he had revealed to her, which was something she had never known about him. "Is it so important for you to be perfect?" she asked curiously.

He regarded her unflinchingly, then put the paperweight down and stepped nearer. "I used to think so. I don't anymore, and you know why? Because of you. You let me know it's okay to be uncertain or feel blue or even inadequate sometimes. Because the past few weeks you've been there for me, as a sounding board and as a friend, every time I've needed you. And that's meant a lot."

She swallowed hard, shaken by the raw emotion she heard in his voice, the yearning light she saw in his eyes. "To me, too, Ethan. You've helped me with Babe and made her feel better, but that doesn't mean— You were there when we talked to my father. We can't...."

At the hesitation in her low voice, her unwillingness to commit to him, to enter this no-win situation, his glance narrowed shrewdly. His mouth thinned unhappily. "I see," he summed up his view of her actions tersely. "I've been a help to you. But not enough of a comfort to risk your parents' wrath and start seeing me again?"

"Not enough to start World War III," she countered more calmly than she felt, tamping down her guilt that she was letting him down and reminding him the animosity wasn't all one-sided. "Your father isn't well, Ethan." *And lately, mine hasn't been looking so good, either.*

"So, what happens if we preserve the peace and do what everyone else seems to want?" he asked unhappily, stepping toward her, narrowing the distance between them yet another pace. "What then, Amanda? Will everyone be happy and content? Or will the two of us just grow old feeling cheated because we didn't act on our heart's desires when we had a chance?"

She kept her face expressionless while her heartbeat clattered in her chest. She'd never known him to be so open, to speak so freely, so hell-bent on expressing what was in his heart. The thought she might be the impetus behind this newfound candor, as well as the recipient, was heady knowledge, indeed.

Needing to argue with him, to maintain her emotional distance, she countered, "We can't just discount our families' feelings about this, Ethan."

"Why not," he retorted, just as determinedly, "if it means the two of us ultimately end up with what we want."

The depth of his masculine impatience was even more disturbing than his steady gaze. Riveting her eyes on him, she asked with a cool matter-of-factness she couldn't begin to feel, "And what do you want?"

He closed the distance between them until they stood toe-to-toe without dropping his gaze. "I want you," he said precisely. "To say to hell with everyone and everything else and pick up again where we left off years ago before my father interfered in our lives."

Part of her wanted that, too, so badly, but she also knew it wasn't that simple, no matter how easy he could make it sound. "And when there's hell to pay for doing just that?" she challenged.

He shrugged uncaringly. "Then there's hell to pay. It won't be the first time either of us has ever been on the hot seat, and it sure won't be the last."

He made such a persuasive argument. But she knew she couldn't rush into anything, tempting as his offer was. Or let him seduce her now. Lifting her hair away from her face, she turned and stalked away from him. "I need time to think."

He followed her, not halting until his breath fell warmly on the back of her head. "How much time?" he asked gruffly in a voice that let her know there were limits on how long he was willing to wait for her, or any woman.

"I don't know." She turned to him, adjusting the soft cashmere scarf around her neck. "But I do know I need some time, so I'm going home now, Ethan. Alone." Although privately she doubted even a full year away from him at this point would change what she was beginning to feel.

He sighed, thrust both his hands in his pockets, and studied her wordlessly. "You're sure that's what you want?" He seemed convinced it wasn't what she needed.

"Yes. I'll talk to you soon," she promised briskly, moving for the door before her resolve faltered.

"Yes," he said, with equal determination. "You will talk to me soon." And his statement had a promise in it.

THE DOORBELL RANG at seven-thirty. Amanda had barely had time to get home and change into cords and a soft turtleneck sweater. Her boot-shaped house slippers in hand, she dashed down the stairs. "Coming!" No doubt about it, this pursuit of Ethan's had left her all mixed up, ready to capitulate, and yet frightened, too. It was easier to be alone than to risk being hurt. To even think about giving her heart to someone was even harder. But that was what he wanted from her, was determined to get.

Glancing through the peephole, she saw Ethan standing there, his arms full of packages, four beautiful leis around his neck. Despite the frigidness of the winter weather, he was wearing a Hawaiian print shirt and white cotton deck pants. She opened the door, not nearly as exasperated as she was pretending to be. "I thought I told you I wasn't going to play this game with you."

"It's no game," he said, moving past her as if she had invited him in. He set down his packages on the parson's table in the front hall, and turned to face her. He rubbed his hands together to warm them and shivered. "Damn but it's getting cold out there."

"Try wearing a coat," she advised dryly.

"And spoil the mood?"

"Which is?"

"Can't you guess?" Taking one of the fragrant orchid leis from around his neck, he slipped it over hers, and then with the same mesmerizing economy of motion added a second one to the first. *"South Pacific."*

The play that had brought them together...the reading of a scene from it had forced him to give her a first kiss.

Pushing the sensual memories aside, she concentrated on what he had in his arms. "What's in the sack?"

"Typical Polynesian fare. I didn't know what you liked so I got a little bit of everything. And—" he reached into a sack and withdrew a videocassette "—the movie version of *South Pacific.*"

Without warning, so many memories came rushing back at her. She had loved him and hated him and desired him madly but never had she been immune to him, and that, she feared, would not change. Whatever the reason, he was destined to make her feel, and more importantly, determined to bring her out of the self-protective cocoon she had spun around herself and her heart.

Suddenly she wasn't sure that was such a bad thing.

His hand touched her chin. At his prompting, she lifted her face to his. "Say you'll spend this evening with me."

She knew she shouldn't. There were still many reasons why they should remain apart. But she also realized he gave her a kind of happiness no one else ever had, a sense of being alive that had never been duplicated by any other man. "I'll probably regret this tomorrow," she warned as she gave in.

"I don't think so," he said. He slid the cassette into the VCR while she went to get some plates. "But even if you do," he said as she returned and dropped down beside him on the sofa, "it'll have been worth it."

"Oh yeah?" she retorted playfully, amused he could be so sure of himself. "Says who?"

"Says me," he replied confidently. "And I know a thing or two about you."

So he did. The movie brought forth tons of memories, most of them about the people in their theatre arts class who had tried out for the play with varying degrees of success. "Remember how awful Betty Lundgren's singing was?" he asked, helping himself to more rice and ginger-spiced chicken from the nearly empty cardboard containers scattered across her coffee table.

"She was tone-deaf as sure as I'm sitting here," Amanda said, savoring yet another bite of the fresh coconut he'd brought.

"And remember what a great dancer Ron Rhodes was?"

"Yeah. And also that he couldn't remember two lines in a row no matter how much Mrs. Wharton coached him."

They both laughed and Amanda continued, "I thought for sure she was going to start screaming that last time when he gave up on the professor's part and auditioned for the part of Luther Billis instead."

"I know," Ethan chuckled, remembering, too. "But that was nothing compared to the look on her face when she made me get up and read for the lead with you."

The mention of that brought forth memories of their first kiss. Fighting the impact of those thoughts, Amanda shook her head and said, "She was so mean sometimes—"

He picked up a chunk of fresh pineapple from his plate and put the juicy morsel against her lips. She tasted the flavor of his skin as much as the succulent bit of fruit.

"And you were so pretty," he said softly. "That's why I kissed you like that, you know. Not so much to make her mad, as everyone thought, but because . . ."

His words trailed off and she fell silent. It was an effort to choke out the words, yet she had to know, now that they were telling the truth. "Because why?" What had he been feeling that day?

He sighed and placed his palm on the side of her face. "Because the chance was there. And because I'd been daydreaming about doing it for such a long time."

An overwhelming feeling of déjà vu stole over her once again. She drew back and releasing a shaky breath, warned, "You're doing it to me again."

"Doing what?" His words may have been innocent but his look was not.

She angled him a grin despite herself. "Encouraging me to take leave of my senses."

"Is that so bad?" he asked, mirroring her wry knowing tone.

Sometimes, she thought, coming back to reality with a bang. *Yes, it was.* "It is when it just won't work," she said softly.

He was silent. Not giving up exactly, just thoughtful. Finally he drew back. "Maybe we are rushing things," he said gently, meshing his fingers with hers. "Maybe we should just take one day at a time, go a little slower, give everyone time to adjust to the idea of us as . . . friends."

And perhaps even lovers, she thought. She knew that was what he wanted. What she was beginning to want if she were honest. She just wasn't sure it was right. There was so much more to being with someone than just the cozy evenings spent alone with each other or the pleasurable act of making love. Passion faded, no matter how strong it was, and there had to be something else, a foundation of mutual friends and shared values, to fall back on once that happened. She wasn't sure they would ever have that. "It's late." She was doing the right thing, she knew she was.

"And I've got to go." He stood reluctantly.

She watched as he pressed the eject button and took the cartridge out of her VCR and snapped it back in its rental case. "Thanks for the movie. Dinner."

He grinned, unrepentant, as she thrust her hands in the pockets of her cords and walked him to the front door. "Even if I did barge my way in."

She looked up at him to say good-night, still sorting through her welter of feelings and wondering what to do about them. And was reminded again how Ethan went after anything he wanted, full force. Could she stand up to his incredible will indefinitely? Did she even want to?

Chapter Twelve

"Great news, the wedding is on again!" Heather announced Sunday evening as she dropped Babe off at home.

"That's wonderful!" Amanda said, giving Heather a hug.

"You should've seen their reconciliation, Mom. It was so romantic," Babe continued as she lugged her suitcase in the front door. "Tim came over to the sorority house last night around midnight, and he brought this guitar player with him, and he stood under Heather's window and sang love songs to her."

"He can't carry a tune, either," Heather said, blushing.

"It must have been some evening," Amanda said. She wondered how she would feel if a man made such an unabashed display of his love for her.

"Yeah, it was." Heather dashed tears from beneath her eyes. She looked incredibly happy. "Is it going to be too much trouble to have the wedding as scheduled?"

"No, not at all. You just worry about making things right with Tim and keeping them that way."

"I will."

Amanda looked back at her daughter. "And how was your weekend?"

Babe grinned, suddenly looking as exuberant as her "adopted" big sister. "Wonderful. Heather's sorority is really neat, Mom. We had so much fun. And we met some really cute guys—"

"Little brothers of some of the fraternities there," Heather supplied when Amanda sent them both a puzzled look.

"Most of them were tall, too, and gosh, they were so nice."

Heather grinned and tapped Babe on the head. "They all thought you were nice, too." To Amanda, she explained dryly, "I don't think one of them went home without her phone number or address, so if you start getting piles of mail for her and endless phone calls, you'll know why."

They laughed and chatted some more, then Amanda walked Heather out to her car while Babe ran upstairs to call her girl-friends and tell them all about her weekend at the university. "I can't thank you enough for doing that for Babe," Amanda said, her gratitude deep and heartfelt.

"I enjoyed it, believe me. And I think it was good for Babe, too. Having all those boys chasing her made her aware of how attractive she is."

"I've tried to tell her—"

"I know, and so have I, but somehow it never really sinks in until a guy looks at you like you're the most incredible woman in the whole wide world."

True, Amanda thought. Like the way Ethan looked at her... If only their parents could get along as well as their girls!

Fortunately he hadn't pursued her the rest of the weekend. Af-ter their chaste goodnight to each other Friday evening, he hadn't called again. Part of her was happy about that, relieved to have some space. She'd put the time alone to good use, cleaning her kitchen cabinets, relining the shelves, getting clothes to the clean-ers, her grocery shopping done. She'd even had time to nap on Sunday afternoon and take in a movie. But through it all, she'd remained lonely and vaguely restless, and she knew, with as much irritation as surprise, that the reason for her mood was Ethan. Fortunately, with Babe returning home, there was plenty to do—stories to hear. By the time she got to bed Sunday evening she was exhausted once again. And yet thoughts of Ethan kept her awake long after she'd thought she should be asleep.

"I HEARD THE GIRLS had a great weekend together," Ethan said, stopping by Amanda's office early the next morning. "And that the wedding is still on."

He looked great for a Monday, fresh and rested. Ready to take on the demands of a full business week. Whereas she was still confused, restless, yearning for what she knew she shouldn't want.

"Yes." Amanda confirmed what he'd told her to be true as she riffled through the stacks of To Do lists on her desk. Finally she found what she was looking for and handed him the copy with his name penciled lightly across the top. "I've made up a schedule of events for this week, so you'll know where you're supposed to be, and when."

"Thanks." He whistled, scanning the itinerary.

Being careful not to brush hands with him, Amanda handed him a second schedule. "This is Heather's calendar. As you can see she has a number of showers to attend. Not to mention a last-minute fitting on her wedding dress, and the rehearsal dinner. I scheduled everything around her classes."

"And the honeymoon, did the two of them ever decide where they wanted to go?"

"They've delayed it a month, until spring break."

Ethan paused, then said slowly, after a moment, "Considering the fact Heather and Tim are both still in school this semester, that's probably for the best."

Yes, Amanda thought, agreeing with his premise for an entirely different reason: they'll get to see more of the islands that way instead of spending all their time in a hotel room, in bed. Unable to share with him the erotic line of her bemused thoughts, she cleared her throat and continued in a more businesslike tone. "In the meantime, they're spending the weekend after the wedding at a hotel here in town."

Ethan nodded approvingly. "That's prudent of them. What about their condo?"

"Phil Summerfield told me it was all set for the kids to move into. They've furnished it with rental stuff for the moment, but when the kids are settled and have time to shop for furniture, the Summerfields are going to give that to them, too."

"They're being very generous," Ethan admitted grudgingly.

"Everyone wants them to be happy," Amanda said. If only she and Ethan had had half as much support for their relationship, they might have made a go of it, too. But it was too late to look back.

"So, what about you? How's your schedule looking this week?" Ethan asked, very low.

"Busy."

He studied her wordlessly for a moment, seeing easily through her charade of aloofness. "You can't keep putting us on hold forever," he warned softly.

A shiver of anticipation crept down her spine. She remembered the way it had felt to be kissed and held by him and knew her resistance was dipping dangerously low. Moreover, he knew it, too. "Is that what you think I'm doing?" With effort, she met his direct look.

His brows rose in silent discord. "Isn't it?"

She had no reply for that, nothing except her promise to herself not to rush into anything.

"I care about you, Amanda, and I think you care about me, and one of these days you're going to realize that."

She lifted her head. They stared at each other silently. He wasn't touching her, and yet despite his restraint, she felt caressed, every inch of her. "And until then?" she whispered, realizing yet again how very much she wanted to be free to kiss him.

"I'll be close by." And on that promise, he turned and left, schedule in hand.

"HEATHER, YOU STAND HERE. And Tim, you'll need to be to her right," the minister said.

Amanda stood in the foreground, watching the Holbrook-Summerfield rehearsal with moist eyes. She didn't know what it was about weddings, but seeing people that happy, that hopeful, reduced her to tears of shared joy every time.

Ethan slipped back to stand beside her. "If you're this misty-eyed during the rehearsal, I can't imagine how emotional you're going to be during the actual ceremony."

She elbowed him gently in the ribs. When he'd practiced escorting Heather up the aisle a few minutes ago he'd looked unabashedly sentimental himself. Which probably explained why he was teasing her now—to get his mind off his own spiraling emotions. It must be hard to lose your only child, she thought. Harder still, because he was alone.

"How're the preparations for the rehearsal dinner going?"

Amanda smiled and glanced at her watch. "Everything should be all set. I'm going over to the hotel to check it out in five minutes."

He frowned at the news she would soon depart. "I'd come with you, but—"

"You'd better stay."

"Okay, I'll follow with Heather and the other guests."

"Sounds good. See you there."

Unfortunately the rehearsal dinner wasn't all set, it was a nightmare. Amanda gasped as she stepped inside the banquet room. "What happened here?" she asked the maître d' in shock. The room looked like the interior of a gag gift shop that was over inventory. The tackiest fuchsia and orange cupids, bows and arrowed hearts, and valentines were all over the place. Purple and red balloons billowed from the center of every tablecloth. A huge yellow-and-black banner read Best Wishes Heather and Tim. There was a giant ice sculpture in the middle of the room of two people embracing that was almost obscene, or it would have been if the fronts of their bodies hadn't been so tightly intertwined.

The maître d' gave her a scornful look. "As far as I know, everything was done precisely as ordered, Mrs. Stratton."

Then he didn't know much. "I didn't order any of this! Where are the festive red-and-white centerpieces I asked for? The party favors and napkins engraved with Heather's and Tim's names? Everything should have been here! The room should have looked tasteful and elegant, with a very subtle Valentine's Day motif. Not like a burlesque show dive."

The maître d' sniffed. "All I can tell you is the decorations arrived at four o'clock today, and each firm that brought something in had strict instructions on what to do."

Amanda glanced at her watch. This was a nightmare. Obviously someone had set her up, wanted her to look bad. But who? Why? Could it have been Ethan's father?

"Mrs. Stratton, your guests will be arriving soon."

"There's no way they can see this, any of it!" Amanda swore. Frantic for a solution, she turned to him, "Do you have another banquet room available?"

"Sorry. We're booked."

"All right then, get everyone available in here. And quickly! Bring laundry carts or whatever, but we've got to get rid of all this stuff before anyone sees it!"

Galvanized into action, Amanda rolled up her sleeves and got busy. All the centerpieces were dumped into a central laundry bin, along with the banner and the balloons. The hideous ice sculpture was carted off to the hotel kitchen.

No sooner had she run back to the banquet hall than Ethan arrived. He looked at the empty room, with the white tableclothes, the plain white china and his face fell. "This is where it's to be held?" Clearly he'd expected a lot more.

Sweat was beading on Amanda's brow. "I don't have any time to explain. I need your help." To the maître d', she said, "Guests will be arriving any minute. I don't care what you do. Stall them. Let them all have a drink in the bar, but don't let anyone in this room—not anyone until we get back!"

As they sped toward Ethan's car, she explained what had happened. He was both sympathetic and angry, vowing to get to the bottom of the mix-up. Too upset to be worried about revenge at that point, Amanda just wanted to salvage what she could.

They stopped at the closest florist shop and ran inside. Amanda bought a dozen vases, every flower they had in stock, and assorted greenery, and charged it all to her business account. Taking two of the florist's employees with them in their van, they led the way back to the hotel.

There, she learned from the disgruntled maître d' the guests were in the bar and had flooded over into the lobby. It wasn't a situation the hotel appreciated.

"Hang on. We'll be ready for them in a few minutes."

Working feverishly, Amanda, Ethan and their two drafted assistants went to work. Soon every table had a lovely floral centerpiece done in a rainbow of colors. There were still no personalized napkins, no banner, but it was the best they could do. "What about the food" Amanda asked. "Was the menu changed, too?"

"No. That was the same."

She heaved a sigh of relief. "Thank God for small miracles. You can send in the guests now." She turned to Ethan. "I'll apologize to Heather and Tim later for the mix-up and I am sorry."

"I am, too. I'm also damn mad at whoever's behind it." He paused. "You don't think the Summerfields had a hand in this, do you? After all, they wanted to pay for the rehearsal dinner and I wouldn't let them—you don't think they wanted to go ahead and decorate on their own?"

Had she not been to their ranch for the barbecue, Amanda might have been inclined to suspect them. But she knew even their taste wasn't that abominable. "If that had been the case, Ethan, I would've known. They would've worked through me to try and control the decorations or have some input in the party. No, this was set up, not to hurt Heather, but to make me look bad. I'm sure of it."

"Why?"

"Because it was done too smoothly, without my office knowing anything at all about it. Because my name was mentioned specifically in every transaction, written on all the paperwork the maître d' saw."

Ethan frowned. "You don't think my father..."

Remembering how Harrison had set her up before to look bad in Ethan's eyes, Amanda blanched. She'd had an uneasy feeling about him ever since. But as to whether Harrison would be moved to meddle with decorations...somehow the idea of that just didn't fit. She had an idea he would consider that women's work. "I don't know," she said finally, in answer to Ethan's question about his father. She looked up at him earnestly. "As much as he wants me out of your life, I don't think he'd do anything to hurt Heather."

Ethan frowned. "Then who?"

They turned in unison, to see Charlene framed in the doorway. Her eyes grew wide with surprise as she looked at the tastefully if remarkably austere interior of the room. Glancing over at Ethan, she composed herself, but it was too late, they'd already seen her shock, knew she had expected something entirely different.

Ethan and Amanda exchanged a glance. They both knew who the culprit was. Ethan swore, soft and low. "I don't know why I didn't see this coming."

"Please." She caught his arm. "Don't cause a scene. You've got to think of Heather."

"I am, and that's precisely why I don't intend to let her get away with this. You can come or not. Your choice." He started for Charlene.

Considering the woman had just tried to ruin her business reputation—and at Heather's emotional expense—Amanda followed him, then watched as Ethan pulled Charlene out of a group. "I'd like to speak to you, if I may."

Charlene turned wide, innocent eyes on him. "Certainly."

Ethan turned back to Amanda, a look of devilish enjoyment mixing with his anger, now that the situation was under control. "Where'd you say that sculpture went?"

Out of the corner of her eye, Amanda saw Charlene blanch slightly. "In the kitchen."

"Great. Charlene." He took hold of her wrist when it looked as if she would bolt. "I've got something to show you."

"It is uncouth," Charlene agreed, pink-cheeked, when they halted in front of the melting sculpture moments later. "I don't blame you for not wanting it at the party. Amanda, how could you? Don't you have any taste?"

"I didn't order it," Amanda said bluntly.

"Then who did?" Charlene countered haughtily, glaring at Amanda as if this were all her fault. "Certainly not Ethan."

"Come on, Charlene," Ethan continued, an impatient edge to his deep voice. "We saw the look on your face when you entered. You were the only guest surprised with the decorations—or shall we say lack of them. I already know you're behind it. What I want to know is why."

She assumed a petulant look. Seeing it would do her no good to lie, she sighed and finally confessed, "Someone had to shake some sense into you."

He stared at her uncomprehendingly. "What the hell are you talking about?"

"Oh, Ethan, for heaven's sake, stop thinking with your hormones and start thinking with your brain!" Charlene retorted, her disdainful tone rising above the clink of pots and pans, the murmur of voices. "You can't get involved with this . . . this caterer!"

Amanda knew she should have been royally offended by Charlene's snobbish attitude, and she was. But she was also still glowing from the great way she and Ethan had worked together to save the day. If she hadn't known it before, she knew it now; even under duress, they made a great team.

Nevertheless, Charlene still had to be dealt with. No one, no matter how rich or how cultured, walked all over her and got away with it.

"First of all," Amanda sighed, correcting the other woman firmly, "I'm a consultant, not a caterer."

Charlene shrugged, the distinction mattering not a whit to her. "Whatever," she said, her pinched white nostrils flaring. "You're not in Ethan's class."

"And what class is that, Charlene?" Ethan shot back ferociously, his voice rising angrily as the chefs in the hotel kitchen turned around to stare. "Is it money that makes a person good? Or a certain amount of blue blood running in his veins? Is it connections or power or social status?"

Charlene stared at Amanda haughtily, then turned to Ethan persuasively. "It's all of that. It's . . . it's knowing you were born to be better than most people. Knowing you're above most people. Oh, Ethan, I can't explain it. I just know that you have it and I have it and Iris had it and she—" Charlene pointed an accusing finger at Amanda "—doesn't."

If it hadn't been so sad, it would have been hysterical. "Well, whatever it is that you have," Amanda said, dusting off her hands, "I'm certainly glad you've got it and I don't."

Charlene turned bright red and whirled on Ethan. "Are you going to let your hired help talk to me this way?" she demanded, insulted.

"I'm not only going to let her, I'm going to goad her on."

Charlene's aristocratic face went from red to white. She patted a strand of her frosted hair back into place. "I don't have to stand here and be insulted."

"Then don't," Ethan said firmly, his look not to be crossed. "Go home."

Her eyes flashing, Charlene glared over at him. "I have never ever been so insulted in my life! I won't forget this, Ethan Holbrook!"

"Neither will I," he retorted sagely, not the least bit disturbed by Charlene's anger.

"If Iris could see you now, she'd turn over in her grave," Charlene continued to rant.

"If she would disapprove—which I doubt, since she always wanted me to happy—then it would be her problem," Ethan volleyed back sternly. "Amanda is part of my life now, Charlene, whether you or anyone else likes it or not. You got that?"

She gave him a withering stare, then without another word turned on her heel and fled. Behind them, the kitchen staff began to clap. Amanda turned to Ethan, in awe of the way he had jumped to her defense. He really did care about her, she realized with amazement, and he didn't care who knew about it. Maybe, she thought in growing wonder, they could conquer anything. "Thanks," she said quietly.

He took her into his arms and hugged her hard, then drew back to look down into her face. "I'm just sorry you had to go through that."

"Don't be," she said. Because now I know how you really feel about me, that you're willing to fight public opinion, anything, and anyone, just to be with me, and that changes everything. It meant they had a chance. She knew now where they were headed, and she was more and more certain it was the right thing, for both of them.

"HEATHER TOLD ME you sent Mimi to help out with the bridal shower Charlene is giving for Heather," Ethan said, the following evening.

"Yes, I did," Amanda admitted with a smile. She hadn't had any time alone with Ethan since he'd gotten rid of Charlene last night. She was glad, even though it was the end of a very long day for her, that they were going to have some time alone. More important still was the fact he had sought her out personally, rather than simply picked up the phone and called. Which meant he wanted to see her, be alone with her, too.

Going back to his earlier question, she said, "Under the circumstances, considering the way you threw her out of the hotel last night, I thought it might be easier if Charlene and I didn't run into each other." She still glowed whenever she thought of the way Ethan had jumped to her defense.

He frowned, his mind apparently still on the society matron. "She wouldn't give your sister a hard time, would she?"

Amanda shrugged, not really worried. "If she did, I have no doubt Mimi could handle her. When I talked to Mimi a while ago, she said everything was going smoothly and that the shower at Charlene's house was almost over. Heather has enough gifts to last her a lifetime. And Iris's friends were enchanted with your daughter, how much a lady she is now that she's all grown up."

Ethan sighed and thrust his hands into the pockets of his trousers. He looked at the To Do list on her desk for Heather's wedding, with all the items scratched out. "It's almost over, isn't it?" he said, the corners of his mouth turning down slightly.

"The wedding?" She had a feeling there was more on his mind, that he had come there not just to see her, to make sure everything was okay, but to talk to her alone. She put down the gift from the Summerfield shower she'd been describing on paper, and set aside her pen. It was important Heather have a complete accounting of all gifts sent, so she would be able to write proper thank-you notes later on, but not so important she didn't have time to talk to Ethan.

"That and my tenure as a parent." He swallowed hard. "I didn't expect it to be up so soon."

None of us do, Amanda thought. Going to his side, she touched his arm lightly, in a consoling gesture. "She still needs you."

Ethan traced the stainless-steel edge of a toaster, and examined a twelve-speed blender. "Not the way she did," he said disconsolately. "She's not ever going to need me that way again."

Amanda heard the emotion in his voice and her heart went out to him. She took his hand in hers, and after squeezing it briefly, led him over to the satin sofa on the other side of the room. "Feeling a little sorry for yourself tonight?" she prodded as she kicked off her heels and curled up beside him on the sofa.

He shrugged listlessly and looked irritated with himself as he admitted, "Maybe."

She smiled, knowing only one way to get him out of that mood: distract him. Gentler still, she asked, "Want some company?"

He hesitated. "What about Babe?"

"She's spending the night with my folks. I knew I was going to have to work late tonight, not to mention all day tomorrow, so I arranged for her to spend the night with them. They'll get her off to school for me. All I'll have to manage is the wedding."

"You've been a real trooper through all this." His hand tightened over hers as he bestowed the heartfelt compliment. "I don't know if I could've gotten through the past few weeks without you. Your moral support has proved indispensable to me. Just knowing you were here...that I could call you anytime and talk to you...made me feel so much better."

"I'm glad," she said softly, meaning it. She also knew what he didn't—that what he was going through right now was experienced by everyone. "And as for your depression about Heather getting married tomorrow," she comforted kindly, "it'll fade."

"I know, I know." He was silent a long moment, staring morosely out into space. She sat beside him, glad it was late, that they were completely alone in the office, talking openly. "It's not just that," he continued wistfully.

"What then?"

"I'm worried about not seeing you."

His confession caught her by surprise.

"I've come to count on that, Amanda. More than I knew. I don't want our friendship to end just because your job is done. I want to keep seeing you."

The words she had so yearned to hear brought an aura of magic to the night. "I want that, too," she said simply, achingly aware that sometime in the past twenty-four hours all the fears she'd ever had about the depth of his commitment to her, about their ability to stand up to outside intervention, had melted away. She knew in her heart what they had was very special. Too special to give up, ever.

"I feel like we've wasted so much time," he murmured, drawing her into her arms and crushing her against him. Hand beneath her chin, he lifted her face to his. He kissed her passionately, and she clung to him, feeling a rush of pleasure invade her soul.

"So do I," she whispered back. Years and years of it.

"Oh God, Amanda, I want you," he whispered, the warmth of his skin feeling so good, so right, pressed against the length of hers. She needed more of that warmth.

"I want you now." He rubbed his jaw against her hair, and planted tiny kisses across her temple, down to her ear. His hold on her tightened inexorably as he whispered fiercely, "I want you in my life." Thumbs beneath her chin, he lifted her face to his, so she might see the tenderness and affection in his eyes. "I want you to be part of me. Not just for tonight or this year or next but forever . . . always."

This should have happened years ago, she thought. But it hadn't. It was happening now. And this time she wasn't going to turn away or let anything or anyone else drive them apart. "Oh, Ethan," she whispered brokenly, tears of happiness flooding her eyes, "I want that, too." *I want what we never had.*

He whispered her name and drew her closer still, until she was sitting on his lap, her arms wreathed around his neck, and then he was kissing her again, ruthlessly this time, evocatively. Until they were shifting again, sliding back, rolling so he was astride her. The weight of him pushed her down into the cushions and warmed her from head to toe. The hardness of his body, the scent of him, the taste of him, were all she knew. All she wanted. And again she wrapped her arms around his neck and pulled him down until her eager mouth met his. She answered his tender caresses with all the love she had to give, accepting his affection in return. He plied her mouth with kisses, until there wasn't a cell that hadn't been touched, tasted, stroked. On fire with desire, she moaned and strained closer, aware of the scratchiness of his wool trousers against her nylon-clad thighs, that her skirt was pushed somewhere up around her waist.

Wanting, needing more, she tugged his jacket off, and then his tie. Unwilling to break the contact, aware of the ludicrousness of their decision to do otherwise, they laughed as she pulled the tail of his shirt out and slipped her hands beneath, to the plane of warm firm skin and solid male muscle. The contact was delicious, electric. Moving her hands around, she touched him from waist to neck, and then slowly, slowly, began to undo the buttons.

Eyes darkening to pewter, he watched her. Together, awkwardly but lovingly, they helped him out of his shirt. He tossed it aside with an impatient oath that had them laughing once again. And then the laughter faded as he touched his mouth to hers once more.

The joining of lips was wild, stormy, passionate. She arched into him, wanting his touch, needing. The yearning grew. He bared her to the waist, button by button, peeling off first her blouse, and then her lacy bra. She gasped as his thumb and forefinger encircled the ripe, rosy peak, then worried it to a hard nub, and he circled it with his mouth and tongue. Insides pulsing, eyes closed, heart filled to bursting, she closed her eyes, and let him touch, let him taste.

Impatient, they dispensed with the rest of their clothes, moving more quickly now. Not stopping until they were free of encumbrances, free to be together for the very first time. He touched her with tenderness and reverence. She touched him with shyness and passion. Gentleness faded and it was all unassailable demand and hot, pulsing need. No matter how much or how often they touched, no matter how much or how often or how deeply they kissed, they couldn't get enough of each other. He reached out and pulled her against him, rolling so they were lying on their sides. He took her mouth fiercely, lifted her hips and found that most intimate part of her. Found it until she moved shamelessly, wantonly, against him. Touched her until she discovered him in exactly the same way.

And then he was turning her again, shifting, rolling her onto her back and wedging a space between her knees. "Now?" he asked, throbbing against her.

She held him tightly, so her bare breasts were crushed hard against his chest. "Now," she said, wanting him as she had never wanted anyone. And then they merged, body to body, heart to heart, lovingly, passionately, toward the edge. She learned what she had been looking for, yearning for. And when it was over, for the very first time in her life, she felt completely, utterly fulfilled.

ETHAN THOUGHT LIFE couldn't get much better, after the night—or at least most of the night—that he had spent holding Amanda in his arms. But his daughter's wedding disproved that, he realized, as the reception came to life around him. There was a very special pleasure in seeing his child grow up, healthy and productive, seeing her in love and being brave enough, daring enough, to merge her life with the man of her dreams. "The wedding was beautiful, wasn't it?" Amanda said, coming over to join him as the guests began to leave the reception.

"Yes, it was," Ethan said. Although he and Amanda had agreed earlier not to let anyone know about them just yet, for fear it would spark unpleasant reactions and spoil Heather's wedding, he found it was not such an easy promise to keep. Particularly when every time he looked at her he remembered the white-hot pleasure of holding her in his arms, and being a part of her. Sweeter still was the ability to talk to her, to say whatever was on his mind and know she would not only understand but somehow find a way to make him feel better.

He turned to Amanda. "I can't wait to get you alone."

From the way she blushed he knew she felt the same. Unfortunately she was given no opportunity to say so, for his father came over to join them, too. "Amanda, you are to be commended for a very fine job," Harrison said.

At his father's unexpected praise, Amanda glowed. "Thank you."

His expression sobering, his dad looked at him. "I've invited a few of our closest friends over to my place for a nightcap. I think you should be there, too. And Amanda, I'd like it very much if you could join us also.''

After a day of socializing, that was the last place Ethan wanted to be, but he knew it would be rude to refuse. As for Amanda, he assumed she would refuse. But then he watched as something flickered in her eyes and, without warning, a silent message seemed to pass back and forth between his father and Amanda. After yet another moment, she nodded cordially. ''Thank you, sir. I'd like that very much.''

''You're sure this is okay with you?'' Ethan asked as the two of them walked away. Their closeness was so new, so fragile, he didn't want anything—especially a careless remark from his father—to spoil it.

''I'm sure,'' Amanda said firmly, not meeting his eyes until after that had been said. ''Shall I meet you there?''

''Let's take the same car. We can leave yours here and get it later.''

She hesitated only a moment before agreeing.

Once back at his father's house, drinks were served all around. The videotape of the wedding was replayed on a huge screen in the den.

No sooner had it started than Ethan saw his father glance at Amanda, waiting until she felt his steady stare and returned his look. He nodded slightly in the direction of the door, then got up and exited unobtrusively. After a moment, Amanda followed.

Ethan sat there, wondering what was going on. Both worried and curious, he followed. His father and Amanda were in his father's study, at the rear of the house. The door had been shut most of the way, but Ethan could hear voices coming through the narrow opening.

''I want to thank you for helping me out,'' his father said. ''I couldn't have done it myself.''

There was a ripping sound and then Amanda's low, incredulous, ''Sir, this is way too much money!''

Money! What the hell was Amanda doing taking money from his father? ''Nonsense, you earned it,'' his father replied gruffly.

''But—''

''We had an agreement, remember? You've done what I asked, and done it well. Not even Ethan knows anything about it.''

Anger course through him as he wondered what the two had hidden from him. In the den, the conversation continued. "You asked me not to tell him." Amanda's voice was defensive.

"Because he probably would've objected—" his father retorted scornfully.

"I hate deceiving him," Amanda countered with genuine regret.

"There was no other way," he heard his father reply autocratically. "You're going to have to trust me on this."

Silence.

"You've also been a true friend to him," his father continued lauding her efforts, "seeing that his friendship with that money-hungry Charlene Davenport was broken up."

Charlene! Ethan thought. What did Amanda have to do with her?

"Wait a minute," Amanda protested vehemently, "I didn't engineer that."

"I know, she did it to herself. Ethan told me about the decorations for the rehearsal dinner. But nonetheless, you were there for him, standing by. Making yourself available to him as a friend, and I appreciate it. Now, we better get back to the party before we're missed."

Ethan's hands clenched at his side. Not wanting to be seen eavesdropping, he stepped back out of sight. First, Amanda passed—she was tucking a check into the bodice of her dress—and then moments later, more slowly with the aid of his cane, his father. He waited until the coast was clear, then went into the study. Front and center on his father's desk was his checkbook. Feeling like the worst kind of sneak, yet determined to know, Ethan went over to the desk. He flipped open the cover, to the last entry. The check was made out to Amanda, for the sum of one hundred and fifty thousand dollars.

Ethan stared at it disbelievingly, his heart pounding in his chest. What the hell was going on?

Why was his father giving Amanda money? What were they in cahoots about? His father couldn't have paid her to distract him, to keep him away from Charlene. But what other reason could they have had for exchanging money on the sly? God knew his father had conned Amanda into accepting money from him once. Was it possible he'd done it again?

Nausea hit him like hammer blows in his stomach. This was like a bad dream. One he'd never had any wish to repeat.

Ethan balled his hands into fists. He had to talk to Amanda. Had to find out what was going on.

Going back into the den, he sat down beside her. The videotape of the wedding was still playing and held most of the guests entranced.

Not realizing anything was up, Amanda smiled at him. "Where were you?"

"I needed a breath of fresh air," he lied, not about to have a scene there. He forced a smile. "Ready to leave?"

She nodded, looking glad he'd asked. "It has been a long day."

Yes, it had, Ethan thought grimly, but it wasn't over yet.

AMANDA KNEW SOMETHING was wrong; she'd noticed the change in Ethan when he came back from "getting some air" at his father's house. She thought she knew what it was, too. The fact Heather was married now had finally hit him—probably while he was watching the videotape of the wedding. Either that or he was just exhausted after a trying day and almost no sleep last night.

With dismay, she noticed the passing street signs. "Ethan, my condo's the other way."

"I know," he said expressionlessly, keeping his eyes on the road. "We're not going there. We're going to my place."

As much as she would've liked to go home with him again, to offer whatever comfort she could, she knew it was not possible. "I need to get home. I can't stay with you tonight. Babe—"

"I didn't ask you to stay the night," Ethan interrupted curtly. "I just want to talk to you."

Beneath the controlled civility, he seemed angry. Very angry. Amanda looked out the window uneasily. Was it possible he knew about her part in his father's wedding gift to the happy couple and was angry because he felt it was too lavish a present? Or because she had been sworn to secrecy until after the cars were presented on Monday? She would just have to wait for Ethan to tell her if this was so. At any rate, she supposed it was a misunderstanding that could be cleared up fairly easily.

Ethan pulled up in front of his home. He got out and circled around to her side, his manner so edgy her whole body chilled. Maybe there was something else wrong, she thought. Maybe his father had found out they had been together the previous night and had said something to him. Something rude. "What's wrong?" she asked the moment they entered his home. She was trying very hard not to jump to any conclusions.

"Suppose you pull that check out and tell me," he snapped.

Amanda's jaw dropped. If he'd seen her tuck the check in her bodice, he had to have been out in the hall outside his father's study. She stared at him incredulously, beginning to feel angry herself. "You eavesdropped?" she demanded, stunned.

"I was curious about what you were up to with my father."

The way he said that made her feel like she'd been condemned. She swallowed, knowing he did have a point—she had hid that from him, but only on direct orders from a client. Surely once Ethan understood that, he'd calm down and forgive her the duplicity. "He asked me to do him a favor—"

"Yeah, so?" Ethan interrupted in a bitter voice. "You could have turned him down."

"Yes, I could've." Amanda met his look equably. "But I needed the extra money for Babe's college education."

Ethan swore profusely and stalked away from her. He ripped off his bow tie in one savage motion. "Like you needed it before for your father's business?"

The color drained from her face. "Just what are you accusing me of doing?" she snapped out.

"I'm not sure," he bit back in the same aggrieved tone. "What exactly does a woman have to do today to earn upward of one hundred and fifty thousand dollars?"

He'd looked at the checkbook, too. At the realization, she felt her face turn blotchy, with patches of heat and cold. "I told your father it was too much."

"Yeah, I heard."

"But he insisted on paying me a commission."

"A rather hefty one at that, wouldn't you say?"

She found his sarcasm insulting. Her spine stiffened. "Most of that money is for the cars. I'm to pay the dealers when I go to pick up the cars."

Without warning, he did a doubletake and his brow furrowed. "Cars?" He looked at her in confusion.

He wasn't the only one who was having trouble following this. "Yes," she bit out, overenunciating each and every word. "Your father hired me to find and purchase two Mercedes convertibles, one for Heather and one for Tim. I also had to find out what their favorite colors for cars were without letting them know why. He would've done it himself, if he didn't have so much trouble getting around these days. He wanted me to comparison shop and wheel and deal until I got him the very best price. What did you think he paid me for?"

Ethan reddened. He shook his head and didn't answer.

Amanda did a quick replay of her conversation with his father. The answer hit her as soon as she remembered what had been said. She stared at him. "Maybe you better tell me what you thought."

Ethan tugged at his collar uncomfortably. "I think I'd better not."

But suddenly he didn't have to. She knew what his father had said—those odd remarks about keeping Ethan away from Charlene—and what Ethan must've thought. Was it possible Harrison had engineered the whole thing, just to set her up, to make Ethan think the worst of her again due to circumstantial evidence? She knew by what Harrison had done to her before, he certainly was capable of it. And knowing that, she also knew what Ethan thought. "You think I slept with you to keep you away from Charlene, and then accepted money for it, is that it?"

He said nothing in response.

A red mist swam before her eyes. Amanda turned on her heel. "I've got to get out of here."

"Wait," he caught her arm, apparently having come to his senses. "Look, I'm sorry. Okay? I made a mistake."

"Sorry doesn't cut it, Ethan, not if you think I can be bought that easily." Tears stung her eyes. "How could you?"

His body tensed. "I didn't want to."

"Yeah, sure."

The grim look around his eyes deepened. "But I remembered what happened before."

"And you thought it could happen again," she interjected softly, savagely. "Well, maybe you're right. Maybe it can happen again." She sure felt like she'd been set up, by a master.

Not that it mattered now what Harrison Holbrook did or didn't do. Her affair with his son was over, and this time it wouldn't be resurrected.

Chapter Thirteen

"Honey, are you all right?" Amanda's mother demanded the second she got in the door. "What's going on? Babe called us. She said you'd been up half the night crying."

"It's that damn Ethan Holbrook again, isn't it?" her father swore, shrugging out of his overcoat. "He's hurt you."

Embarrassed to be caught still in her bathrobe at 10:00 a.m., with her eyes swollen and her hair a mess, Amanda turned away from her parents. She picked up her cold cup of coffee and padded out to the kitchen, her rubber-soled slippers making swishing noises on the tile. She wasn't up to dealing with this. "Mom, Dad, please—" Still stung by her own culpability, she fought a new flow of tears. "I know you mean well, but you've got to stay out of this."

"How can I stay out of it?" her father thundered, trodding after her. "With you looking like you've just been run over by a truck. Damn those Holbrooks." He slammed his fist into his open palm. "I'll make them pay for hurting you."

Harrison probably deserved to be punished for his part in this, but she knew Ethan was just as much a victim of their parents' feud. Putting a hand to his arm, she stopped her father as he started to pick up the phone. "Ethan didn't mean to hurt me, Daddy. It was all a big misunderstanding." A misunderstanding that, nevertheless, had let her know exactly how little he still trusted her. And realizing that, she knew it really was over. It had to be.

"I'll bet he didn't mean to hurt you," her father grumbled irately.

Amanda knew the only way to get her father to calm down, to keep him from going over and punching Ethan out, was to give him all the details, humiliating as they were. If only she hadn't been so gullible where his father was concerned! But she had been and now she had to pay for her naiveté. Swallowing hard, she continued, "His father hired me to help buy a very lavish wedding gift for his granddaughter and her new husband."

"So?" her mother said, helping herself to a cup of coffee.

"So Ethan saw me accepting money from his father for the gift last night after the wedding and assumed it was like the first time," she explained in weary exasperation.

"What first time?" her father countered forcefully, even more upset. "When have you ever accepted money from Harrison Holbrook?" Realizing the enormity of her slip, she paled and bit her lip. "Dammit, Amanda, you tell me or I'll go and ask him myself!" her father swore, glowering even more. Her mother gaped at her, aghast, and with one hand, backed into a nearby kitchen chair.

Knowing he meant what he said finally provoked her to tell him what she hadn't revealed to him in all these years. Her father, receiving the news, was dumbfounded. "You mean Harrison Holbrook made the loan to me that started the Webster Group!" he repeated incredulously.

Amanda nodded, tears in her eyes, knowing she deserved his rebuke.

"And you not only never said a word about it, but you helped deceive me?"

Amanda was flooded with guilt and remorse. She stared at him forlornly. "I—I knew you'd never accept the money if you knew where it came from. And Mr. Holbrook said he really wanted to help."

"My own daughter, betraying me."

Getting up again, her mother stepped between them and tried to intervene, to no avail. Her father shrugged them both off. "I'm going over to see Harrison Holbrook and give him a piece of my mind!" The two women watched helplessly as he stormed out.

Knowing her father's mood was dangerous, Amanda dashed for the phone. "I've got to call Ethan. Maybe he can get there in time to stop this!"

She punched the number for his private line in with trembling fingers. Fortunately for them both, he was home. She spilled the words out hurriedly, knowing she sounded hysterical. After listening to her, he said brusquely, "I'm on my way."

Amanda hung up the phone and dashed up the stairs to dress. Finished, she ran back down and reached for her purse and car keys. "I'm going over there, too."

"I'm going with you," her mother said.

Ethan's car pulled in the drive the same time as Amanda's. They rushed toward the door together, but even as they approached Harrison's house they could hear the voices inside, shouting. "Thank God you've come," Harrison's houseman said, letting them in. "I was about to call you."

"It won't be necessary," Ethan said. He followed the voices into the living room, with Amanda and her mother close on his heels.

Harrison was leaning on his cane, trembling visibly from head to foot. His face almost purple with rage, he looked at Ethan. "Get this cretin out of my house!" he shouted.

Ethan stepped between the two men. "I have to agree with my father, Mr. Webster, this doesn't seem like a good idea," Ethan said.

Amanda's father responded with an obscenity, the likes of which she'd never heard, then turned back to Harrison. "You went too far this time, using my daughter," he threatened.

"I was trying to help you."

Her father winced, as if in physical pain, and put a hand to his right side, just beneath his ribs. "Assuage your guilty conscience, maybe," he retorted angrily.

His hands and legs trembling uncontrollably with the side effects of his disease, Harrison Holbrook backed into a chair and shook his head disparagingly. "You always were an overly emotional fool," he rasped.

"At least I have feelings for people." Her father countered once again. "Unlike you and your son."

Amanda moved forward beseechingly. "Dad—"

"Stay out of it, Amanda. This man has used you—our family—for the last . . . oh, God." Her father doubled over in pain.

"Dad, what is it?" Amanda said, taking in the sudden gray-white color of his skin and the beads of perspiration shining on his face. Without warning, a trickle of blood oozed from the corner of his mouth. In the background, her mother screamed. Her father grappled in his pocket for a handkerchief and, not finding it, collapsed on the floor.

Behind her, Ethan swore and moved swiftly for the phone. "I'll call an ambulance," he announced.

Harrison fell silent, looking as shocked and dismayed at Amanda's father's collapse as everyone else.

The room was deathly silent as they all waited for the ambulance to come, the argument of moments before all but forgotten. Only her mother spoke in soothing murmurs to her father, as she knelt by his side. *Not my father,* Amanda thought, repeated the words over and over in her head. *Please, God, don't let anything happen to my father.*

When the emergency squad arrived, her mother rode with her father in the ambulance. Ethan insisted on escorting Amanda to the hospital. "You're not in any shape to drive."

Knowing what he said was true, she felt like she might faint at any time; she tucked her trembling hands in the pockets of her jeans and didn't argue.

Neither of them spoke during the interminable ride to the hospital. There seemed nothing to say. Once there, time passed in a blur of antiseptic hospital smells and hushed sounds. Finally, an hour after her father had been admitted, the doctor came in to the waiting room to see them. "Mrs. Webster, your husband has a bleeding ulcer. We've stabilized him, but he's going to need to stay here for a few days. Has he been under any unusual stress recently?"

Her relief showing on her face, her mother looked at Ethan. "Yes, quite a bit, actually," she said, giving Ethan a pointed, angry look.

The doctor picked up on the new tenseness in the room. "Maybe we'd better talk alone," he said.

Amanda and Ethan moved obediently out into the hall. "I'm sorry," Ethan said.

Heavy-hearted, she stood in the polished hall, wrestling with her own guilt for her father's illness. "I know you are, but that doesn't change anything, does it?"

"I shouldn't have fought with you last night. I shouldn't have jumped to conclusions."

"But you did."

"It won't happen again," he reiterated firmly.

"Oh, Ethan, if you believe that, you really are fooling yourself. Besides, even if that were true, even if I could get you to believe in me through thick and thin, there's still the issue of our families. They hate each other."

He expelled a breath of exasperation. "So, we'll work on changing it. It's past time this feud came to an end, anyway."

She moved away from him, never more potently aware of the differences between them. He was dressed as elegantly as always in a suit and tie; she in a worn sweatshirt, sneakers and jeans. She pushed the toe of her sneaker against the shiny waxed surface of the floor until it bent. "You saw our fathers together. No matter how much we want it, it just isn't possible."

He was silent, studying the remorse and listlessness on her face. Finally he crossed his arms over his chest. "So we'll give them no choice but to accept us as a couple."

She closed her eyes and tipped her head back, until it rested against the wall. If only it were that simple. Slowly, using all the strength she possessed, she opened her eyes once again and faced him. "And do what in the meantime?" she queried softly, virulently. "Do we ruin their respective healths? Cause stress to both our children? Wait for one of us to get a stress-related ulcer, too, or for your father to collapse?" He blanched at the imagery her words evoked, and she continued, "Ethan, as much as I'd like our...feelings for each other to be able to exist in a vacuum, it just isn't possible." She knew that now.

The betrayal he felt was stamped in the harsh, unforgiving lines of his face. "Meaning what, Amanda, you won't fight my father or yours?"

"No, not anymore. I won't prolong this war."

His jaw set angrily. He leaned toward her, being careful to keep his voice down despite the emotions pouring hotly through him. "You're making a mistake."

Was she? Right now she couldn't judge. She only knew she hadn't had nearly enough sleep or anything to eat, that Babe was still home alone, no doubt wondering what had happened to all of them, and Mimi—who hadn't been home earlier—still needed to be called. "I'm exhausted. I'm going to go and check in with my mother and telephone my sister and my daughter, and then, if I'm not needed, go home and get some sleep."

"Tonight—"

"I'll be back here at the hospital, with my father."

After a moment, he nodded. She knew he was unhappy with her. She also knew there was no helping it. For the moment, her first loyalty had to be to her family. As did his.

"How's Lloyd Webster?" Harrison asked the moment Ethan returned to the mansion.

"Stable." Ethan loosened his tie and took a seat opposite his father. He was glad to see his father had recovered from the argument. His color was good, and the trembling in his hands and legs had lessened to a slight twitch every now and then. "But he has a bleeding ulcer. He'll be in the hospital a while."

His father's eyes darkened, but that was the only change of expression on his impassive face. "I'm sorry to hear that," he said finally.

Ethan looked at his father, wondering if he had ever really known this man at all. "Are you?" he volleyed back quietly, working to keep his temper at a manageable level.

Harrison raised his snowy white brows. "What's that supposed to mean?"

"When did you start caring about people, their families?"

After a lengthy pause, his father warned, "That bleeding-heart girlfriend of yours is beginning to muddle your judgment, son."

Ethan pushed from his chair and jerked at the knot of his tie. If only he'd followed his instincts and had gotten to Amanda earlier today, before her parents had. He might have circumvented this whole ugly mess. Instead, knowing what a horrendous schedule she'd been keeping trying to make his daughter's wedding happen, he'd decided to let her sleep late, if possible, and call her around noon, go over and pick her up, take her somewhere elegant and quiet for lunch, somewhere they could talk, make amends. Settle this foolishness that had sprung up between them. But he hadn't and now he didn't know if he would ever be able to make her see reason, to get her to think past the feud to what was right for the two of them.

Hell, he didn't know. Maybe it was selfish of him to want to be with her. But how could loving anyone be wrong? They simply had to get through this, work things out. In time, everyone would accept them; they would give them no choice. And even if they

didn't, what would it matter if only he and Amanda were together?

"Maybe you should stop seeing her," his father continued.

Ethan turned to his father, furious now. "Why, because she's
helping me see clearly for the first time? Because she makes me see
everything in terms of human cost whether I want to or not? You
can't manage a business without taking into account the human
factor, Dad. You can't go around treating people the way you have
and still expect the business to thrive."

His father sat, unflinching. "Meaning what? You still can't get
good technical people to come and work for us?"

Ethan stared at his father in disgust. Business was always first
with him. "No," he said wearily, figuring they might as well get
this out in the open, too, since they were already arguing, "no
matter what salary we offer, we can't get good technical people to
come to work for us. And with the history of this company, the
periodic layoffs and unexpected firings, it's no wonder." As an
outsider, he wouldn't have wanted to risk taking a job at HCI. Nor,
like Amanda, would he have wanted anything to do with his
scheming, selfish father.

It was becoming clear he had a choice. Stay loyal to his father,
during the last days of his life; make the most of the time they had
left and later do things his own way; and lose Amanda, and maybe
even the company he was supposed to inherit. Or say to hell with
his dad and please himself and feel guilty as sin the rest of his days.
Some choice. Either way was bound to bring him much unhappiness.

"So what now?" Harrison asked, thumping the end of his cane
on the floor. "You're just going to give up trying to get HCI back
on track, is that it?"

Ethan moved around restlessly, still undecided about what to do,
who to hurt, his father or Amanda. "I didn't say that," he reiterated tiredly. Turning back to his father, he said honestly, "I want
to save our company from going down the tubes. But if I'm to do
that, I have to do it my way, Dad. With no interference from you."

Harrison's mouth thinned. "I can't give you that kind of control."

Ethan sighed. He'd been afraid it would come down to this, with
his father refusing to give an inch. He knew they couldn't keep
fighting; that would destroy his father's health, too. Almost as

much as watching the company he'd built fall into ruin. Ethan sighed wearily. Maybe it would help if he weren't family. Maybe there was a chance his dad would listen to an outsider. God knew he'd done everything he could to try and get his dad to change course before it was too late. "Then I can't work for you any longer," he said sadly. "I'll have my resignation on your desk this afternoon."

"Ethan..." His father's voice stopped him before he opened the door. Hearing the pain in that low timbre, Ethan turned around. "You really mean that, don't you?" his father said.

Ethan nodded. He knew if he was ever to have a relationship with Amanda, things were going to have to change. And this was just the start.

His father remained silent. "I could take you up on this threat, you know," he said angrily. "Let you resign. Then what would you do?"

Ethan shrugged. "Work for someone else. Maybe start my own company. Does it matter?"

For a moment, he didn't think it did. Hurting as much as Harrison, he regarded his father resolutely. *I'm doing the right thing,* he told himself sternly. *If I stay we'll only argue more, and that stress will aggravate his condition. I don't want to watch my father's health fail any more and know that my inability to get through to him is the cause. I just can't do it.*

If only there was another way.... But there isn't and you know it.

Even though his heart was breaking, Ethan knew what he had to do. Slowly he turned and started for the door.

Realizing he was serious about quitting the company, Harrison interjected heavily, with great remorse, "All right, Ethan. You win. I'll—have my resignation on your desk first thing this afternoon."

Ethan turned around slowly, stunned, until they were face-to-face again. He knew what an effort it was for his father to relinquish control—of anything. "You mean it?" he asked slowly, almost afraid to trust it.

His father rubbed his hand over the handle of his cane and said gruffly, "It's what I've been working for all these years—to have something to give to you in terms of inheritance. It'd be foolish not to do so now."

Ethan studied him carefully. "Even if you think I'll throw it all down the drain?"

"You won't disappoint me," his father said certainly.

If only Amanda could've been that sure, Ethan thought, troubled.

"TALKING TO ME about Amanda won't do any good," Lloyd Webster said from his hospital bed when Ethan arrived to see him several days later. "I know she's been avoiding your calls. I know why. And frankly I think she's doing the right thing."

"Because of the feud between our two families," Ethan ascertained, relieved to see Lloyd looking so well.

"And other reasons," Lloyd affirmed stubbornly.

Ethan studied his father's nemesis, knowing if he could just get Lloyd to listen and cooperate it would lessen the stress on all of them. "What if it could end?" he proposed softly.

Lloyd's glance narrowed. "Stop trying to steal my employees, then."

"I never did that, my father did, and he's resigned, effective two days ago. You have my word, no one will make an offer to any of your employees on behalf of HCI again." Amanda's father arched his brow skeptically, and Ethan continued, "I've come up with an even better solution."

"Look, son—"

"Just hear me out. Then I'll go, I swear." Taking his silence as permission to continue, Ethan said, "Neither HCI nor the Webster Group has thrived during the past few years. Given the current marketplace and your company's difficulty in continuing to finance the day-to-day operation of your development lab, that's not likely to change unless something drastic is done for both."

"Like what?" Lloyd asked gruffly.

He was listening, that was something. "I think we should combine the two, absorb your think tank back into our corporation. We've got the funds. You've got the talent."

Lloyd snorted in disbelief. "You've got to be kidding."

Ethan leaned forward earnestly. "I've never been more serious. A company needs two mind-sets to thrive—the hard-edged business sense we Holbrooks have in abundance, and the technical creativity and excellent people-management skills the Webster Group possesses."

"It's crazy."

"It'll work, if you just give it a chance. Give me a chance." And when it did, the stress on both his father and Lloyd Webster would ease, which would be better for both men's increasingly precarious health, not to mention the personal tension between the two families.

To Ethan's disappointment, Lloyd refused to give his proposal even the slightest consideration. He shook his head firmly, rejecting the offer out of hand. "I want nothing to do with your father, son. I want nothing to do with you."

"I TOLD YOU he wanted something from us," Amanda's father said with grim satisfaction after filling her in on what Ethan had just done.

Amanda shook her head, feeling the information was almost more than she could possibly absorb. Maybe she was culpable as her father and Harrison Holbrook both seemed to think. Maybe she should have seen this coming. Certainly Ethan had indicated from the outset he'd had business problems. Was this what he'd had in mind all along? she wondered, upset. Was that why he'd been so good to her, in the hopes she would be able to soften up her father to accept the offer he planned to give? Or had the brainstorming of this latest business ploy of his come later, when HCI's ploy to steal all the Webster Group's best employees had failed miserably?

Not that it really mattered, she realized as she said a quick goodbye to her father and exited his hospital room, so he wouldn't see how upset and distressed she was and be further upset himself. Either way, she had been used, betrayed. And the sooner she had it out with Ethan about this, the better.

"How COULD YOU DO something like that without talking to me first?" she demanded irately, after bursting into Ethan's office unannounced.

Ethan had been working late. He looked tired and drawn. His shirtsleeves were rolled up above his forearms, his tie loosened to midchest. He tossed down his pen and pushed away from his desk.

She watched the pen bounce as it hit the stack of papers he'd been working on.

"I tried, but you wouldn't return my calls, remember?" He defended himself as he came around the desk to talk to her, face-to-face.

Suddenly he was too close to her, the scent of his skin and his after-shave too enticing. She paced away from him. "You know my father's been under stress." She continued her accusations, unabated.

"Yes, I know that." Ethan rested both his hands on his hips. "This will ease it. If he comes to his senses and accepts my offer for a truce, that is."

She whirled to face him, hating the way he broke highly charged emotional matters down into a distant quandary, one he apparently felt they both should have been willfully oblivious to. "You're so coldly analytical."

He didn't even try to deny it, rather, shrugged his broad shoulders acceptingly. "In business, you have to be."

And what about in affairs of the heart? she wanted to ask, but didn't. *Did you ever truly want to be close to me or were you just using me as a way to soften up my father?* And considering how little he trusted her, what did it matter, anyway? They had no future together, and as such, this meeting was pointless. Knowing they would only inflict more pain on each other if she stayed, she turned defiantly toward the exit.

He moved to block her way. "Amanda—don't go. Please." He held out a hand beseechingly. "We need to talk."

"Do we?"

"You know we do," he said softly. He tried to take her into his arms; still feeling betrayed, she resisted. "Combining our two companies would be a way to end the feud. If that were over, we could be together."

She knew what he was proposing was hopeless. Her father might someday merge his business with another company, but it wouldn't be HCI. "Even if the two companies merged, our fathers would still hate each other."

"That would change, given time."

Once Amanda had been naive enough to think that time solved everything. But now she was old enough to know better. She had been married to Alex for five years, and during that time, her ex-husband's family had never accepted her. Nor would their opinion have changed if she had stayed married to him. To them, she would always have been a gold digger. To Ethan's father she was a gullible fool. She would never be good enough for his son, and one day, even if they did manage to get together, that animosity would also break them apart. Loving him the way she did, she knew it was too much pain to risk. "You're fooling yourself if you think that," she replied disparagingly.

"And you're a fool if you refuse to even try to make this work so we can be together!" he shot back angrily.

Frustrated tears stung her eyes. "I want it to work, too, but I'm a realist. Couples have enough problems working out the everyday details of a relationship without adding this kind of pressure." A pressure that would not only destroy her own self-esteem and sense of well-being, but Babe's as well.

"Meaning what?" He closed in on her and took her by the shoulders when she would have turned away. "That you don't care enough about me to even try? That you don't care enough about me to brave our families' disapproval, or to make the necessary sacrifices and adjustments to forge a successful relationship?"

The way he put it made her sound selfish when she was just being logical. She sighed wearily and closed her eyes against his relentlessly searching gaze. "I just don't believe in beating my head against a brick wall," she whispered on a fresh wave of pain. It hurt bad enough, letting him go now. She knew the pain would be unendurable if she let herself get any closer to him, only to have to end it again.

His grip softened, without warning becoming as persuasive as his low voice. "Ignoring our problems won't make them go away."

Amanda shook her head ruefully, knowing even if they didn't want to, they had to be brave enough to face the truth, to think about what was, not what they wanted. "Maybe not," she said softly, her low voice as determined and pragmatic as his had been persuasive, "but if we avoid each other, and our families do the same, maybe we can at least avoid World War III."

He shook his head and released her, angry now as he moved away from her. "I thought you were different from Iris. I thought you were stronger, but you're not. You're just like her. You fold at the first signs of difficulty, run from problems rather than acknowledge them and try to work them out."

Tears blurred her eyes. This wasn't how she had wanted their relationship to end, with them not even being friends. "That's unfair. I have tried to work this out!"

He gave her a stern, uncompromising look. "Not hard enough," he said flatly.

It really was over between them. Knowing there was nothing else to say, feeling like her heart was breaking, she turned on her heel and left.

Chapter Fourteen

"You did the smart thing, breaking up with Ethan that way. You've
got to stop beating yourself up about it," Mimi said.

Amanda looked up from the proofs of the wedding photos from
Heather and Tim's wedding. The two of them looked so happy.
And Ethan had, too. If only she could go back, recapture that
special night, before all the problems had started.

"He was only using you, anyway, to try and get to Dad's company. Dad said so," Mimi continued authoritatively.

Amanda knew it looked that way. At first, knowing how the
hard-edged Holbrook family operated, especially when it came to
business, she too had assumed Ethan had had that in mind all
along. Now that she'd had time to think about it, however, she
wasn't so sure.

Ethan was as hard-nosed a businessman as his father, but he also
was very direct and honest, in ways his father was not. If he'd had
that in mind, she felt he would've talked to her about it earlier, or
hinted at his wish in some way. He hadn't. He'd only tried to buy
her father's company to end the feud, to pave the way for an
eventual reconciliation between the two families, and to make
things easier between the two of them. How could she resent him
for that?

Realizing Mimi still had serious doubts about Ethan's character, Amanda sighed. She could see it was going to take some per-
suading to make her protective older sister believe she knew what
she was doing. She also knew she wanted at least one person from
her family on her side in this, and right now, considering her father's scathing opinion of the Holbrook's, Mimi was the likeliest

candidate. Deciding for the moment to play devil's advocate, she asked doubtfully, "If my breaking up with him was so right, then why doesn't it feel like the right thing?" Why did she still feel like her heart was breaking? Why wasn't the hurt getting better instead of worse?

As always, her sister had an answer for everything. "Because you're depressed, that's why." Mimi unwrapped another set of proofs from the Holbrook-Summerfield wedding, and after perusing them cursorily, handed them over to Amanda for a look. "And that's natural," Mimi continued pragmatically, "after any breakup. The important thing to remember is the two of you had no real future together. Not with our families feeling the way they do about each other."

A week or two ago, Amanda would've agreed with that. Now that time had passed and she'd seen what the power of love could do for two clans as disparate as the patrician Holbrooks and the flashy Summerfields, she realized she was beginning to feel very differently. If those families could manage to come together for the sake of their kids, then so could theirs. "We could have changed that," Amanda said stubbornly.

Mimi sent her a skeptical glance, then opened the third box of proofs. "I thought you'd already tried."

"Maybe not hard enough," Amanda retorted grimly, the proofs in front of her forgotten, her mind already racing ahead. Why hadn't she thought of this sooner? Why hadn't she tried?

"Amanda, where are you going?" Mimi asked with exasperation.

Her mind made up, Amanda didn't bother to turn around as she answered simply, "Out. Hold the fort down until I get back."

"What about the proofs?"

"Hang on to them. I'll get them to Ethan and Heather later." Right now she had more important things to do.

"I HAVE NOTHING TO SAY to Mrs. Stratton. Tell her to go away," Harrison Holbrook said.

Not about to be thwarted again, Amanda momentarily "forgot" her good manners, followed the sound of the autocratic voice, and pushed her way into the room. What she saw brought her up short. Harrison Holbrook was stretched out on a chaise lounge, a wool blanket drawn over his lap, pillows propped behind his back.

He looked so drawn and ill she stopped short where she was. Maybe this wasn't a good time, she thought guiltily, knowing how stress was likely to exacerbate any illness. But then, when would be a good time? Sooner or later, this feud had to stop. Only then would some of the tension end, she told herself firmly. "Mr. Holbrook?"

"You weren't invited in," he advised icily, the strength in his voice unabated.

"I'm in, anyway. And I'm not leaving until we talk."

Harrison rolled his eyes and murmured something undecipherable in a disparaging voice. He lifted his head and swung his legs around to the front of the chaise. Throwing off the blanket, he reached for his cane. "Just like your father, I see. Over-emotional and impulsive." With a shaky hand, he planted the cane on the floor, and after another moment, pushed himself up. Watching him maneuver his way with difficulty across the floor to a straight-backed wing chair, she was tempted, out of kindness, just to forget the whole thing. But she knew she couldn't do that. What had to be said was more important than anyone's immediate comfort. "Maybe I am," she retorted softly, moving uninvited to the wing chair opposite Ethan's imposing father, "but that doesn't change our need to talk."

Harrison harumphed. "Speak for yourself," he muttered, then glanced at his houseman. "You can leave us alone. Shut the doors." He waited until the servant withdrew before he turned back to her. "Spit it out and be done with it then."

Amanda leaned forward earnestly, her legs crossed demurely at the knee. She hardly knew where to start. "You never liked me."

His eyes narrowed intolerantly. "I don't know you well enough to like or dislike you." She flinched, and he continued in the same steady yet emotionally annihilating tone, "I think you're a fine bridal consultant. You did a wonderful job ordering the cars."

So he approved of her on the servant level, Amanda thought, taking a deeply in-drawn breath. That was something.

"I also think you're wrong for my son."

His matter-of-fact pronouncement hurt, much more than she had expected. Amanda battled the urge to cry. "Is that why you gave me the check the night of the wedding," she asked in a slightly less steady voice, "when Ethan was around, because you wanted him to get the wrong idea, to jump to conclusions—again?"

Harrison shrugged as if it were of no consequence either way and did not answer.

"That was a lousy thing to do."

"I'm sure Ethan agrees with you, but I was just protecting my own. Trying to save us all from heartache."

At his roundabout admission of guilt, Amanda was silent. She thought of her ex-husband Alex and his family, how they had looked down on her during all the years she had been married to their playboy son. She'd thought she couldn't take being called a gold digger again, having her character besmirched or questioned every time she turned around. And as far as her past relationship with Alex went, that was still true. But it wasn't true for Ethan. For Ethan, she would risk anything—even her heart, just to be with him again.

Maybe he had wanted to buy her family's company all along, but he hadn't romanced her for that reason. On the contrary, he hadn't seen that one thing had anything to do with the other. It hadn't really occurred to him to tell her about that.

Nor would she have wanted to know about it, she realized now. She liked the fact that he enjoyed his work, that he was good at it, but there her interest in it ended. She had no wish to influence the way he did business at HCI any more than he wished to tell her how to run Moonlight and Memories. And that was the way it should be. They had been building a relationship, not a bridge between two companies. The latter had been incidental. And it probably would have happened inevitably, whether she had been involved with Ethan or not.

Realizing that freed her to act from her heart. She faced Ethan's father with every ounce of courage she possessed, knowing it was now or never, that she either took the plunge and sacrificed what remained of her pride or spent the rest of her life wondering what if. "What would it take for me to prove to you that I can be worthy of your son, that the fact we're from two different worlds does not matter?"

Harrison's eyes narrowed shrewdly. "Are you telling me you plan to marry my son?" His voice carried no particular inflection, but his level gaze oozed disapproval.

She'd done so well up until now. She couldn't, wouldn't, let him scare her off with this long-suffering act of his. "I'm telling you I love him, and that I want to keep seeing him." She didn't know about marriage. It hadn't come up. Nor was she so sure, considering all that had happened, if it ever would. But maybe that wasn't so important, either. Not if she could just be with him again.

He gave her a thin-lipped smile and offered a silent rebuff. "How does Ethan feel?"

I wish I knew.

She was so afraid she'd blown it with him, by letting her family loyalty get in the way of their being together. She fought the urge to look down at the clasped hands in her lap. "I don't know. I haven't talked to him yet."

"But you think he'll take you back?" Harrison weighed the possibility solemnly, without the least encouragement on his patrician face.

Amanda gestured helplessly, and her voice dropped significantly. "I don't know that, either."

Harrison sighed. "Marriage is hard enough under the best of circumstances. If you and Ethan married, you'd be living your life in the middle of a war zone. You understand that, don't you?"

Yes, she did, now more than ever. But it would be worth it to her, if only she could be with Ethan. She swallowed hard. "I can take that chance."

He shook his head. "I can't. I'm sorry."

She'd never felt so desolate as she did at that moment.

"If you're asking for my blessing about this," Harrison concluded with steely indifference to her feelings, "for a truce, you've come to the wrong person."

Amanda didn't know why she was surprised. Ethan's father had never approved of her before. He wasn't likely to change his mind now, especially after the way she had behaved, walking out on Ethan because he'd tried to do what was right in a business sense for both families, both companies.

Of course, she wasn't the only person at fault here. Ethan hadn't displayed much more faith in her, assuming the worst about her when he saw that check his father had handed her. But that, too, was understandable, given the mitigating circumstances. Their lack of trust in each other went back to one thing, the history of animosity and opposing values of both families.

She had so hoped she could get Ethan's father to, if not accept her, at least admit she was an okay person. But he hadn't, not in the way she wanted, as a potential romantic partner for his son.

She could still go to Ethan, of course. Tell him how she felt about him, that she wanted to try again, but would that really change anything? Would they be able to find happiness despite the odds if they tried again? Or would they just be asking for more unhappiness? She was willing to sacrifice her relationship with her family to be with him, but what about Ethan? His father was older than hers, and he was ill. He might not have all that much time left on this earth. How could she ask Ethan to sacrifice his relationship with his father to be with her? As much as she wanted to, she knew she couldn't.

So what was the answer? Amanda had to admit she didn't know, and maybe never would. . . .

THE REST OF THE DAY continued without incident. Heather came in to pick up the proofs of her wedding pictures. Glancing through the glossy photos, all of which were of exquisite quality, she moaned, "I'll never be able to decide which ones to pick."

"You can call me if you need help," Amanda said.

"I know." Heather smiled, then said, more shyly, "How are you? I mean, I know, I heard—Daddy told me the two of you weren't seeing each other anymore."

"I'm fine," *Or at least I would be if I could somehow find my way back to Ethan.*

Heather didn't look as if she believed her as she searched her face. "He misses you," she said softly.

Hope made her pulse quicken. "He said that?"

"No, not exactly," Heather admitted shyly, "but I can tell."

Sure, Amanda thought. That was why he hadn't called or tried to contact her in any way.

"He's always working," Heather continued. "And he never does that unless he's upset," Heather finished worriedly.

"I'm sure he'll get over it," Amanda said, for lack of anything better. She felt so foolish, standing there with her heart practically on her sleeve, mooning over a guy she would never, could never, have, yet wanted with all her heart and soul.

"Well, I better go," Heather said reluctantly. She glanced at her watch. "As usual, I've got a class."

Amanda nodded. "Have fun with the pictures."

The afternoon dragged on. Amanda met with several clients, and set up appointments with two more brides who wanted perfect June weddings. Although her outward demeanor was as pleasant and personable as always, inside she felt as if she were just going through the motions, and she couldn't wait to go home. She was just packing up her briefcase when Mimi trotted in, carrying a lavish bouquet of forget-me-nots. "Delivery for you."

"They're beautiful," Amanda breathed, impressed, feeling almost afraid to hope. "Was there a card?" she asked.

Mimi shook her head no. "Must've been an oversight on the part of the florist." She exited with a shrug.

Maybe, Amanda thought, and yet...forget-me-nots symbolized true love. Could they be from Ethan, or were they just from a grateful client?

Still feeling afraid to hope, because she wanted them to be from Ethan so badly, she picked up her phone and dialed her sister's office. With effort, she kept her voice calm. "Do you know which florist brought those flowers?"

"No, but I'll check for you and let you know."

No sooner had Amanda hung up the phone than her secretary came in, an enormous bouquet of red chrysanthemums in her hand. She grinned at Amanda. "You sure are popular today."

Breathing in the fragrance of the blossoms, Amanda checked for a card. Again, there was none. She thought about what the lovely flowers were supposed to symbolize—sharing. And again she wondered, was it possible?

Her heart pounding with the implications, she looked up, to see Ethan standing in the door, a bouquet of rosemary in his hand. He'd never looked more handsome, or less sure of himself. And that gave her pause, too. "These are for you," he said softly, walking closer as an explosion of emotion shot through her system.

Their hands brushed as he gave her the flowers. She thought about what the bouquet of rosemary symbolized, commitment and fidelity. Judging from the look in his eyes, that seemed to be what he was feeling. She gestured to the two bouquets in vases on her desk, and said in a revealingly throaty voice, "The others—"

"Are from me, too," he acknowledged, taking her hand in his and drawing her to her feet. "I was trying to tell you something."

True love, commitment and fidelity, sharing...it sounded like he was working up to something she very much wanted to hear. Her emotions soaring, she waited mutely for him to continue.

"But maybe you'd better read this first." Releasing his light grasp on her, he reached into his suit pocket and withdrew a sheaf of papers. "It's the first of many documents, but I think you'll see where we're going with it." His eyes held hers, and for the first time she saw his uncertainty more than matched her own.

Reluctantly she tore her eyes from his and gazed down at the typed papers. As recognition dawned, she murmured, stunned, "This is a contract between HCI and the Webster Group."

His eyes shone with satisfaction as he elaborated, "It took some doing, but your father has finally agreed to do some development work for us in his lab. We're going to underwrite all costs and share equally in the profits of any technology created, but retain the companies as two separate, independent units. He'll manage his, I'll manage mine."

She marveled at the compromise he'd negotiated. Knowing her father's attitude, she knew how difficult that must have been. "Oh, Ethan, that's wonderful," she said, feeling absurdly like she might cry.

He beamed at her praise as she handed the papers back. Still exuding calmness, he folded them into thirds and put them back in his inner suit-coat pocket. "I thought so. Your dad seemed pretty pleased, too."

Suddenly her heart was beating very, very fast. Was that all he'd come to tell her, that the feud had ended? At least partially? "When did you work all this out?"

"The agreement was finalized a little while ago, although I've been talking to your father on and off for several weeks. He's not such a bad guy, you know? I think he likes me, too—at least a little bit, now that we've gotten to know each other better."

She swallowed hard, her pleasure over that news lessened by what she hadn't yet told him. What he had to know before this reconciliation went any further. "I wish I could say the same for your dad." Briefly, sadly, she detailed her unsuccessful visit to the elder Holbrook.

Ethan was pleased she'd gone to see his father, and to her surprise, not so concerned about the unhappy result. "He's more stubborn, but he'll come around."

She studied him warily, still almost afraid to hope for a reconciliation after all that had happened. "You seem awfully sure of that."

He wrapped his arms around her waist and drew her against him. "I'm sure of only one thing," he said hoarsely, "and that's my feelings for you, Amanda. I love you."

The words she had yearned to hear filled her heart with joy. She threw her arms around his neck and hugged him tightly. "Oh, Ethan, I love you, too," she gasped in a broken voice as tears of happiness slid in a river down her face.

He kissed her tenderly. "I wish it could be, but it won't be easy—"

"True love never is." She smiled through her tears.

"But we'll find a way to make it work, anyway," he promised, tightening his hold on her affectionately. "No matter how long it takes, or what we have to go through."

"I promise not to let my loyalty to my family interfere with my feelings for you." If she had done that, she never would have walked out on him before.

"And I promise you I'll be more sensitive to your closeness to your family, although—" he paused "—even with all that's happened, our families may still disapprove."

Amanda shrugged, joyously aware this didn't seem the insurmountable problem it had been, not anymore, not when they were back together. "That's their problem, not ours. We have better things to think about."

He grinned, his priorities as firmly in place as her own. "I couldn't agree more."

"Besides, once they see how happy we are, how right for each other, they'll come around," she said softly. She knew it in her heart and soul. "It might take time—"

"But that we've got," he said as he kissed her thoroughly and they embraced. And that was the last either of them said for a very, very long time.

Chapter Fifteen

"Mom, you look beautiful!" Babe said.

Amanda looked at herself in the mirror. In a tea-length gown of white satin, with an embroidery overlay, she felt beautiful. And happier than she could remember. Her heart brimming with love, she turned to embrace her daughter. "Thanks."

"Nervous?" Babe asked softly.

Amanda nodded. "A bit."

"You shouldn't be," Babe advised her happily. "Ethan loves you very much, you know."

Amanda smiled. Of that, she was very sure. "I know." And he loved Babe, too; in fact, had become the devoted father she had always wanted but never been blessed with.

The strains of the wedding march sounded in the distance. Babe picked up her bouquet and handed Amanda hers. "Are you ready?" she asked. "Grandpa is waiting outside."

Tears of happiness shimmering in her eyes, Amanda nodded. She went out to join her father.

The ceremony was beautiful, more so because both their families were in attendance, the reception that followed an even more festive affair. "Whoever would've thought," Ethan murmured hours later, as the two of them danced to the strains of Cole Porter, "you could put both our families in a room and not have it end in chaos."

"I know," Amanda murmured happily, looking up into her new husband's face. "A year ago it wouldn't have been possible."

"But we didn't rush. We were patient." He sighed, adding, "As hard as it was, we stuck with our decision of a long engagement to give everyone time to adjust to the idea of our being together."

"And they have adjusted," Amanda agreed with contentment, looking over at the table where her mother and Ethan's father were chatting as if they had been lifelong friends. Farther on down the same table, Mimi and her husband were talking to Phil Summerfield and his wife.

"As well as held on to their health," Ethan said.

Amanda waved at her father, who was across the room, talking to some of the other guests. "And both companies are flourishing under the new agreement between HCI and the Webster Group."

Ethan nodded thoughtfully, a look of satisfaction coming onto his face. "It was a long time coming. It feels good to have the feud over."

"And our family around us," Amanda added with heartfelt satisfaction. Across the dance floor, she saw her new stepdaughter and son-in-law, cozily ensconced in each other's arms. "Heather and Tim look happy tonight."

Ethan smiled fondly, following her glance. "They should. They have everything going for them."

Amanda knew what he meant. To everyone's relief, Tim had turned out to be a good, honest businessman. As a result, the reputation of Summerfield Construction was slowly turning around. Heather loved her work as an interior designer. The Summerfields had toned down slightly under Heather's gentle tutelage and the example she set, but had still retained, and would always have, the "down home" warmth and gregariousness.

"Speaking of our daughters," Ethan interjected in a pleased tone. "Have you noticed how many young men have asked Babe to dance tonight?"

"Almost everyone here that's remotely close to her age," Amanda noted with approval. She looked back at Ethan, so resplendent in his black stroller tuxedo, crisp white shirt and striped gray tie. "And that's due to Heather, more than anyone. She helped Babe realize it was great to be tall, to just be herself."

Ethan smiled, his hold on her tightening affectionately as he murmured, "Heather always wanted a baby sister. Now she has one."

"And I have the husband I always wanted," Amanda murmured, content.

"We have it all," Ethan agreed, bending slightly to touch his lips to hers, then linger ardently. "Because," he finished softly, "We have each other."

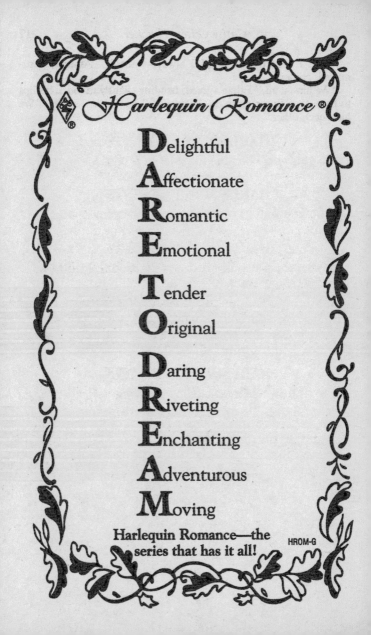

Harlequin Romance®

Delightful

Affectionate

Romantic

Emotional

Tender

Original

Daring

Riveting

Enchanting

Adventurous

Moving

Harlequin Romance—the
series that has it all!

HROM-G

HARLEQUIN ◆ PRESENTS®

HARLEQUIN PRESENTS
men you won't be able to resist falling in love with...

HARLEQUIN PRESENTS
women who have feelings just like your own...

HARLEQUIN PRESENTS
powerful passion in exotic international settings...

HARLEQUIN PRESENTS
intense, dramatic stories that will keep you turning
to the very last page...

HARLEQUIN PRESENTS
The world's bestselling romance series!

Harlequin® Historical

If you're a serious fan of historical romance, then you're in luck!

Harlequin Historicals brings you stories by bestselling authors, rising new stars and talented first-timers.

Ruth Langan & Theresa Michaels
Mary McBride & Cheryl St. John
Margaret Moore & Merline Lovelace
Julie Tetel & Nina Beaumont
Susan Amarillas & Ana Seymour
Deborah Simmons & Linda Castle
Cassandra Austin & Emily French
Miranda Jarrett & Suzanne Barclay
DeLoras Scott & Laurie Grant…

You'll never run out of favorites.

Harlequin Historicals…they're too good to miss!

LOOK FOR OUR FOUR FABULOUS MEN!

Each month some of today's bestselling authors bring four new fabulous men to Harlequin American Romance. Whether they're rebel ranchers, millionaire power brokers or sexy single dads, they're all gallant princes—and they're all ready to sweep you into lighthearted fantasies and contemporary fairy tales where anything is possible and where all your dreams come true!

You don't even have to make a wish...Harlequin American Romance will grant your every desire!

Look for Harlequin American Romance wherever Harlequin books are sold!

SPECIAL EDITION

Stories of love and life, these powerful
novels are tales that you can identify with—
romances with "something special" added in!

Fall in love with the stories of authors such
as **Nora Roberts, Diana Palmer, Ginna Gray**
and many more of your special favorites—as
well as wonderful new voices!

Special Edition brings you
entertainment for the heart!

SSE-GEN

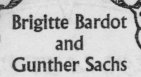

Brigitte Bardot
and
Gunther Sachs

In 1966 Brigitte Bardot, then aged thirty-one, was visiting a St. Tropez restaurant when she met German millionaire industrialist Gunther Sachs, who was thirty-three. They both described the experience as love and lust at first sight!

They enjoyed a five-week courtship with all the trimmings: Lear jets, speedboats, a Rolls Royce and a Bavarian château. One evening Sachs even flew in a mambo combo from Trinidad for Brigitte's dancing enjoyment after a caviar and Dom Perignon candlelight supper.

Miss Bardot stated, "I have never known a man like him. I feel mad, serene, wonderstruck. I have arrived at the end of a long journey. I'm living a fairy tale and he is my Prince Charming."

Similarly, Sachs said, "Since knowing Brigitte, I have the feeling I can succeed at anything."

To avoid the paparazzi (the French press) at the wedding, the couple flew to Los Angeles, only to be met by over 100 reporters at Los Angeles Airport. They chartered a jet and flew on to Las Vegas, where they were married at the home of Las Vegas attorney G. William Coulthard. Their double-ring civil ceremony was conducted by Judge John Mowbray.

B-BARDOT